Praise for the *Stoker's*

'Hopstaken and Prusi have done their homework and
produced a pleasing period penny dreadful.'
Publishers Weekly on *Stoker's Wilde*

'Historical details and supernatural monsters abound, but
it is the odd couple of Wilde and Stoker,
with their diametrically opposed personalities and
interesting quirks, that drives this story. Pass this
volume on to readers who are hungry for more
historical stories with a supernatural frame.'
Booklist on *Stoker's Wilde*

'A fun throwback to classic horror […] this tale stars
fictionalized versions of both Stoker and Wilde,
brought together through circumstance to hunt the
undead throughout England [...] This husband-and-wife
writing team offer a solid choice for fans of vampire
lore and atmospheric, historical horror.'
Library Journal on *Stoker's Wilde*

'A piece of work that is more original and creative
than any novel I have read in years.'
High Fever Books on *Stoker's Wilde*

'*Stoker's Wilde* is immensely entertaining and
engrossing […] an utter delight.'
The Haunted Reading Room on *Stoker's Wilde*

STEVEN HOPSTAKEN & MELISSA PRUSI

LAND OF THE DEAD

A Stoker's Wilde Novel

This is a **FLAME TREE PRESS** book

FLAME TREE PRESS
6 Melbray Mews, London, SW6 3NS, UK
flametreepress.com

US sales, distribution and warehouse:
Simon & Schuster
simonandschuster.biz

UK distribution and warehouse:
Marston Book Services Ltd
marston.co.uk

Thanks to the Flame Tree Press team, including:
Taylor Bentley, Frances Bodiam, Federica Ciaravella,
Don D'Auria, Chris Herbert, Josie Karani, Mike Spender,
Cat Taylor, Maria Tissot, Nick Wells, Gillian Whitaker.

The cover is created by Flame Tree Studio with
thanks to Nik Keevil and Shutterstock.com.
The font families used are Avenir and Bembo.

Flame Tree Press is an imprint of Flame Tree Publishing Ltd
flametreepublishing.com

A copy of the CIP data for this book is available from the British Library
and the Library of Congress.

3 5 7 9 8 6 4 2

HB ISBN: 978-1-78758-643-7
PB ISBN: 978-1-78758-641-3
ebook ISBN: 978-1-78758-644-4

Printed and bound in Great Britain by Clays Ltd, Elcograf S.p.A.

STEVEN HOPSTAKEN & MELISSA PRUSI

LAND OF THE DEAD

A *Stoker's Wilde* Novel

FLAME TREE PRESS
London & New York

WHITE WORM SOCIETY
ARCHIVIST'S NOTE

This collection pertains to the London Spiritual Invasion of 1883–1884 and the destruction of the first White Worm Society.

Queen Elizabeth created the first society in 1599 to protect the Empire from ungodly occult powers. A satanic cult had summoned a wyrm – a giant serpentlike creature – and it was terrorising a village.

The Queen dispatched a force of her best knights to vanquish the creature and bring the cult to justice. By the time they reached the village, the wyrm had killed more than twenty villagers and sent the rest fleeing for their lives. The knights found the beast in a cave, with the cult worshipping it and bringing it captured peasants for sacrifice.

The knights quickly overpowered the cult and turned their attention to the wyrm. Half a dozen of the valiant force lost their lives before Sir Walter Raleigh leapt upon its back and drove a silver sword – rumoured to be Excalibur – through its skull.

The cult members were imprisoned in the Tower of London and interrogated. They revealed the wyrm came from another place called 'the Realm'. The Realm exists alongside our world, but is not part of it. Her Majesty decreed the creation of a society to investigate and stop incursions from this other world.

Shrouded in a veil of secrecy, the first White Worm Society valiantly battled the supernatural for almost three centuries. They faced their greatest challenge by far when the Order of the Golden Dawn, led by the madman Richard Wilkins (known to his followers as the Black Bishop), opened a new gate into the Realm and unleashed its evil back into our world.

Thanks to the courage of Bram Stoker, Oscar Wilde, and their compatriots, his plan failed. They sealed the gate and Wilkins died at the hands of a monster he thought was under his control. However, that was not the only incursion into our world from the Realm, and as Mr. Stoker would say, the dead travel fast.

The following exhibits relate how the Land of the Dead encroached upon our living world and the havoc that it wreaked, including the destruction of the original White Worm Society. These entries are, for the most part, arranged in chronological order, with needless passages and multiple entries on the same subject removed.

    — Acting White Worm Archivist, 15th of June 1885

REPORT FROM WHITE WORM SOCIETY AGENT CORA CHASE

Date: 4th of December 1882
Subject: Bram Stoker and Dr. Victor Mueller

I have been tasked with recruiting Bram Stoker to once again help the White Worm Society stop an evil man wielding supernatural power.

This time it is Dr. Victor Mueller.

Public records show Dr. Mueller purchased the scientific library and laboratory of Dr. James Lind, who died in 1812. Lind was a pioneer in anatomical research and a mentor to Mary Shelley. It's been said that Lind was the inspiration for the character of Dr. Frankenstein in her novel, *Frankenstein: The Modern Prometheus*, written in 1818.

Mueller, the son of a wealthy German industrialist, left Berlin in 1867, at which point he vanished from the public records.

We first took an interest in him when he aligned himself with Reverend Richard Wilkins, the Black Bishop. After the Black Bishop was defeated, the White Worm Society and the Queen's Guard raided Dr. Mueller's Edinburgh laboratory, only to find that he had fled the country.

His lab contained fresh corpses, electrical equipment and notes on restoring 'the life force' to the dead.

We also discovered his correspondence with Wilkins, which revealed Mueller was conducting scientific research at Wilkins' request, as well as procuring specimens of an occult nature for him.

Wilkins rewarded Mueller with pints of vampire blood, and a sample of Bram Stoker's hybrid blood, for use in his own research.

Because Stoker was given vampire blood as a child to save his life, he developed an immunity to vampirism, which Mueller believed could be used to extend human life without the negative effects of becoming fully a vampire.

Mueller surfaced again in Germany in 1881 to collect his inheritance when his father died. This made him one of the richest men in Europe. He then disappeared from the public eye once more.

Recent reports place him in Finland, where we believe he is attempting to resurrect the dead.

Which leads us directly to Mr. Stoker. I went to the Lyceum Theatre, where he works today, but found it prudent to first speak with his employer, Henry Irving.

As stated in the 'Black Bishop Incident Report,' Mr. Irving is a vampire, albeit an unusual one. He seems to possess a soul and wishes to regain his humanity.

He had also been a friend of Richard Wilkins (never suspecting his friend's nefarious intentions), and assumed the task of settling Wilkins' affairs after his death. From Wilkins' correspondence, Irving discovered Mueller was researching the properties of vampire blood and the unique effects of Stoker's human/vampire co-mingled blood.

He then contacted Dr. Mueller in hopes his research could cure Irving's vampirism. Because of this, I felt he would be more receptive than Mr. Stoker to the idea of working with us as a means to his own ends.

I found him in his office, and briefly explained the situation.

"We must stop him, Mr. Irving," I said. "Surely you can see that. But if there is anything in his research that can help you cure your affliction, I will ensure that information is shared with you. The White Worms are as eager as you are to find a cure for vampirism."

He seemed sceptical, but what choice did he have? He was no longer in contact with Mueller, so his efforts there were at a standstill.

"Very well, Miss Chase. But you know that Bram will be harder to convince."

Although Stoker at times mistrusts the White Worm Society's objectives, he does owe me a debt of gratitude for saving his life in the American West and I hoped he would at least be willing to listen to our proposal.

Mr. Irving called him into the office.

"Not you again!" he exclaimed. "Honestly, Miss Chase, while I appreciate all you did for us in America, I wish the White Worms would just leave us alone. Oh, and Florence would like her journal back."

"Please, listen to what she has to say," Mr. Irving said.

He reluctantly took a seat. "I already gave your London office my records from our American misadventures," he said. "What do you want now?"

I got right down to it, giving him a brief history of Mueller. "His experiments are growing ever more dangerous," I concluded. "We can't allow him to continue."

"What makes you think I can help?"

"We intercepted a letter he wrote to you, Mr. Stoker." I handed it to him and he read it.

Here is the letter in its entirety:

Dear Mr. Stoker,

You don't know me, but I have been corresponding with Henry Irving concerning the magical properties of his blood and, by extension, yours. I assure you, Henry did not betray your confidence about your condition; that information I gained from the Black Bishop.

I am doing important scientific work that will revolutionise medicine. In time, my work could lead to the cure of all diseases and even of death itself!

I would like to buy a sample of your blood. I believe it is the key to reanimation without the nasty side effects of vampirism. If you agree to this, it can be to the benefit of all mankind.

I have enclosed the address of my solicitor and he can deliver me the sample. I thank you in advance.

Sincerely,

Dr. Victor Mueller

"Absolutely not," he said. "I will play no part in yet another madman's schemes."

"Obviously, we don't want you to give him your blood," I told him. "There's no telling what he would do with it. But we can use you to set a trap for him. All you need to do is set up a meeting and we'll do the rest."

"Aren't there any Finnish theatre managers you could press into service?" he asked.

"Not one with the blood he wants, or your ability to sense supernatural activity which that blood gives you," I said.

Side note: I first met Mr. Stoker when he was helping the U.S. government track down vampire outlaws in the Western Territories of

America. (See 'The California Incident' report.) His unique blood has given him the power to see where supernatural creatures are and have been. He could be a great asset to the White Worms and we should continue efforts to recruit him to our ranks.

I told Mr. Stoker I understood his reluctance to help us, but Dr. Mueller had to be stopped as he does not feel bound by any laws of God or man in his pursuit of scientific advances.

"He's creating monsters that are terrorising Finland," Mr. Irving added. "We can't let that go unchecked. And perhaps his research…"

"Yes, yes, I know," Mr. Stoker said. "This might lead to your cure."

With Mr. Irving's pleading, Mr. Stoker relented. He agreed to help us catch Mueller, but said it would be the last favor he would ever do for the White Worm Society.

FROM THE DIARY OF OSCAR WILDE, 8TH OF JANUARY 1883

Dear yours truly,

Bram stopped by my flat today, more flustered than usual. He told me the White Worms have coerced him into taking on a mission for them. It shocked me to learn they want to use him as bait to catch a madman, a former cohort of Reverend Wilkins.

"At first I was only to deliver a blood sample to his solicitor."

"Heavens, not your blood? The last time that was released in the wild, I found myself down the gullet of a giant worm!"

"It wasn't my actual blood, Oscar. We brought him some plain, ordinary blood. Besides, he's not interested in the Realm, he just wants to bring the dead back to life."

"Oh, is that all? Carry on then."

"Apparently, the solicitor got cold feet about the assignment and never delivered the vial. Lawyers aren't normally tasked with carrying blood across international borders, after all. Now Mueller's asked me to meet him in Finland, and the blasted Worms want me to go. They need to lure him out so they can nab him."

"Ah, he can't get his hands on the milk, so he wants the cow!"

"Aye, that's what I'm afraid of. I told him with a production at the theatre just mounting, the earliest we could meet would be the first week of February. The White Worms are planning my voyage now. They will be offering me protection and will be there to grab Mueller when we meet."

I told him he should refuse to go. After all, he has a wife and child to think about. Gallivanting through Finland in the winter is dangerous in itself. Throw in a mad scientist who's raising the dead, and it seems like, well, just the sort of trouble that tends to find Stoker – and, by extension, me. Besides, I believe the Finns wear enormous fur coats in the winter, and this will make Stoker look even more ursine than usual and a hunter could shoot him.

"The mad scientist is the reason I should go," he said. "There are reports he is creating some sort of monster up there. And then there is the fact he helped the Black Bishop with his nefarious plans. He should be brought to justice for that, if nothing else."

So there you have it. I could not talk him out of it and may have helped talk him into it. Not even my charms can work against his stubbornness.

He made me promise to look after Florrie and little Noel should things go south in the north, which I am happy to do.

I told him my engagement to Constance is back on the calendar.

He did not seem as happy as I would have liked at hearing the news. In fact, I think I saw him roll his eyes.

He did offer his congratulations and said that Florence would be over the moon at the news. I can always count on Florrie to be in my corner.

He departed into the cold and left me alone to ponder his journey further. A feeling came over me, like the dread I felt the day I met Derrick. He was so beautiful and so talented that I coveted him from the first. I couldn't have known then that his obsession with eternal youth would lead me into the clutches of the Black Bishop and his vampire cult, but I seem to have a sixth sense for these things.

I felt the same shiver down my spine today, and it was telling me this might not end well for Bram. I hope I am wrong; alas, I seldom am.

FROM THE JOURNAL OF BRAM STOKER, 8TH OF FEBRUARY 1883

1:00 p.m.

Our ship has pulled into port near the town of Kokkola, on the west coast of Finland. Our time at sea was most arduous. February is not the best time for such a journey. The North Sea was treacherous, and the Baltic was not much better. The Gulf of Bothnia was partially frozen over and we had to navigate around many ice floes.

Stepping on deck even for a moment for fresh air turned my red beard white with ice and chilled me to the bone even through the many layers of my fur coat.

Normally I have good sea legs; however, the large swells bounced us up and down vigorously for most of the journey, leaving me green around the gills as the sailors say.

Onboard with me were four White Worm 'operatives', as they call themselves.

There is Mr. Blackwood, a tall gentleman with curly black hair. He shares my love of the theatre and we spent many a night on the voyage talking about plays and the world of acting. The others tell me Mr. Blackwood has studied karate in Japan and can break a thick board with his bare hands – imagine that.

The others include Mr. Fry, who is a large, muscular man I assume is along should things get rough. He doesn't say much but is pleasant enough.

Mr. Cantor is shorter, five eight or so, and is in charge of firearms. I am told he is a decorated soldier with many heroic deeds to his name.

And finally, the man in charge, Errol Hammond. He is the current director of the White Worm Society. I suppose this must be a particularly important mission to have him along; however, I simply don't like the man. He is very ill-tempered and is often chastising his men for the smallest infractions: a loose tie, an unpolished shoe and the like.

We are alone at sea except for the captain and a small crew, so one would think protocol could wait until we get to shore. He is a small man and one gets the impression all his bluster is making up for his lack of stature.

I suspect he, like me, is fighting seasickness and that may affect his mood. Still, there is something not right about him and I do my best not to socialise with him if I don't have to.

★　★　★

9th of February, 3:15 p.m.

I was happy to set foot on shore despite the freezing temperatures and strong north wind.

The town is very charming, with many colourful wooden buildings of Swedish and Finnish design.

We checked in to the Hotel Kala, and after freshening up in our rooms, met in the lobby downstairs. A fire roared in the large stone fireplace and we ordered some brandy.

We discussed strategy for bringing in Mueller during our rendezvous tomorrow.

"We will be covertly sitting in the dining room posing as locals," Hammond informed me. "I've asked the hotelier to not seat other guests in the hour before and during the meeting time. When he sits down to talk with you, hear him out for a bit. See if he tells you what his plans are for your blood and if he is working with others."

I very much doubted Mueller would offer up this information at our first meeting and said as much.

"Maybe so," Hammond said. "As he thinks his work will benefit the world, he might let you in on the details. Make him feel comfortable, and when you think the time is right, give us a signal by scratching your ear. Then, Mr. Blackwood and Mr. Fry will grab him."

I've retired to my room for the night, happy to sleep in a big feather bed without the sea rolling beneath it.

I still feel much trepidation about the meeting tomorrow. It should be a simple task for five men to take in Mueller, but I know how these things can go pear-shaped, especially with my cursed luck.

REPORT FROM WHITE WORM SOCIETY AGENT BRENT BLACKWOOD

Date: 10 February 1883
Subject: Mueller Investigation

I am sorry to report our current mission to capture Dr. Victor Mueller has taken a turn for the worse.

We had stationed ourselves in the Hotel Kala tearoom. Bram Stoker was waiting to meet with Dr. Mueller and would gain as much information as he could before we apprehended him.

Agent Cantor and I dressed as local fishermen and sat at a table in the corner of the room eating our lunch.

Agent Fry and Director Hammond were also dressed as locals, with Mr. Hammond sitting in an adjacent corner and Fry in the lobby standing guard over the rear entrance to the room.

All of us had a good line of sight on Stoker near the centre of the room.

The rest of the tables were empty, as was the dining room except for the occasional entrance and exit of the waiter.

The room itself had a large wall of windows showing the rear garden of the hotel, which had a path cleared of snow for carriages and horse-drawn sleighs to drop off passengers. A single door in the centre of the wall of windows led to the back garden. We were told this was the entrance most locals used when visiting the restaurant, while those staying at the hotel used the lobby entrance. A small kitchen to the right had no exit or entrance except through the dining room.

It had stopped snowing, and the sky was clear, giving us a brightly lit view of the outside.

When the appointed meeting time grew near, a horse-drawn sledge came down the path. This was not the normal open style of sledge but an enclosed box, like the horse-drawn carriages police use to round up drunks. A very tall man sat on top driving the horses and he pulled them to a stop in front of the door.

I immediately thought this mode of transportation was odd and snapped to attention.

The driver jumped down and, with barely a glance towards the tearoom, went to the back of the sledge and opened the rear doors.

Mr. Stoker jumped up from his seat as if he, too, sensed something was wrong.

"There are supernatural things in there!" he shouted. Hammond also sprang to his feet and came to Stoker's side.

"What do you see?" Hammond asked.

"I see a green glow when something supernatural is nearby. I can see it now, shining through a knothole in the box. It's very bright!"

I had heard about Mr. Stoker's supernatural vision, so this revelation made me rush to the window with my pistol drawn. Mr. Cantor did the same.

Four men came tumbling out of the back of the sledge, falling onto the snowy ground and then staggered to their feet as if they were drunk.

The driver returned to the top of the box, took the reins and drove away as the men stumbled towards the windows of the tearoom.

These men, if I could call them that, were dressed in torn, ragged clothing and had yellow, waxy skin. Their eyes were pale white and their lips dark black. They lurched towards us slowly, moaning and gasping.

Mr. Cantor and I ran to secure the door, and Mr. Fry came running in from the lobby to join us.

"My God, what are those things?" Mr. Hammond asked Mr. Stoker.

"I haven't a clue," Mr. Stoker said. "I have never seen such creatures before – and I have seen many supernatural things."

Mr. Cantor went out the door, gun drawn, and shot one square in the chest. It jerked upon the bullet hitting it, but kept moving forward with the other three creatures.

Mr. Fry and I joined him in the yard and fired many rounds into them, to no avail.

They pushed past us and crashed through the wall of windows, apparently not feeling the shards of glass that were now sticking into their waxy skin. They did not bleed as such, but yellowish-green fluid dribbled out slowly from the cuts and bullet wounds.

"Fall back!" I heard Director Hammond yell. He was quickly ushering Stoker towards the lobby door for safety.

We re-entered the dining room and kept firing. Mr. Cantor hit one in the head, splattering its brains, and it dropped to the ground. "Aim for the head," Cantor yelled.

Fry was out of bullets at this point and was fighting one hand to hand. The creature tried to bite him, but Fry's strength held him at arm's length.

I put a bullet in the head of Mr. Fry's assailant and that dropped him to the floor.

I turned to see Mr. Cantor trying to reload his pistol as one of the creatures clawed at him, ripping flesh from his face. Cantor stumbled back and dropped his gun and bullets.

I too found I was out of bullets and began to reload. One lunged at me and I used a *mae geri* (front kick) to push him back.

Mr. Fry jumped the one clawing Mr. Cantor and twisted its head so forcefully he snapped its neck and it fell dead.

The last creature stumbled its way past me and, finding food on a table, began to savagely eat it like an animal, seemingly uninterested in us now that it had found sustenance.

I walked up to it and put a bullet in the back of its head, killing it – or re-killing it, I should say, as I would later find out these were reanimated corpses.

During this melee, we had lost track of the Director and Mr. Stoker.

We rushed into the lobby to find the Director unconscious and Mr. Stoker gone.

The hotel manager was cowering behind the front desk. He told us a tall man had pummelled Mr. Hammond on the head and put a hypodermic needle into Mr. Stoker's neck. The man dragged Mr. Stoker out the front door and into his sledge.

I am ashamed to say we have lost Mr. Stoker, kidnapped in broad daylight right under our noses.

We revived Director Hammond, and he is recovering from his blow to the head. Mr. Cantor is tending his scratches, which are quite deep. Fry and I are no worse for wear.

I suspect Dr. Mueller has Mr. Stoker now and we will do our best to track and rescue him, hopefully before Mueller gets his hands on Stoker's blood.

—End Report—

REPORT FROM BRAM STOKER: ENLISTED TO HELP WW SOCIETY IN THE MATTER OF DR. VICTOR MUELLER

Date: 13 February 1883

I will do my best to document my recollections here, though my brain is still foggy. I will endeavour not to embellish or sensationalise the events, as anyone might do after such a strange and harrowing experience.

My last memory from the Hotel Kala is being rushed into the lobby by Director Hammond. I had just enough time to see the alarmed face of the hotel manager, then I heard a thud behind me.

The next thing I knew, I awoke in blackness. I did not know how much time had passed. I was in a compartment of some kind, and it was in motion. Later, I would find out that I was in the box the creatures had poured out of earlier. It smelt like decay and death, but I was wrapped up warmly in blankets and the ride was smooth. From the pain in my neck I assumed someone had drugged me with a hypodermic needle, but I did not recall that or how I came to be in the sledge.

I was in and out of my drugged state, but I tried to listen for clues as to where I was along my journey. There were cracks and holes in the box, and though my hands and feet were bound, I manoeuvred myself to peer through them. We had left Kokkola behind, and were passing through a landscape of snowy fields and rolling hills, with no landmarks to help me determine our location. I cannot be sure how long we glided along, but it was quite a while, as darkness fell and we were still travelling.

At some point, the sleigh stopped. I heard the driver jump down and come to the back. He opened the doors and dragged me out. In my drugged state, I had little fight in me.

I discovered we were not at our ultimate destination, but that he was transferring me into an open-air sledge that was harnessed to two reindeer.

He wrapped me up in fur blankets and the world went dark again. I fell asleep at some point and when I awoke, I could hear the ocean surf. I then feared he might transfer me to a ship, but we soon stopped and he lifted and carried me out of the sleigh. I am not a slight man, over six feet tall and well over fourteen stone, but this man lifted me like I was a child.

I heard the creaking sound of wooden doors opening and I was carried into a building and laid down on a cot where I lost consciousness once again, despite my best efforts to stay awake and alert.

When I awoke, it was morning. I was no longer bound, and I clawed away the blankets covering my face and sat up. I was on a cot in a corner of a large, open room with high ceilings. With its walls of stone and a ceiling of wide wooden beams, the building looked to be old, maybe even medieval. The only windows to speak of were small and up near the ceiling.

I could hear crashing waves that sounded like they were far away, as though we might be on a cliff above the ocean. I could also hear a rushing stream and creaking that sounded as if it could be a mill wheel.

An enormous fireplace at the far end of the room provided heat. There was a laboratory table in the middle of the room. On it was a rectangular object, about six feet long, covered with a blanket. Water was seeping out from under the blanket and dripping to the floor. I assumed the object was a block of ice that was melting from the heat of the fireplace. It struck me as strange, even in a room full of strange things.

It was most definitely a laboratory. I recognised modern scientific apparatuses throughout – glass beakers, Bunsen burners, and the like – as well as quite a bit of electrical equipment that I could not identify but that looked out of place in an ancient building. Wires ran along the ceiling and walls and it was then I saw the place was lit entirely with Edison bulbs. I am not sure how Mueller was generating the electricity, as I was certain we were in the middle of nowhere.

"Ah, you are awake, Mr. Stoker." I turned around to see a short man with thinning white hair entering the room. He was wearing rose-coloured spectacles and a white lab coat, looking very much the part of a scientist. "I am Dr. Mueller," he said with the slightest hint of a German accent.

He walked over to me on the cot and held his hand out for me to shake it, which I ignored.

"What do you want with me?" I asked.

"For you to keep your word," he said. "I plan to keep my part of the bargain. My solicitor will arrange for payment for a pint of your blood. Had you kept your part of the deal, I wouldn't have had to resort to such extreme measures. I knew from my work with the Black Bishop that the White Worms would try their utmost to interfere in my business."

The tall man who had brought me there entered with a tray of food. "Your breakfast, master," he said, putting it down on a nearby table.

"Please, have something to eat, Mr. Stoker. I so rudely interrupted your lunch yesterday and you must be famished." He pulled out a chair at the table and gestured me to sit in it.

I was hungry, so I reluctantly accepted the invitation. I knew Mr. Hammond and his men would be searching for me, so it was best to comply, if only to play for time.

Mueller sat down to join me at the table. "I'm afraid Risto is not much of a cook, but I hope this is to your taste."

It was cheese, dried fruit and bread. I eyed the bread knife for a moment but, remembering how strong Risto was, decided against any sudden moves. I looked around the room once again, to see if I could find some avenue of escape.

He assumed I was marvelling at his handiwork and, with pride, said, "All electric lights. The bulbs are of my own design. All powered by the mill wheel and a supplemental kerosene dynamo."

"Impressive," I said. In other circumstances, I likely would have found this fascinating, but as things were, I had little interest in humouring my kidnapper's desire to show off his handiwork. I quickly got to the matter at hand. "To what purpose do you wish to use my blood?"

He did not seem to mind the change of subject. In fact, a smile spread across his small face. It reminded me of smiles I have seen before on the smug faces of other madmen. "Why, to bring the dead back to life, of course."

I remembered the mindless creatures that had attacked us. "To create monsters, then? Why would you do such a thing – killing people just to bring them back to do your bidding!"

"I did not kill those men I experimented on. There was an accident in a lumber camp near here. A large tree came down and killed them. It was a fortuitous opportunity that provided me with my subjects. Those things I sent were failed experiments, sadly fit only as a diversion," he said. "I can, and have, done better. You have already met my first success." His eyes looked up to Risto, who was standing next to the table staring off into space like a dutiful servant.

I looked at Risto in bewilderment, which Mueller took for wonder.

"Yes, I returned him from the dead. As you can see, he is a functioning, live human being, capable of thought and speech. He can be taught and learn. He is my crowning achievement, my Adam."

I have to admit, my bewilderment did indeed turn to wonder.

"I found him drowned in the river. Washed right up to my mill wheel like a gift from God. Decomposition had not even set in yet. He was perfect."

Mueller jumped from the table and went over to Risto, intently studying his face.

"When I discovered there were such things as living-dead vampires, I began to wonder if we could use them to conquer death itself. Could we use vampire blood to restore life? Could I eliminate the negative traits of vampires and harness the good? I have corresponded with Henry Irving about that very thing."

"Yes," I said. "He has been looking for centuries for something similar and has not found it. Even Henry, who has managed to quell his appetites, still has darker impulses that he struggles daily to control. You cannot split the monster from the host."

"Ah, but I have. I have, using your blood to create a serum! Those other things you saw – I brought them back with vampire blood and electricity. They are mindless, drooling creatures with no impulse but to feed. But when I used my technique with *your* blood – the sample given to me by Reverend Wilkins – I created Risto. He lives! He really lives!"

He circled Risto, who remained motionless. Mueller pointed to Risto like a lab specimen as he blathered on.

"I administer the vampire blood, then your blood, then electricity, and life is restored. They retain some vampiric traits, not only life but super strength. Risto here is as strong as five men, is impervious to the cold and has great resistance to pain. Yet he does not need to feed on blood; he lives on food like any human. And as you saw, he has all his strength in the daylight. None of the bad vampire traits remain."

"But your entire endeavour is the height of arrogance. What right do you have to play God?" I asked. Such things must be said, though madmen never listen.

"If God did not want this *he* would stop me, or *he* is no god," Mueller said, sounding very much like the Black Bishop at that moment. "It is the culmination of my life's work. Why settle for easing ailments when you can stop death itself?"

It suddenly occurred to me that Risto was not triggering my sense of the supernatural. He did not give off that telltale green glow as those other Mueller creations had. Maybe Mueller *had* purged the vampire out.

He sat back down at the table. "Mr. Stoker, your blood could save thousands of lives. It could reunite parents with their dead children. Do you not want to be part of the greatest discovery in history?"

"I have met people with grandiose ideas like yours before. It never ends well."

"Tomorrow I plan to resurrect the love of my life. My wife, Charlotte." He went to the object on the lab table and pulled off the blanket. A naked woman was suspended in a block of ice.

"With your blood, Mr. Stoker, we will bring her back from the dead!"

He told me Charlotte had been his assistant, even when he had been working for the Black Bishop. She was a scientist herself and was all on board with the raising of the dead.

When they were chased out of Scotland, they came here, where they had set up a laboratory. The cold conditions were ideal for storing dead bodies, and they had built an icehouse nearby for such a task. The remote location kept them safe from prying eyes.

But last year Charlotte had an accident, tripping down the stairs and breaking her neck. She had been on ice ever since.

I spent the rest of the day listening to Mueller's megalomaniacal prattle and examining the laboratory as closely as I could, both to provide detail in my report and to seek some means of escape. But I was forced to admit to myself that even if I managed to slip out of the lab, I had no idea where I was. I would either freeze to death or be swiftly recaptured by Risto before I could make it to safety.

The next morning, after Charlotte had thawed, Mueller went to work repairing her neck the best he could. I wondered if his procedure could regrow severed spinal cords, and he assured me it would.

Once satisfied with his wife's condition, he took a pint of blood from me and divided some of it among various beakers, adding chemicals. (The bottles were not labelled and I'm afraid I cannot identify what exactly he used.) At several points, he shocked the solution with electricity.

Later that morning he injected the body with vampire blood, then the 'Stoker Serum' as he called it. (He seemed to think I would be flattered.) Then he hooked electrodes to her wrists and ankles.

Risto was his assistant in all of this, bringing him chemicals and surgical tools. I just observed, and though I suppose I had a chance to make my escape while they were busy prepping Mrs. Mueller, I have to admit I wanted to see if it could be done. Does that make me as much of a madman as he?

Risto went to the far wall where there was a board of electrical switches and dials.

Dr. Mueller finished checking the connections to Charlotte, then took a moment to wipe his brow.

Even knowing he had done it in the past, it did not seem to me that he could restore the lifeless corpse on the table to life. The body was slightly bloated, the skin yellowed and showing signs of decay. Her hair, which looked as though it was once a golden blond, was grey and thin. Stitches from Dr. Mueller's restorative surgery ran up both sides of her neck and oozed a greenish-yellow pus.

Mueller put on a pair of dark goggles and instructed me to not look

directly at the sparks that were to come, "Staring at them too long can lead to permanent damage to your eyesight."

He stepped back away from the table and shouted, "Now, Risto! Now!"

Risto pulled a lever down and there was a sudden firework of sparks on the board that ran down the wires into the corpse on the table.

The body lurched and flopped, as I have seen when shocks are applied to dead frogs. But this had never resulted in bringing them back to life.

The light bulbs dimmed, smoke started to form at the connections at the wrists and ankles. It was a most horrific sight, and at that moment I thought it to be all folly.

Then we were plunged into darkness for a moment, yet the room was lit from an eerie glow emanating from Charlotte's corpse.

"Stop, now, Risto!" Mueller shouted.

Risto pulled the switch back up and the light above us flickered back on.

For more than a minute, we all just stood there staring at the body. Mueller seemed despondent. Maybe it hadn't worked.

But then Charlotte Mueller's eyes opened! She took in a big gasp of air. Then another. Then another. It...*she* was breathing.

Mueller gently raised her to a sitting position. She looked around the room, but a cloudy veil was over her eyes, seemingly obscuring her vision. We watched in amazement as the veil lifted, revealing blue irises. With every breath she took, her cheeks regained their rosy hue. Even her hair was transforming back to its golden lustre.

"Can you stand, my dear?" Mueller asked, gently helping her off the table.

Her legs were shaky, and Mueller held her up. She clung to him, frightened. After a moment, she found her footing and pushed herself away from Mueller like a toddler wanting the freedom to take her first steps.

She held her hands out and examined them in wonderment. Then her gaze made its way down her naked body, which was still filling with life: skin becoming flush with blood and growing a more natural pink, muscles gaining tone and strength.

She put her fingers to her face and felt her cheeks and lips. Then her neck. Small ruby jewels of blood appeared around the stitches on her neck, which had been oozing greenish pus only moments before.

She opened her mouth as though she had just discovered it was there and puffed out air. She made an *ah* sound, and it surprised and delighted her.

Her trancelike wonder at her rebirth was interrupted by Mueller, who was clumsily trying to put a robe on her. This frightened her and she flinched away from him. She turned and looked at him, her eyes wide with horror.

"Charlotte, my love, it is me, Victor. You are safe now."

She backed away from him like a startled fawn.

"Don't you recognise me?" Mueller said, slowly moving towards her. "Search your memory. It is me."

Risto rushed over to Mueller. "Remember, when you brought me back, I had to learn to talk again. I was like a child."

"That was because you were an imbecile to begin with," Mueller said angrily. "Charlotte is highly educated and has a brilliant mind!" He regained his composure and added, "She is just in shock. She will remember."

He continued to walk forward. She continued to back away.

It was then I regained my senses and thought this might be a good time to make my escape.

Mueller grabbed Charlotte's wrist, and she shrieked and screamed. She broke away from Mueller and hid behind Risto for protection.

I took the diversion to dash for the door.

"You fool, stop him!" Mueller yelled at Risto, and in an instant he was blocking my escape. He punched me down to the floor with a fist to my jaw.

I lay on the ground fighting to keep my consciousness. I looked up with blurry eyes and saw Mueller trying to restrain Charlotte, who was growling and scratching at him like an animal.

Risto ran over. "No, master, she is just frightened!"

Charlotte bit Mueller's hand until he let go from the pain. He slapped her hard with his other hand.

She ran to Risto once again for protection, this time clinging to him.

"Charlotte," Mueller pleaded. "I am sorry I hit you. Come here. Come to me, I am your husband, don't you recognise me?"

She held on more tightly to Risto, hissing at Mueller like a cat.

I tried to stand, but dizziness overtook me, and I dropped to my knees.

"Do not hurt her," Risto said, calmly but forcefully.

"I'm not going to hurt her! I brought her to life!" Mueller screamed. "Give her to me!"

Risto pushed her behind him and lunged at Mueller.

I started to lose consciousness, my mouth full of blood from Risto's blow. I fell flat on my face and blacked out for a moment.

I came around for a second and saw Risto on his knees holding Mueller and sobbing. "I killed him! I killed my father!"

Charlotte ran up to console him and my eyelids closed once more and the world went black.

I was awakened by an icy wind on my face, which quickly revived me. It was dark. I was once more in the reindeer sledge. Risto was driving with Charlotte by his side. Neither one was wearing a coat, but Charlotte was dressed in men's clothes.

They had me wrapped warmly in my fur coat and blankets.

We drove for at least an hour more before we came to the lights of a farmhouse. Risto pulled the sleigh to a stop and told me to get out.

"Please do not come looking for us," he said. "We have a right to live our own lives."

He pulled off into the darkness and that is the last I saw of them.

The farmer gave me a ride back towards Kokkola. We met Hammond and his men on the trail back.

As for Mueller's lab, it shouldn't be too hard to find. You are looking for an old monastery near the sea. It is on a river with a mill. When you find it, please destroy my blood. I know you will be tempted to salvage Mueller's research, but I think no good can come from it. Just as the supernatural disturbs the natural order of things, I now know science can be bent to the will of a madman in similar ways.

—End Report—

REPORT FROM WHITE WORM SOCIETY AGENT BRENT BLACKWOOD

Date: 9 March 1883
Subject: Mueller Investigation

We have at last located Dr. Mueller's laboratory near Pirskari on the coast of Finland. Unfortunately, it has burned down to the ground. The stone walls have collapsed into a pile of rubble which would be very difficult to excavate given the size of the stones and remote location of the site.

There were still hot embers when we arrived, leading me to believe the fire was recent, perhaps only days ago. Whether it was set ablaze by an unattended fire in the fireplace or purposely by Mueller is unknown. Since retrieval of the body is not likely, we have to assume the worst: that Dr. Mueller may still be alive.

We shall return to London at once and await further instructions or reassignment.

—End Report—

FROM THE JOURNAL OF CONSTANCE LLOYD, 10TH OF DECEMBER 1883

Oscar and I have finally pinned down a date for our nuptials.

We have set a date thrice before, only to have Oscar get cold feet each time. Now the event will be this May, and he assures me he will not reschedule.

Oscar's mother is even more thrilled than I am at the news. Lady Wilde is adamant that we settle down and start a family. I haven't the heart to tell her I have been told by my physician that I cannot conceive and not to get my hopes up on such matters.

I am ambivalent about motherhood, so this news did not devastate me, but I think Oscar wants children. It is admittedly quite charming how he fawns over the Stokers' boy, Noel. I suspect he would make a better father than a husband, for I have my eyes open going into this marriage and accept Oscar for who he is.

Which is not to say that I am not as excited as any bride-to-be, or as determined to make my marriage a success. I love Oscar, deeply and passionately, and believe he feels the same for me. But I am not the type of woman who will subsume herself completely in her husband's needs and happiness. I, too, have ambitions and interests, which I value and intend to pursue. Oscar completely supports me in this, as I support his dreams and goals.

Oscar tells me not being married could affect his chances at employment with respectable publications. He hopes to become an editor for a magazine or publishing house to supplement his income while he works on his plays and poetry.

I wish to find work as a writer, and Oscar has been most encouraging in my endeavours.

Our union shall be an artistic marriage, born of our shared passion for ideas, each other and all things beautiful.

Had I doubted Oscar's love for me, I would not after today when he said he 'wanted to confess all'.

I had heard all the gossip about Oscar and his friends, of course, but hearing the actual truth was even more bizarre.

He came to the house I share with my grandfather, which he almost never does because he hates the wallpaper and its lack of artistic furnishings.

He seemed nervous and uncharacteristically silent. I expected the worst, that he was there to call off the wedding once again.

He sipped tea out of a cup he had brought with him, since he refused to drink tea from my grandfather's copper mugs, the only drinking vessels we owned.

"I'm afraid my hesitance to settle upon a date has been more than just cold feet," he said. "I love you and wish to commit fully to our life together; however, there are a few things of which I must make you aware. I do not want there to be any secrets between us going forward."

"Agreed," I said. "Let's go into this with eyes open, as it were."

He paused for a moment to collect his thoughts, then finally said, "As you know, I am a lover of beautiful things. I am an advocate of the Aesthetic movement and, as such, seek to surround myself with beautiful art and even more beautiful people, such as yourself."

I thanked him, quite demurely.

"Yes, well then, you might have heard through gossip circles that I from time to time might seek the company of beautiful men as well as women."

He paused again.

"Go on," I encouraged.

"I may have, in the past, in seeking new ideas of beauty, pushed the boundaries of what polite society would call moral protocol."

"I have heard this about you, yes," I admitted.

"Let me assure you, all my dalliances are in the past now that I am with you. I will remain faithful, but I thought we should…I should put it all out on the table."

"So you have made love to men, as well as women?" I asked, more to see him squirm than for a confirmation.

"More like experimentation," he said. "But, yes. If you find my past is not something you can live with, I understand."

"What is in the past is the past," I assured him. "I myself have experimented."

"Oh, I was hoping you would…wait, what?" he said as though the last part of my sentence had just caught up to his brain.

"Yes, in school. Many girls do it. I see it as nothing more than quenching curiosity, a rite of passage, as it were."

"Indeed," he said. "Well, there you have it." He seemed a bit dazed by the news.

"I am glad you told me, Oscar. We need not speak of it again and I will keep your secret if you keep mine."

He smiled in relief and hugged and kissed me. After a moment, he broke away.

"There is more, I'm afraid," he said. "While we are in this happy moment of confession, I need to tell you everything."

Again one hears rumours, but they did not prepare me for the full extent of the truth. Apparently, supernatural monsters are real and have plagued Oscar and his friends for some time.

He told me that Bram Stoker was fed vampire blood at an early age but not turned into one. This has given him immunity to vampirism, and the power to see supernatural things.

"It was done to save his life, you see," Oscar told me in a long rambling story, which was difficult to follow but quite intriguing.

And apparently, this feeding was done by none other than Henry Irving! Yes, the gifted thespian who I have seen perform so many of Shakespeare's greatest roles is a vampire! Perhaps this is what makes him so charismatic onstage.

"But he is a good vampire. He has been trying to find a cure for it. That's why he fed Bram his blood as a boy. There was a prophecy that feeding a boy vampire blood on his seventh birthday would give his blood powers to cure vampirism, or some such thing, I forget all the details. Suffice to say it didn't work, but it has given Bram the gift of second sight."

"I see," I said, doing my best to sound like I was believing it all, which I was not.

Then he told me a harrowing tale of a madman known as the Black Bishop who tried to use Bram's blood to open the gates of hell.

"He wasn't really a bishop," Oscar explained. "He was clergy though, Vicar of the Close at Salisbury Cathedral. Not really important to the story. In any event, Bram and I stopped him and saved the world."

"Thank you for that," I said. The look on my face betrayed me.

"By your sceptical look, I am getting the impression you don't believe a word I'm saying, but that has never stopped me from talking before and I shall therefore continue."

"Please do," I said, settling back for more of this gripping yarn.

"So this madman," he continued.

"The Black Bishop," I said.

"Yes, he was trying to open a portal to hell, and he had it from yet another prophecy that he could do it at Stonehenge with the blood of a half human, half monster. He tried other monsters at first. A werewolf, for example, seemed to fit the requirement of being man and monster. It didn't work."

"Thank goodness," I said, becoming more enthralled in the tall tale.

"But the werewolf bit my brother, Willie, who was working for the Black Bishop against my advice."

"Oh, no," I said.

"Yes, terrible for Willie, who must now chain himself up once a month."

"So, your brother is a werewolf in this story?"

"Yes, and I assure you it is no mere story. All that I have said is true. I would not make up such an unbelievable tale. My talent would be wasted on a penny dreadful. In any event, it was Bram's blood that turned out to be the final thing needed to open the portal. Stoker always gets himself into these things and somehow drags me along."

He then went on to tell me Bram and he have been targeted by vampires ever since. They even fought them in America while on tour there. This story was more outlandish than the last.

"We again saved the world, or at the very least America."

I was willing to take this story as a fanciful creation from a fanciful man, but what he said next connected it to my real life and rang a bell, as it were.

"The White Worm Society – they are charged by the Queen to keep the Empire safe from these things – have been pestering us to join their ranks."

"The White Worm Society, you say?" He obviously saw the colour go from my face.

"Yes, you have heard of them?"

I stood up on shaky legs, and he steadied me.

"Constance, are you all right?"

"I have heard of them. My father worked for them. He told me it was just a social club for men who collect old books. He handled their legal matters." I walked over to my desk and retrieved my father's journal from the drawer.

"My father left me this when he died. It is written in a code I cannot decipher, except for the one phrase on the spine of the journal in English, 'White Worm Society'."

I handed it to Oscar, and he thumbed through it.

"Ah, not really in code, this is Taylor shorthand," he explained. "Which I am a bit rusty on, but it should be easy enough to translate, if you would like me to do so."

He put the book down and said, "There is another thing I must tell you, something I learned from a White Worm operative. I was sworn to secrecy, but I cannot keep this from you."

He walked me back to my chair and sat me down.

"Your father did not die of a heart attack on a trip to Paris. He was killed on a mission for the White Worms, exploring a place called 'the Realm', a world where these supernatural creatures come from."

A lifetime of memories of my father came flooding back to my mind. His frequent trips abroad, which required him taking many maps and camping supplies with him. I thought it odd even then that a barrister would need to be so supplied for a business trip.

His library filled with old books on the occult mixed among his law books.

The strange men stopping by the house and talking to him in his study in hushed voices.

"Go on, Oscar, tell me everything again. This time I will listen with an open mind."

He did, and it changed my world forever. I feel even closer to Oscar now. We share a terrible secret, but at least we are no longer alone in the world and can face it together.

LETTER FROM AGATHA POWELL TO SARAH CAWLEY, 23RD OF JANUARY 1884

Archivist's note: The White Worm Society was aware of the rise of spiritualism in England and the number of people claiming the ability to contact the dead. At this time, Lorna Bow was still under the influence of her uncle, Leonard Pith, who was running a séance parlour. The Society had no reason to suspect they were anything but the typical charlatans. Little did they know the extraordinary power Lorna would exhibit in coming months. Below is an example of one of their séances.

Dear Sarah,

Thank you for your letter, and I do hope that your Gregory is feeling better. My mother always said that eating a bowl of figs could help with that sort of problem, and if that fails perhaps a bit of strychnine.

And speaking of my mother, I have the most wondrous story to relate. You know how dreadfully I have missed her since she passed last year. I've never forgiven myself for not rushing to her side immediately when she took ill. By the time I realised how serious it was, it was too late, and I arrived mere hours after she drew her final breath. It has haunted me that we left so much unsaid between us.

Recently, an acquaintance of mine told me about her visit to a séance parlour where she had communicated with her late husband. Well, you might think me silly, Sarah, but I decided it could not hurt to try it myself, and I set an appointment. This acquaintance, Mrs. Benchley, agreed to accompany me, as I did not want to go alone, and I felt Walter would not approve.

The séance parlour is in a modest row house on Merlin Street in Clerkenwell. We arrived at the appointed hour and were admitted by a meek little lass of no more than twelve. She took our coats and ushered us into a sunny but slightly shabby sitting room where another girl, a little older than the first, bade us sit and offered us tea.

A man entered and greeted Mrs. Benchley warmly, then introduced himself to me as Mr. Pith, the proprietor. He was thin and dressed in an impeccably tailored black suit. His dark eyes glittered from a narrow, pale face, beneath a thick head of black hair, going slightly to grey. A scarlet cravat was the only splash of colour about the man.

"I understand you wish to speak to your mother today," he said. "Our medium has extraordinary abilities. She will try her best and is often successful, as she was for Mrs. Benchley here, but you understand we cannot always make contact the first time we try. The spirit world takes skill and subtlety to navigate, and our loved ones who have passed are often reluctant to be drawn back into earthly affairs."

I assured him that my mother would have no such reticence and would happily speak with me if his medium could only bring us together. He smiled vaguely and patted my arm, murmuring, "Of course, of course," then turned to greet an elderly couple who had just been ushered into the room. Moments later, another woman was admitted, and we all settled, politely sipping tea, while Mr. Pith described what was to come.

"Our medium, Lorna, is preparing herself – physically and spiritually – for the séance. When she is ready, we shall enter the parlour. Please do not speak, so as not to disturb the aura she has created around herself. The more sensitive among you may feel this aura as you enter the room. It is difficult to describe, at once charged with energy and peacefully soothing. But do not worry if you cannot detect the aura; it does not mean you will not be able to speak to your loved one."

Mrs. Benchley caught my eye. She had told me that she had experienced just such an aura on her last visit, and I felt a thrill of anticipation.

He told us that Lorna would be at the far end of the table when we entered the room, and that I was to sit to her left with Mrs. Benchley beside me. The Wickhams would be across from us, and the other woman, Miss Haverford, would sit directly opposite Lorna. "You will move quickly and quietly to your seats," he instructed. "Please be careful, as the room is only dimly lit. Anything brighter would be detrimental to our purpose, as our spirit friends are frightened by the harsh light of our world."

I thought of my mother and hoped that she would not be frightened by being called forth. Perhaps this had been a selfish idea. But I could not stop now.

"Lorna will try to reach each of your loved ones in turn. Contact can sometimes take a good long while to be achieved. Sometimes it's not possible at all. I ask that each of you concentrate, and focus your thoughts on the spirit world, even when it is not your turn. The combined energy of all in the room can help the spirits to 'cross over', so to speak. If you all help each other, it's better for everyone."

We all nodded to each other fervently; all for one and one for all, as the musketeers said.

"Do not be frightened by anything you see or hear," Mr. Pith continued. "The spirits are rarely angry, and Lorna is particularly skilled at calming them down if they are. And it's even more unusual for a spirit to take a form corporeal enough to do damage to anyone or anything in the physical realm."

"But not impossible?" Mr. Wickham asked, incredulously.

"I have seen it," Mr. Pith admitted. "I probably shouldn't even mention it, it's that rare. But in good conscience I feel everyone should know that it is a possibility, though a faint one."

I felt a bit of apprehension at that. I knew my mother would not become angry or violent, but had no idea who the others might be there to contact. They all seemed to be people of good breeding, but still, one never knows these days.

"There will probably be physical manifestations of the spirits," Mr. Pith said. "They might cause the table to shake, for instance. Or you might feel a breeze. If we're lucky, we may get some ectoplasm to prove they were really here."

"Ectoplasm?" Miss Haverford asked.

"Yes. It's a substance the spirits can leave behind. Kind of slimy or jellylike. Fascinating stuff. It's been studied by the leading researchers in England, and they've determined that it's quite harmless."

At that point, a pretty flaxen-haired girl came into the room. "Lorna is ready to begin now, Mr. Pith," she said quietly.

He stood, and we all followed suit. Looking around at us, he said,

"We shall now enter the parlour. Remember what I said: quickly but quietly."

The girl held the door as we all followed Mr. Pith out of the sitting room and down the dimly lit hall towards a closed door. As we approached, the door swung open silently and seemingly of its own accord, which was quite unnerving. At the threshold, Mr. Pith stood aside and ushered me in. "Down the table to the seat on Lorna's left, please, Mrs. Powell," he reminded me quietly.

It was not a large room, and much of the space was taken up by an oblong table with six chairs around it. A dark wood cabinet stood in the corner, though I could barely make it out as the curtains were shut tight and the room was lit only by three candles spaced along the table, which was draped in a scarlet cloth.

At the end of the table sat Lorna, our medium. I was taken aback by her youth – she couldn't have been more than sixteen years old! Her ginger hair hung in wild curls, framing a pale face. Her eyes remained closed, her face impassive, while we all moved to our places. She made no sign that she was even aware of our presence as I hastened to my assigned seat, which was cushioned in faded red velvet.

When the last of us had entered the room, I heard the soft snick of the door closing and glanced up to see that the young woman who had ushered us in had pushed it shut. The room grew even darker without the dim light of the hall, and I could barely make out the young woman taking up a post on one side of the door while Mr. Pith stood on the other, his hands folded in front of him.

Once we were all seated and the last creaking and scraping of chairs died away, Lorna opened her eyes and gazed around the table. Her glance settled upon my companion. "'Tis a pleasure to see you again, Mrs. Benchley," she said, her voice soft and girlish.

"Thank you, Lorna," she replied. "Though you needn't trouble yourself with me today. I'm just here in support of my friend, Mrs. Powell." She patted my hand.

"How kind," Lorna murmured. "Nevertheless, your husband says to tell you he hopes your ankle is feeling better soon, and to be sure to put it up as soon as you get home."

"Oh my," Mrs. Benchley said, her eyes wide. She had told me on our way over that she had twisted her ankle just the day before while coming down the stairs. "Tell him I certainly will."

Lorna's face took on a dreamy expression. "No need," she said. "He heard and sends you his love."

At that moment, Mrs. Benchley let out a soft cry and her hand flew to her face. "I just felt something!"

Lorna smiled again, a twinkle in her eye. "I believe he just gave you a wee kiss, Mrs. Benchley. The spirits can sometimes be a bit bold in showing their affections, even in front of strangers."

Mrs. Benchley blushed, and the others smiled and exchanged excited glances. Lorna turned her attention to the older couple.

"You are the Wickhams, I believe. Mr. Pith tells me you are hoping to contact your son."

They nodded eagerly, and Mr. Wickham spoke. "Alistair. He was a lieutenant in the army, stationed in India. He died of malaria."

"You have my sympathies," Lorna murmured. "Let us see if we can reach Alistair. If we could all join hands."

She laid her hands on the table and I eagerly grasped one while Mr. Wickham hesitantly took the other. On my left, Mrs. Benchley squeezed my hand, and I looked around to see that the circle was unbroken all around the table.

Lorna closed her eyes again. "I seek the spirit of Alistair Wickham," she said. I don't know what I expected, but her voice was as soft and conversational as if she were simply talking to those of us at the table. "Lieutenant Alistair Wickham," she reiterated, then after a pause, said, "No, Cyrus, your parents aren't here today and I don't have time to chat with you, I'm afraid. Lieutenant Wickham, if you're there, your parents—"

The table jumped! Miss Haverford let out a short scream, and Mrs. Wickham cried, "Alistair!" I was afraid the candles would tip over, but the holders were heavy and probably selected especially for their stability, so they stayed upright.

"It's not Alistair, I'm afraid, Mrs. Wickham," Lorna murmured. "Cyrus! I told you your parents aren't here today. I'm sorry, but please behave yourself!"

The table rattled again briefly, but then settled down.

"Thank you, Cyrus," Lorna continued. "Lieutenant Wickham, can you hear me? If you're there, please give me a sign." She sat silently for a moment, swaying slightly, her brow furrowed. "I'm hearing music. I can't quite make out the tune." She hummed a low note.

"Is it 'There Is a Tavern in the Town'?" Mrs. Wickham asked. "That was always his favourite."

"Perhaps. I don't know that song, I'm afraid," Lorna said.

But then, faintly, a tune began to play. It sounded like a violin, coming from far away, like one might hear the distant notes of an orchestra before one gets to the hall where they are playing. As we all listened, astonished, Mr. Wickham started humming, then sang, "Drinks his wine 'mid laughter free, and never, never thinks of me."

"It's him!" whispered Mrs. Wickham.

"Hello, Lieutenant," Lorna said, her eyes still closed and a faint smile upon her lips. The music faded away. "Your parents are delighted to hear from you, I think."

"Yes, Alistair!" Mrs. Wickham cried. "Oh, we've missed you so!"

Lorna listened for a moment, then said, "He has missed you as well. He says he is sorry to have caused you grief."

"Oh, no! He mustn't blame himself!" said Mr. Wickham. "We... well, we just wish he had not died so far from home."

"Yes," Lorna said. "He is grieved by that himself. The fever... what's that, Lieutenant? The fever brought him delusions. He thought for a while that he was at home, with his mother tending to him. Ah, how sad he was when he realised where he really was."

Mrs. Wickham let out a little sob.

"Don't cry, Mother!" Lorna said, and astonishingly her voice had deepened and lost its girlish tones. "I am beyond all pain now. And we shall be together again someday."

Mr. Wickham was blinking back tears. I did not even realise I was weeping as well until a tear slid down my cheek.

The Wickhams and their son exchanged a few more words, but I shan't intrude upon their privacy further by sharing them. After a bit, Lorna drew in a sharp breath and her head lolled forward for a moment. When she spoke again, her voice had returned to normal. "Ah, yes, rest now, Lieutenant." She inhaled deeply and opened her eyes. "He is gone. Contact is wearying to the spirits, and they cannot maintain it for long. But he wants you to know that speaking to you gave him peace, and you are welcome to contact him again at any time."

The Wickhams gazed at each other a moment, silently sharing their mingled grief and joy, but they did not break the circle of joined hands around the table.

Then Lorna turned to me.

"Mrs. Powell," she said. "'Tis your mother you wish to speak to, is that correct?"

I was suddenly nervous. "Perhaps Miss Haverford should go next," I said in a rush.

"Oh, I'm not here to contact anyone," she said. "I just wanted to see what it was like. And I'm so glad I came!" She gaped at Lorna, awestruck.

"Your mother's name?" Lorna asked kindly.

"Sybil Potts," I said quietly.

Lorna closed her eyes again. "I seek the spirit of Sybil Potts." Mrs. Benchley squeezed my hand reassuringly. "Mrs. Potts, can you hear me?"

The table rattled again. "Not now, Cyrus!" I muttered. It stopped.

"Mrs. Potts. Sybil Potts," Lorna continued. "Is that you, Mrs. Potts? Don't be shy."

"Mother!" I cried. "Please talk to me! I'm sorry I didn't some sooner! Before you…before you died."

"Oh, I don't think she's angry with you, Mrs. Powell," Lorna said. "Just a bit nervous. Afraid this is some kind of devilry, perhaps. That happens sometimes."

Well, Mother was never that religious, truth be told, but perhaps death gave her a new perspective.

I called out to her again. "Oh no, Mother! It's all right! If Lieutenant Wickham is still about, ask him – he and his parents just had such a nice talk."

Lorna smiled faintly. "She is talking to someone, but I can't hear…. Oh! Hello, Mrs. Potts."

I almost clapped my hands in relief, but that would have broken the circle.

"Mother! Oh, I've so longed to speak to you! I miss you every day, and will never forgive myself for not rushing straight to your bedside when you fell ill."

When Lorna spoke again, it was in Mother's Kentish accent. "Please don't blame yourself, my dear. It happened much more quickly than anyone could have expected."

"Yes, but I did not have time to say goodbye! To tell you one more time how dear you are to me!"

"Ah, not half as dear as you are to me, darling daughter," Lorna said.

"Were you…was there much pain?" I asked.

"Barely any," she reassured me. I don't think this was true, but Mother never liked to complain. "I hardly knew what was happening. Now, Agatha, is Walter there with you?"

"No, Mother. I…well, I did not tell him I was coming here."

"Good, good. And tell me, did you find the money?"

I was taken aback, as you can imagine. Mother had never really spoken to me about money before.

"What money?" I asked.

"I set a little by for you. So you have a bit of your own, you know. Didn't I tell you?"

I shook my head, confused. "No, Mother, you didn't."

"Well, a woman needs something of her own, doesn't she? I hid it for you. Under the mattress, I think. Or it might be in the sugar tin, or a hatbox."

"You don't remember?" I asked.

"Well, I moved it around from time to time, just in case."

"In case of what?"

"Oh, I don't know. It just seemed prudent at the time. I'm having difficulty remembering, now, some things from my earthly existence."

"But you're sure you hid some money?"

"Yes, yes." But Lorna's voice was growing fainter.

"Mother!" I called. "Please hang on."

It was no use. Lorna's head lolled forward, and when she raised it she was Lorna again. "I'm sorry, Mrs. Powell. She ran out of steam, so to speak. It's even more of a strain for the older folks." She withdrew her hands from the circle and we all followed suit.

I sat there, stunned. "She never said a word to me about money," I said, more to myself than to anyone else.

"Have you disposed of her home and belongings?" Mr. Wickham asked. His wife shushed him, scandalised.

"Alfred! That's personal!"

"Apologies, madam," he said.

"I haven't, actually," I said. "Walter is keen to put the house on the market, but I have not yet had the heart to go through her things."

"Well, for heaven's sake, my dear, do poke around for that money," Mrs. Benchley said. "After all, she clearly wanted you to have it."

I nodded absently. I wondered why she didn't just leave me a sum in her will, though of course I immediately realised that any bequest would belong as much – if not more – to Walter than to me. Why was she so keen that I have something of my own? Did she not trust Walter to look after my best interests?

It's all so puzzling, Sarah! I have started going through Mother's things and, though I've thoroughly searched the three places she suggested, nothing has turned up. Obviously, she had more hiding places than she told me about. I shall persist.

Do write soon, my friend.

Affectionately,

Agatha

LETTER FROM LADY WILDE TO RICHARD BURTON, 2ND OF FEBRUARY 1884

Dear Richard,

I do hope this finds you well. I have just received some terrible news and I have no one else in whom I can confide. It is of a supernatural nature, you see, and so few of my friends understand such things the way that you do.

For once it is not Oscar who causes me worry, but Willie. He came to me earlier today to confess all, and it has sent me into such a state of concern I felt I needed to put it all down on paper at once.

For the past few months, he has been living on his own in a very dilapidated house in an unsavoury part of town. I have implored him to move in with me, as I have plenty of room in my apartment, but he will not hear of it. I worry about him living in such a dangerous neighbourhood and I fear he falls into drink most days.

Oscar pays his rent and tells me it is good for Willie to be on his own at this time in his life. However, I cannot help think that had I kept an eye on Willie, none of what I am about to relate would have ever happened.

He came by for tea today. He had gin on his breath, so I was especially happy to get some tea and food in him.

He waited until the housemaid was out of the room before telling me.

"Mother, I'm afraid I have some rather bad news."

I braced myself, because the last time he had bad news it was that he would not become a barrister and instead was going to be a journalist.

This was worse than being a journalist, but not by much.

"I suppose Oscar filled you in on all the details about the Black Bishop, with himself the hero of the tale."

"He has," I said. I know they called you in to help in the aftermath of that dreadful incident, Richard, so I shan't go into the details here.

"Well, I tried to steer clear of that complete fiasco," Willie continued. "But I found myself briefly in the Bishop's employ, inadvertently, of course. Had I known that Lord Wotton was in league with an evil madman bent on taking over the British Empire, I might not have taken the position as his secretary."

"Yes, Oscar mentioned you had been drawn into the Bishop's circle."

"What he probably didn't mention...." He paused. "Do you remember when we all went down to Greystones to investigate that werewolf?"

I did, of course, and I trust you do too, Richard.

"Well, Lord Wotton and the Black Bishop procured a werewolf hoping to use it to open something, I forget what exactly."

"The gates of hell," I said. "Oscar filled me in on that as well."

"Yes, that is it. Well, it did not work. I, being expendable, was conscripted to help wrangle the beast, and the damn thing bit me. Bad luck that."

He pulled a flask of gin out of his pocket and added a splash to his teacup with a shaky hand.

"Are you telling me...." I gasped at the thought. "You have this affliction now?"

He nodded. "It's not the most horrible thing, really. I only need to deal with it on full moons."

I was stunned.

"Oscar rented me a house with a cellar and I am careful to chain myself up, when I can remember to look at the calendar. So, I haven't hurt anyone as yet."

He then burst into tears, and I rushed over to comfort him.

"Oh, Mother, what have I done with my worthless life?" He sobbed as I held him close to my bosom.

"Thank you for telling me. I can help you. The Roma folk are cursed with these creatures, and they have remedies that some think can cure the curse."

He sniffed loudly, but his sobbing had ceased.

"And let's not forget science," I said. "They are coming out with new cures for all sorts of ailments."

"They can't cure measles, I don't think they have a grasp on lycanthropy." He laughed and regained his composure. I dried his tears with a handkerchief like I did when he was a boy and Oscar had said something mean to him, which was often.

"In the meantime, we will continue to chain you up. What is it like? The transformation, I mean."

"It is terribly painful, from what I can remember. I black out during so have never seen it through. I make sure I am well and truly drunk before then, and I think that helps. Although the hangovers are atrocious."

I then remembered a book I had on the subject that said there were people who had learned to control when they changed. We had seen as much with Captain Abramoff in Greystones. He could change and change back at will, as I reminded Willie.

"That is true," he said, now with some hope in his voice.

"Yes, and if he could, you can as well. Maybe you could even hold the wolf back entirely, even during a full moon."

I sent him home with that book and went to my folklore library to research the matter further. I have found little in my books about the subject, but I am hopeful I can learn more information from fellow scholars. If you have learned anything new in the field recently, please do share it with me at your earliest convenience.

Oh, why must my children suffer so, and trouble their poor mother? I feel I must have failed as a parent somehow, with both of my children being afflicted by the supernatural. Did my dabbling in the occult and women's suffrage bring this on them somehow?

But there is nothing for it now but to press on. I shall continue to look for a cure for my troubled boy.

Please give my best to Isabel and write back when you have a moment. It is in dark times such as these that we need our friends by our sides, even if it is only through the post.

Sincerely,

Speranza

FROM THE DIARY OF LORNA BOW, 10TH OF FEBRUARY 1884

This is my first diary entry. I have wanted to start one for a long while, to set my thoughts and the happenings of my life down on paper. I would write them in a letter if I had anyone to send it to. And so I asked my uncle if I might have a diary, but he thinks such things to be a waste of time, ink and paper.

I had put the thought out of my mind until this blank diary fell right into my hands. It must have been divine intervention, which I never believed in before today.

I was working at Speaker's Corner in Hyde Park, passing out handbills advertising the séance parlour as I do most Sundays. I do not mind doing this since it gets me out of the house and away from my uncle.

It was cold, but a sunny day, and a crowd gathered to listen to a lady on a soapbox ramble on about women's clothes being too tight and impractical. Lots of ladies were there that day. They are always ripe for the picking. We get many gentlemen in the parlour during the week, but Uncle Leonard wants to bring in the wealthy society women he says really control the purse strings.

I stopped and listened to the lady speaker. I had never heard a woman yell and shout like she was doing. She was dressed fancy in a butter-yellow dress with puffed sleeves, and green ribbons trimming the bodice. True to her speech, it fit looser than most of the dresses the rich ladies who come to the parlour wear, and I don't think she was wearing a corset either. Maybe that's what gave her the energy to go on so.

She was very pretty, though her brown hair had come undone by the wind. She was getting much applause from the women and boos and jeers from the men, but she shouted them down.

"We know who wears the trousers in *your* family," one man yelled. "You try'n to be the man of the house?"

"No, but if I were, I would be twice the man that you are!"

I cheered her on for that one, then as I was standing nearby, I sidled over to the man and slipped one of my handbills into his pocket. I hope he shows up someday. It will be a pleasure to take some of his money, maybe tell him something nasty that will put the fear of God into him.

After the speech I made it a point to find the woman in the crowd and give her a handbill as well, hoping she would come to one of my 'communications with the dead'. I'll make sure we let her off easy, though, and send her home with a nice message from her dead grandmother or whoever, something that will make her smile when she thinks about it later.

She read the paper immediately and asked me many questions about it. I told her I have the gift and can talk with spirits and communicate with her loved ones. All for free, of course, as I cannot use my powers to line my pockets. Mr. Pith likes to reel them in with free séances, then hope for their patronage later. They always offer, we never ask. The men during the week we charge, but they are mostly there in hopes of groping one of the 'spirits,' and not to talk to loved ones. Loved ones are how you reel in the big fish.

She asked if we could talk some more. I said I would like that, and she took me to a café outside the park and bought me an orange squeeze. She introduced herself as Constance Lloyd.

I told her I liked what she was wearing, since I'm pretty sure that's what she wanted to hear.

"Thank you," she said. "Practical is no excuse for unfashionable, as my fiancé would say."

I mentioned how much more comfortable her clothes looked than what women usually wear, and she agreed they were. "And even more important," she said, "is how much easier it is to move about when one is not restricted by tight sleeves, corsets, or heavy, wide skirts. Do you know how many women get their dresses caught in factory machinery?"

I told her I didn't.

"Over one hundred every year, and most of the time this results in injury or death. That doesn't happen to men wearing trousers. Even in the home, dangers abound. It is not uncommon for a woman's clothing to catch on fire when she stands too near a fireplace. That very thing happened to my fiancé's sisters – one caught ablaze, and when the other rushed to her aid, she also caught on fire. They both died."

I gasped and told her how tragic this was. I even meant it, though I'll confess that a part of my brain stored that information away to use if she ever brings her fiancé to the parlour.

She asked me if I could read and write, and I told her I could. Then we talked about books. I told her I am partial to Jane Austen and hope to be a writer of novels myself someday. She told me she thought that a very fine ambition.

When I'd finished my orange squeeze, she asked me to come with her to the stationery shop next door where she bought some writing supplies for herself and presented me with a new pen and inkwell and this diary.

It is bound in brown leather and very thick for holding many ideas, and has a lock and key to keep out prying eyes. It is probably the nicest thing anyone has ever given me, and I told her so. Her blue-green eyes twinkled, and she said, "Perhaps someday you will be a famous novelist, maybe even with an idea you first write down in this book. Then I shall be able to say I had some tiny role in your success. So you see, I am really being quite selfish."

She had to run then to meet her fiancé but said she would try to come for a reading when she has the chance.

So, here I am writing down my first thoughts and even in my first entry had an interesting story to relate. I assure you that many interesting things happen to me. Most of them are not good, but I make the best of them.

I suppose now I should tell a bit about myself. My name is Lorna Bow, and I am sixteen. I am an orphan and for the first ten years of my life I lived at Mrs. Roberts' boarding school. I was told that at the age of three I was dropped off by my mother, who said she would return for me.

My mother paid my tuition for the first five years in advance. In all that time, she never visited me and I received not so much as a letter from her. When the money ran out, they assumed she had died or simply abandoned me. Mrs. Roberts kindly let me stay on, and I paid my way by cleaning house.

I was allowed to attend classes and learned to read and write. The other girls tormented me for being poor and not having parents. Despite that, I loved living there and spent my free time reading books from the large library.

My second tragedy in life came when I was ten, and Mrs. Roberts died. After that, I found myself in an orphanage. It was a horrible place where we had no teaching and very few meals. We took in mending and blackened boots to earn our keep, and did little else.

I was certain that was to be my life, when one day Mr. Pith showed up saying he was my uncle come to take me to live with him.

I am not sure if he really is my uncle. He doesn't show me any love an uncle would show a niece, and won't tell me anything about my parents, saying only, "They are dead, so get your head out of the past and put your eyes to the future." And he has picked up many girls from orphanages, saying he was family, but he really puts them to work. Still, in the privacy of the parlour, I am the only one he claims as a niece, and he does not touch me like he does the other girls he 'rescued' over the years, so maybe that is out of genuine family obligation. However, he will hit and yell at me when I cross him, which I seldom do.

The other girls are like sisters to me. There is Molly, who is fourteen, Gwen is twelve and little Nell is ten. As bad as it can be here sometimes, at least I have them.

We do fine, I guess. We have clothes to wear and three meals a day, which is more than I had at the orphanage.

There have been others, but most girls run off when they get old enough, so now I am the oldest of the lot. Being the eldest girl means I get to sit at the table and run the séances. The other girls do the cooking and housework and are the ghosts I call out of the cabinet to make the noises and fling the ectoplasm. Ectoplasm is the stuff that proves the ghost was manifested, and it very much impresses the sceptics. It really is a mixture of gelatine, honey and lemon curd. I'm glad it tastes good because sometimes I get some in my mouth as little Nell's aim is not that good.

For two shillings gentlemen get a shot of gin and are allowed to feel the spirits to prove they are real. Sometimes they take it too far and have to be dealt with as we are a respectable establishment, or at least not as disreputable as they hope we are.

Our big money comes when we can rope in a wealthy widow who wants to fund our 'research into the other side'. We provide a service, Mr. Pith says. We make these old bats happy and we earn our keep. It is honest work, if you think about it. Of course, Mr. Pith is not against a little pickpocketing in the dark or blackmail should we learn something especially scandalous during our readings.

That is all I have the finger strength to write today. I will hide you, dear diary, under the floorboards in the WC until more interesting things happen to me.

FROM THE JOURNAL OF BRAM STOKER, 18TH OF FEBRUARY 1884

6:15 p.m.

Opening night for our new production is this Friday, and I am happy to write the rehearsals have gone rather well. Once again we are doing the Scottish play; perhaps we have gone once too often back to that well, but Henry seems to have a particular affinity for the play and the role. And there is no denying that we have always had much success with it. Perhaps it is the witches or the ghost, but there is something in Macbeth's tragic lust for power that the public responds to on these dark winter nights.

My own nights of late are troubled by nightmares. I dream often of Dr. Hesselius, our comrade who was murdered by the Black Bishop's vampire thugs.

He comes to me with a warning, but I cannot understand what he is saying because it is in Dutch. When I urge him to tell me in English, it is garbled and I still cannot make out the words. I awaken with a start from the dream and then have a terrible time getting back to sleep.

Perhaps I still feel guilt about his death. Had he not come to help us with the vampire threat, he would be alive today. However, without his help we might all be under their control.

Speaking of being under the control of a vampire, Henry has been in a foul mood all month, snapping at the cast and crew for the tiniest of infractions. It is not good for morale and I said as much to him this afternoon in his office.

He agreed he has been on edge and said he will try to manage his outbursts better in the future. He confided in me that he has been having sleepless nights – or rather, days – himself.

"It is becoming increasingly difficult to hold back my vampire nature," he said. His voice was steady, but I saw the apprehension in his eyes. "Last night I found myself out on the street walking towards a woman. I do not remember leaving the theatre or walking the few blocks I had."

This was indeed troubling.

"It was all I could do to force myself back to the theatre. It was not hunger, for I had fed the night before."

Henry now has an ample supply of stored blood procured from Dr. Seward.

"There are nights I do not remember," he said. "What if I have been feeding without knowing it?"

"I do not think that is likely," I assured him. "Surely we would hear about victims in the newspapers or from the White Worms. They monitor such things, and they know where to find you."

"True," he said. His manner eased somewhat and a small smile even returned to his face. "Still, if you wouldn't mind keeping an eye on me when you can...."

I assured him I would, as would Florence, Oscar and Ellen – all his friends who know his secret.

He paused as if the conversation were over, then said, "Oddly, I have had dreams during my daytime sleep. I can't remember the last time I had a dream. Maybe not since becoming a vampire."

I told him of my troubling dreams and asked about his.

"Richard Wilkins calls out to me from beyond. He isn't the horrible Black Bishop he was to become, but the Richard I knew as my friend. He is kind and jovial and tells me, with much joy and passion, that the afterlife is real. Then he suddenly turns monstrous, all fangs, claws and devil horns, and shouts at me that I should cleanse my soul before it is too late."

"That sounds like the Reverend Wilkins I came to know," I said.

"Why these dreams now, after so many years?" He paused, deep in thought. "And at the very time I feel the vampire in me trying to consume me fully."

I told him it was probably just the stress of the new production; however, I too was wondering if it was a portent from the dream world. I do not believe in such things, but until a few years ago I never believed in vampires either, and here I was conversing with one.

More to think about to fuel my restless nights.

REPORT FROM DR. WESLEY PRYCE TO THE PHYSICAL SOCIETY

20 February 1884

My colleagues:

I am happy to report we have shut down another fraudulent séance parlour that tarnishes the good name of spiritualism.

I exposed the establishment run by Leonard Pith today, with the help of Scotland Yard. This parlour has been a thorn in our side, because they were such skilled charlatans. I must admit, they even fooled one of our most esteemed Physical Society colleagues who attended a séance there last spring. They managed to produce ectoplasm with no visible trickery, and we had trouble identifying its make-up in the laboratory.

However, a girl working there became a police informant and revealed their fraudulence. Pith has been bilking people out of their hard-earned money for several years now. She has also accused him of other crimes, including molesting young girls, pickpocketing and running gambling dens. After hearing her story, the police were quite keen to catch him in the act and they contacted us to help prove that Pith's séances are mere trickery.

Extraordinarily, the police force has recently begun employing women as matrons to guard female prisoners, and we recruited one of them to help with the investigation. She and I attended a séance this morning, posing as a married couple grieving the loss of a child.

The Pith ensemble put on quite a show, I must say. After we'd taken our places at the séance table, they drew thick velvet curtains, plunging us into total darkness. One of Pith's girls struck a match, lighting a single candle, which she placed at the centre of the table. The 'spiritualist' – a young woman no more than sixteen years of age – entered and took her place at the table.

She instructed us to each hold one of her hands and complete the circle. She asked why we had come and Mrs. Burwell, the matron, told her we wished to contact our five-year-old daughter who had died of cholera.

The girl closed her eyes and called out for Margaret, the name we had given her for our deceased daughter.

Her voice changed to that of a little girl.

"Mother! Is that you?"

It was a very eerie-sounding voice, and for a moment it almost fooled me. It was very much like the channelling I have witnessed from genuine mediums.

"It's me, Mother, Peggy."

It was then I noticed Mrs. Burwell's face. She seemed quite taken aback by the performance. Her eyes were wide and her mouth agape.

A sudden gust of air blew the candle out.

We were completely in the dark. Then a soft green glow lit the medium's face. I could not tell where the light source was, even knowing it was a trick of some sort. The green light lit our faces as well, and perhaps that stopped me from seeing the source, like how it is difficult to see stage lights while you are in the spotlight. It was well-orchestrated deception indeed.

The medium seemed surprised as well. Her eyes went back into her head so all I could see were the whites. "I miss you and Daddy so very much." She turned and looked at me. "You aren't my daddy! Where's Daddy, Mummy?"

She looked at Mrs. Burwell.

"Wait. You aren't Mummy, Lizzy. Where's Mummy? Why are you so old?"

Then a small child appeared out of the darkness, wrapped in lace and muslin to give her a ghostlike appearance. She too was softly lit with green light, giving her a most ghostly presence.

The medium continued to provide the voice as the girl flitted around the room.

"I am so happy to see you, Lizzy. How is Kitty? Does she miss me?"

Mrs. Burwell just stared at the medium in stunned silence and then whispered to herself, "How does she know that name?"

It was here I jumped to my feet, ran to the curtains and yanked them open, exposing all to the sunlight.

Mrs. Burwell grabbed the little girl as she tried to disappear back into the spirit cabinet from which she had come.

Two uniformed police officers burst into the room. The medium tried to make a run for it, but they apprehended her.

As we left the establishment with the medium, the little ghost and two other girls in tow (Mr. Pith had escaped, I am told), Mrs. Burwell stopped me.

"My name is Elizabeth, and my family *did* call me Lizzy."

"Easy enough for them to guess a nickname," I pointed out. "They knew your first name."

"But I had a sister who died young named Margaret. We called her Peggy."

Again, a common enough nickname for the first name we had selected for our fictional child.

"Yes, but how did she know about Kitty? Peggy's pet cat? And why did she say I wasn't Margaret's mother and looked older? I was thirteen when Peggy died."

I had no explanation, except that maybe someone had tipped them off about a police officer and they'd had time to do a bit of research on her.

Still, I wonder if maybe our little fraudster might have some talent that even she is unaware of.

POLICE REPORT FROM INSPECTOR FREDERICK ABBERLINE

26 February 1884
09:00 a.m.
Interrogation of Molly Gold
– Subject –
Investigation of Leonard Pith's Séance Parlour

On the 20th of February 1884, undercover detectives broke up an illegal séance operation. We conducted our investigation on the tip of an informant, Molly Gold, age fifteen, and with the co-operation of the Physical Society.

The séance parlour's proprietor, Leonard Pith, evaded capture, but we took into custody three girls ages ten to sixteen. The two youngest girls were turned over to an orphanage and the older girl, Lorna Bow, was taken into custody. I had intended to also take Molly to the orphanage, but she was not there and I was unable to locate her.

Today I went to Lorna's cell to find she wasn't there. I asked the sergeant in charge where she had gone and he was surprised to find she was missing.

No one could tell me anything about why, or how she came to be released.

I at once suspected Pith had somehow bribed one of my officers to release her and have set into motion an internal investigation on that matter.

In his youth, Pith had multiple arrests for pickpocketing and assault, but has stayed out of trouble for the last ten years. Then Molly Gold came to us to report Pith's fraudulent séances, as well as his abusive behaviour towards the girls he had working for him, including Molly herself. She returned to the parlour to help us get more information on

Pith and his operation, and we made arrangements to meet regularly when she went out to distribute flyers for the séance business. After finding Lorna missing today, I redoubled my search for Molly and found her in her usual spot, though she wasn't handing out flyers. She was shivering and begging passers-by for a few pence. I bought her a sandwich and a bowl of soup, then brought her in again for questioning. This is her statement.

"I done what you told me," she said. "I didn't think Lorna and the girls would get pinched. I thought we'd get to keep living in the house with Lorna in charge. She's his real niece, after all, so with Pith gone the house would belong to her. You said you would take him away."

I told her we intended to do that as soon as we find him.

"Well, I can tell you exactly where he is: at the house. And if he finds out I'm the one who squealed on him he will kill me! He was already looking at me all shifty since I wasn't pinched with the other girls. I told him I slipped through the spirit cupboard and out the back when the coppers broke up the séance."

I asked her what Pith has been up to since the police raid on the twentieth.

"Hiding, mostly. The woodshed has a secret room in the back behind a fake stack of wood. That's where he hides should the police be looking for him. He didn't know what to do with all his girls being gone. No one is going to go to a séance to feel *him* up. To make things worse for him, yesterday this angry lady came to the parlour and had a big row with him."

"Angry lady?"

"I think she might be Lorna's mum. She was beside herself that Lorna was in jail."

I asked her if she could describe the woman and if she had ever seen her before.

"She was pretty, with red hair like Lorna's. I never slapped eyes on her before and Lorna'd told me she was an orphan like the rest of us, but this woman was the spitting image of Lorna."

I asked her if she could recall what the woman and Pith had talked about.

"Mr. Pith was terrified of this woman. I never seen him back down to a woman before, but he was cowering like a mouse in front of a cat.

She told me to leave the room, and I did, but I stayed within earshot in the back room.

"Mr. Pith kept saying, 'I'm sorry, I'll get her out of jail,' and 'This isn't me fault.' Then, this is the amazing part, I heard her start slapping him! He was crying and begging. It brought joy to my heart it did to hear Mr. Pith in that state. He had done the same to me too many times to count, and here was a woman giving him a good thrashing.

"He said, 'I did what you told me, I raised her and taught her to do séances the best I could.'

"'You were supposed to get her out of the school when the money ran out,' she said. 'Not let her rot in an orphanage!'

"She then must have heard me because she looked right at the spirit box.

"'I know you are still there, child, come out here.'

"I stepped out from behind the curtains and saw he was on his knees and she had her hand around his throat. I could not believe me eyes. She asked me, 'Has this man ever hurt you?'

"I didn't know what to say. I didn't want to make Mr. Pith angry, but I didn't want to make her angry neither. So, I told her the truth.

"'I never did anything to Lorna!' he cried. 'I never touched her – I wouldn't!'

"She turned to me and asked me to take her to where Lorna was, and I did. Then I run off. That's the last I have seen of her, or Mr. Pith. I haven't been back to the parlour. He must be fit to be tied after what she done to him, and I know he'd just take it out on me."

She asked if she could see Lorna, and I told her that Lorna is no longer here. Then I gave her a little more money and sent her on her way.

Later that day, I returned to the séance parlour to find the woman described by Molly is now in charge. Her name is Endora Bow, and Lorna Bow was with her. Mrs. Bow informed me she was the landlady of the property and had fired Mr. Pith. She did not know his current whereabouts.

She showed me a letter signed by the commissioner pardoning Lorna in the séance matter.

Molly Gold had returned to the parlour, but we pretended not to know each other.

After verifying the letter's authenticity, I am now marking this case closed. The police have better things to do than chase down petty criminals such as Pith.

FROM THE DIARY OF LORNA BOW, 26TH OF FEBRUARY 1884

I have been through many hard times in my life, and I seldom give in to despair; however, I was sitting in a jail cell and my friends had been taken to an orphanage. All seemed lost, as I knew Mr. Pith would not come to my aid. I realised that jail was going to be my life now, and that made me sadder than I have ever been.

I sat there for days, and there was never a moment when it was quiet. I could always hear the noises of people talking and moving about in the main room down the hall. Drunks yelling, men and women screaming as coppers dragged them down the hall and slammed them into their cells.

My last day in jail, there were two other women in my cell, both passed out drunk. They smelled bad, even overpowering the stink of the overflowing chamber pots.

Then, in an instant, the world fell silent, eerily quiet as if someone had shut it off. I put an ear between the bars and strained to hear anything.

From the silence, I heard footsteps and jingling keys coming down the hall.

And there she was, a beautiful, tall, ginger-haired woman in a green silk dress. With her was the desk sergeant, who took out his keys and unlocked my cell door. His eyes were glassy, and he swayed as if he were drunk.

"Come, child," she said to me. I stepped out of the cell.

The sergeant just stood there staring off into space.

"Where are the other girls?" she asked me.

"They took them to an orphanage," I said. "I don't know which one."

"Where did the other girls go?" she asked the sergeant.

"St. George's Orphanage," he said in a strange voice, like he was talking in his sleep. "On Cabot Street."

"Let's get your friends and go home," she said. We went down the hall and through the main room where there were many coppers all sitting motionless at their desks, staring off into the distance with the same blank faces as the sergeant.

I just stood there with my mouth open, dumbfounded by the spectacle of it. People frozen like they were in a painting.

We strolled through the police station like we owned the place and made our getaway into the daylight.

I have never felt so free.

I turned to the astonishing woman. "Who are you?" I asked.

"I am your mother, Lorna." As we walked down the police station steps, she turned and waved her hand and the station was once again alive with the sound of people talking and moving about. I knew even then I was witnessing magic, real magic!

As we made our way to Cabot Street, I noticed a streak of grey in her red hair I had not seen before. In the light of day I could see wrinkles around her green eyes, but she was still the most beautiful woman I had ever seen.

"You're my mother, my real mother?" I said. I didn't know whether to be overjoyed or angry at her for abandoning me.

It was as though she were reading my thoughts at that moment, for she said, "I did not want to leave you, but some wicked men were trying to kill us and I had to protect you." We continued down the bustling street as she explained.

"They banished me to another world, and I spent all this time trying to get back to you." We stopped at the steps of the orphanage. "I am here now and will never leave you again."

She held her hand up to the building and closed her eyes, reciting something in a language I did not recognise.

She opened her eyes and said, "Come, let's rescue your friends."

We entered the building and, just like the police station, it seemed like time was standing still. People were frozen in place. "Quickly, we must find them. I cannot hold this spell for too long."

We found Gwen and Nell in the kitchen. They too stood frozen, washing dishes and mopping the floor. "These two," I said.

With a wave of her hand, they came back to the world of the moving. Each jumped in fright at the sight of Mother and me. "Come," I said. "I'll explain later."

We rushed out of the building and into the daylight, and with a second wave of Mother's hand the orphanage sprang back to life.

I watched as she did this and was shocked to see another swath of grey blossom in her hair and more wrinkles deepen in her face. She saw me staring and said, "All magic has a price."

We all returned to the parlour. Mr. Pith was nowhere to be seen and neither was Molly. But a few hours later, she came creeping through the back door. I was so happy to see her and threw my arms around her, but she pulled away and wouldn't look me in the eye at first. Then she confessed she had squealed on Pith. I was mad for a minute, then I thought about how the other girls had it worse than me with Mr. Pith. Maybe they would have been better off in the orphanage instead of at his mercy. I told Molly it was all right.

"It doesn't matter anyway," I said. "Mr. Pith isn't in charge anymore." Then I introduced her to my mother, though they'd already met. Mother thanked her for helping her find me, then sent Molly to the pantry for some much-needed food. I sat down with my mother.

"What are you? How did you do that magic?" I asked her.

"I am a witch, as are you. The power of necromancy is strong in our family and I will show you how to unlock it."

So, dear diary, I started the day as a jailbird and I ended it as a witch! A fair trade, if you ask me.

REPORT TO WHITE WORM SOCIETY

Date: 27 February 1884
Subject: Debriefing of Arthur Conan Doyle regarding the South American Expedition
Attending: Errol Hammond, White Worm Director
Lesley Bainbridge, Secretary

Doyle: First, Mr. Director, let me offer my condolences on your tragic loss. Andrew died bravely, saving my life in a most terrifying situation.

Hammond: That is why we are here today, to get to the bottom of what happened. How did you come to be the sole survivor? How did my son come to his end in this fiasco?

Doyle: Sir, we had no idea of the horrors we would face going into the Realm, and I said as much when we set out. But we felt that if we could keep our wits about us, we could gain valuable information about the Realm and return safely to our own world. We took our best men; we planned meticulously. I felt certain that if we stuck to the plan, we would all make it home safely.

However, I was not in charge of the expedition; Professor Summerlee was, and, if I may be perfectly frank, he was often reckless in his pursuit of knowledge.

Hammond: I put Summerlee in charge. Are you questioning my decision?

Doyle: Summerlee was one of our finest scholars and a brave man. But he took foolish risks. While I am loath to speak ill of the dead, it is my duty to report honestly.

Hammond: Hmmph. Continue.

Doyle: As you know, the White Worm Society approved the expedition after your son, Andrew, discovered a map in an ancient text. He was able to translate the text and decipher the map that showed an entrance into the Realm in the mountains of Bolivia.

Andrew and I set out for South America early last year, arriving in Arica, Chile by steamship on the fifteenth of March. We made our way to La Paz, Bolivia by train, and arrived on the twentieth of March.

Professor Summerlee had much experience with expeditions and was an expert in the flora and fauna of jungle climates. It is for this reason, I am told, the Society put him in charge of our journey.

Also with us were the explorer Lord George Roxson and White Worm Secretary Jeffery Malone, who was to record the journey and help collect and catalogue samples.

An American, Theodore Roosevelt, was also to accompany us. However, he came down with malaria and was forced to stay behind in La Paz to recover.

We hired a guide, an American recommended by Roosevelt, named Rodney Maplewhite.

Mr. Maplewhite had extensive experience as an explorer in South America and told us he had discovered a plateau in Bolivia where he found an entrance into a lost world filled with prehistoric creatures. The animals he described to us could only be as-yet-undiscovered dinosaurs!

If all this wasn't amazing enough on its own, he told us he was unable to return through the opening from which he entered.

He said when he turned to go back there was a wall of solid rock where he had come through just moments before. He was forced to look for another way out.

He took out his journal and showed us drawings of animals he had made; he was a very talented artist. Summerlee recognised the species of the creatures straightaway as iguanodon, stegosaur and a pterodactyl.

"I ran into native people, who were short and hairy," Maplewhite said. "They looked more like apes than humans, but were intelligent and friendly. They showed me a way out." He flipped the pages in his journal to show a map. "A grove of trees by a pond, here by this volcano. Astoundingly, when I went into the cave, I came out in Ireland! I had a hell of a time getting back to Bolivia, I can tell you!"

Lord Roxson thought this all was preposterous.

"It could be true," I said, and I told him I myself had entered the Realm through a cave in France, became lost, then eventually found my way out through another portal that landed me in the centre of Cleveland, Ohio, in America, of all places.

On that journey, I had seen many strange creatures and ancient abandoned temples, but no people or dinosaurs. I only walked twenty miles at the most in the Realm, yet I came out thousands of miles away from where I'd started in our world.

"Both of you are having me on, surely," Roxson said.

Andrew confirmed that based upon his experience, space and time didn't work the same way in the Realm. And we all agreed that, if true, it might save us the long trip back through the jungle.

This new information invigorated Professor Summerlee; he was hoping to be the first to study live dinosaurs. But facing a world of such creatures filled the rest of us with dread. We had weapons, but nothing that could bring down a dinosaur.

However, Summerlee was keen to press on immediately and as he was expedition leader, that is what we did.

We hired José and Miguel, two strapping young Bolivian tin miners who had worked extensively in the region, to guide us and help portage our supplies, and we set off down the river which the natives call Rio Negro, or Black River, towards Maplewhite's plateau.

Just getting there was dangerous in itself. Native tribes attacked us twice, but luckily we were able to scare them off with our rifles. The insects were ferocious, and we were forced to cover our faces with thick layers of mud to protect ourselves.

It took us nearly four weeks to reach the base of the plateau. Our supplies ran low, despite José and Miguel's excellent hunting and fishing skills. Our morale was running low as well, as we started to think that Maplewhite might be a madman leading us to our doom.

But finally, there it was in front of us. The top of the plateau was shrouded in mist. Our journey was far from over as we still had to make our way to the top. On his previous expedition, Maplewhite had followed a small riverbed that zigzagged up to the top, and we set out on this same route. This took us nearly two days.

Halfway up we found refuge in a cave where we slept for the night. In the morning we found that José and Miguel had left us, taking what remained of our food with them back down the mountain. I could not blame them, for we all had thought about turning back. The path was getting narrower and more treacherous as we went. The tiny riverbed was quickly filling up with rain and we had to fight a current of water that was threatening to sweep us back down the mountain.

As we rounded a bend, Summerlee pointed to vultures circling something below. Through my binoculars I saw José's and Miguel's broken bodies near the streambed where we had spent the night. Somewhere in the dark they must have taken a wrong turn and tumbled to their deaths.

As the sun set on the second day, we made it to the top. We were rewarded with a pleasant grassland and a forest of papaya trees. We made camp for the night, dined on papaya and prepared ourselves to enter the Realm in the morning.

We went through the entrance at first dawn. It was a tight fit into the cave, but each of us squeezed in and made our way to the back, which was shrouded in mist.

Despite what we had been told, nothing prepared us for seeing it for ourselves. We emerged from the mist and into a totally new world. The first sensation was an oppressive humidity and heat, and mind you, we were stepping into it from an already warm and moist environment.

The air was thick, as if it contained extra oxygen. We set foot into a swamp that immediately soaked our boots. Maplewhite assured us it wasn't very deep and there was drier land just up ahead.

We stepped out of the swampy jungle onto a massive grassy plain. Each man who left the jungle ahead of me immediately stopped and stared, and when I emerged I saw why: before us was a herd of large, giraffe-like dinosaurs, munching on the tops of the trees that marked the edge of the grassland.

It was of a species Summerlee could not identify, but there was no mistaking it for anything but prehistoric.

A stegosaur was eating grass nearby, seemingly undisturbed by the larger dinosaurs surrounding it. It had a ridge of armour-like scales on its back and a spiked tail that looked quite dangerous.

Before any of us could say anything, Summerlee had run up to the stegosaur and touched it. It gave him a look, then went back to eating.

"The scales are fuzzy," he exclaimed. "Softer than one would suspect."

"Get away from that thing," Roxson yelled. "It could charge at any moment."

"Nonsense," Summerlee said. "It's as tame as a cow."

I was about to point out that even cows can charge when startled, but then noticed the tree eaters were becoming agitated.

"We should get back into the cover of the jungle," I said.

Summerlee ordered Secretary Malone to bring the camera and take a photo of him with the stegosaur.

Malone unpacked his box camera, which required some assembling.

Roxson, Andrew and Maplewhite took my advice and were retreating to the shadows of the jungle with me when suddenly the large plant eaters started to stampede! The ground shook as they moved in our direction, more quickly than I would have thought possible given their size.

Roxson, Andrew, Maplewhite and I were safely out of their path. Summerlee was taking refuge alongside the stegosaur, which the plant eaters were avoiding.

Unfortunately, poor Jeffery had nowhere to run as the dinosaurs trampled him. I last glimpsed him opening his mouth to scream, but could not hear him over the thundering hoofbeats.

As they passed, we could see what had frightened them so: a larger carnivorous dinosaur. It ran on two feet and had an enormous head and a full set of razor-sharp teeth that were snapping at the plant eaters. I would learn later that it was an allosaur, the small cousin to the tyrannosaurus.

As the plant eaters disappeared into the distance, the allosaur turned its attention on the stegosaur – right where Summerlee was hiding. The four of us rushed out of the jungle with our rifles firing, hoping to prevent the loss of another colleague.

Summerlee too had his rifle out. He was at a better angle to fire on the creature and managed to hit it in the neck several times.

But it was the stegosaur that was our best ally. It let out a terrific roar and swept its large, spiked tail into the allosaur's legs, bringing it down and allowing us to finish off the predator in a barrage of bullets.

The stegosaur wandered off, seemingly unfazed by the encounter.

With great sorrow, we located poor Jeffery's body. We buried him on the grassy plain of another world.

I told Summerlee that under the circumstances we should make a straight line to the exit on Maplewhite's map.

"Nonsense," he said. "As tragic as Malone's death is, we should not let it stop us from our primary mission, which is to increase our knowledge of the Realm."

At the very least, I told him, we should do our exploring while walking towards the exit, and he agreed to do so.

Maplewhite pointed towards a smoking volcano in the distance. "It's just to the right," he told us. "I'd say ten miles as the crow flies. But I would stick to the cover of the jungle and not cross the grassland."

Roxson disagreed, saying we could see things coming from a distance better on the plain, and there would be less chance of us catching some prehistoric disease from jungle insects.

It was then I recalled Henry Irving telling me that blood-sucking insects from the Realm are the source of vampirism. While this distinctly was not the part of the Realm described by Irving, it sent a shiver down my spine thinking of all the unknown contagions to which we could be exposing ourselves.

We all agreed to cross the plain and make a straight line towards the exit, collecting as many specimens as we could along the way.

And collect we did. Andrew and Summerlee gathered many strange plants, dinosaur scales, insects and a few small mammals and packed them in jars of formaldehyde.

The sun was setting, and we made camp under a grove of palm trees. We shot what looked like a large, prehistoric hare and had that for dinner.

The stars that night were remarkably bright. There was no moon, and the stars were in a pattern none of us recognised.

"We are on a whole new planet!" Summerlee exclaimed.

He proclaimed the new world Victoria, and we all toasted the monumental occasion with our remaining brandy.

The next morning we set out again, full of hope and wonder.

As we trekked towards the mountain range and its volcano, the landscape changed. We went through a fern forest that provided much-needed shade, and we stopped for a rest.

It was short-lived, however, as the full danger of this new world was upon us once again, this time in the form of tiny dinosaurs, about the size of small chickens.

At first, we paid them no mind, assuming them to be plant eaters. Summerlee approached one to get a closer look and learned too late that it was a carnivore. It lunged at him, biting his calf and clamping down.

The others started after us, and it was all we could do to beat them away with the butts of our rifles. They were moving too fast and too close for us to get a good shot at them. Roxson fired a few rounds into the air and that sent them scurrying away into the shadows of the ferns.

Summerlee's leg was badly damaged, and we dressed it the best that we could with what medical supplies we had.

After that even Summerlee was keen to leave, and we fashioned him a crutch and resumed our march to the volcano.

As we approached the mountains, we could see what looked like large birds circling the volcano. When we drew closer, to our amazement, we saw they were pterodactyls.

"Oh, how I wish I had Malone's camera," Summerlee said, and we continued on our way.

The airborne creatures must have spotted us, for that is when they swooped in.

Roxson took aim and shot at the pterodactyl closest to us. I am not sure if he missed or if the creature's hide was too tough for his bullet to penetrate, but it was the last shot he would fire.

In one smooth motion, the creature glided down and grabbed Roxson with its massive talons and flew off!

Andrew pushed me down to the ground just as one swooped over my head, causing it to miss me by inches before it turned back up to the sky for a second pass.

I heard Summerlee scream as a pterodactyl grabbed him and took him swiftly into the sky.

Maplewhite took shelter between two boulders, while a creature desperately tried to dig him out from the rocks.

Andrew and I ran, but there was no cover for us to run to and we soon found ourselves in the grip of sharp talons.

I could see Summerlee struggling in the pterodactyl's claws ahead of us. The fool took out a pistol and shot the creature in the stomach, causing it to release him. We were now very high up and I feared Summerlee did not survive the fall, but I did not see him land.

The animal carrying Roxson circled and flew away from us, and we quickly lost sight of him. What we did see was horrible; a claw had pierced his side, and he was losing much blood. I cannot say for certain he was killed, but it is highly likely.

The pterodactyls carried Andrew and me ever higher until we reached a large nest of sticks. We were dropped roughly into the empty nest. Then the creatures settled down to eat their prey.

The pterodactyl that had carried me clamped its large beak over my head, and I thought for sure I was moments away from death. Then I heard two shots, startling my carnivore into releasing me.

Andrew was standing there with a pistol, his pterodactyl dead at his feet.

He took aim and shot mine twice in the head, and it dropped dead.

Andrew fell to his knees and I could see he had deep puncture wounds in his stomach and chest. I rushed to help him, but he had already lost consciousness. He died in my arms.

Your son saved my life, Director Hammond. I tried to carry his body out with me, but it quickly became clear that I could not. I too was wounded and losing blood. With great remorse, I left him up there on the mountain.

It took me the better part of a day to climb down. I made my way to the pond and the exit.

I don't remember leaving the Realm, but awoke on a beach in Ireland where two fishermen found me and got me to a doctor.

It is possible Maplewhite may be still alive, as I did not see a creature tear him from his hiding place. But one would think he would have found his way out by now. As for the other two who were carried off, I very much doubt they survived as they too knew the way out.

Hammond: So it would seem. With this new information, I am cancelling all further expeditions into the Realm. We should return to our primary mission, which is to find and close all the entrances and exits.

Furthermore, I partly blame you for this failed mission. You might not have been the leader, but you are a senior member and should have handled Summerlee's recklessness better. You will submit your resignation from the White Worm Society at once.

Doyle: Sir, I understand and will do as you ask, but I implore you not to cancel expeditions. We could learn so much.

Hammond: That is my final word on this matter. Good day.

Doyle: It is a mistake not to learn all we can to fight—

Hammond: I said good day, sir!

FROM THE DIARY OF LORNA BOW, 29TH OF FEBRUARY 1884

I am fully a witch now. I feel different, more so than I did when I became a woman. The only feeling I got with that was cramps.

When I received my witchy powers, I felt them surging through me like sunlight. It is the only way I can explain it. Like sunlight on the skin on a cold winter day, but deep down to my bones and spreading out through my toes and fingertips. It is a wonder I don't glow.

Mother tells me I am one with nature now and can bend it to my will. I can take 'life energy' and redirect it to the sick or dying or even momentarily to the dead.

I would think her mad if I had not seen her perform magic myself.

I should feel bad about what we did to Uncle Leonard Pith tonight. Strangely, I do not.

Earlier this evening Mother told me we were going to 'unleash my powers'. She brought me a robe to wear. It was white cotton. On it were Egyptian symbols, embroidered in golden stitching. The robe was obviously old, threadbare from years of wear with holes here and there.

Mother apologised for the look of it and told me it was ancient. "I wore this for my ceremony, as did my mother for hers and my grandmother before her, and so on, back through the generations. It is over two thousand years old."

I felt proud to wear it, although I didn't like where the holes were since I was naked underneath. "You can wear this over it until the ceremony," she told me, draping a black cloak over my shoulders. She took my face in her hands and smiled at me, and for the first time I really felt like I had a mother.

She took me out into the back garden under the full moon. The garden has a high wall so we have privacy, which was good considering what was about to happen.

It was bitterly cold outside and I could see my breath. My feet were bare, as ordered by Mother. She told me it was important my bare feet touched Mother Earth during the first part of the ceremony.

She told me to wait, and she returned to the house. I stood there, freezing, with my hands tucked under my arms. I could do nothing about my feet, which were going numb on the frozen grass.

To my surprise, Uncle Leonard accompanied her when she returned. He had the same glassy-eyed look the police sergeant had, so I knew he was under a spell.

She commanded him to get on his knees, and he obeyed. She returned to the house once more, then returned with a small clay jar and a silver dagger that sparkled in the moon's light.

She handed me the knife and slipped the cloak off my shoulders, letting it pool on the ground. Even then, I was calm and not really understanding what I was supposed to do.

"Slit his throat," she said. She placed a finger on his neck to show me where to cut.

I thought she was joking, that maybe we were just going to scare him for his past sins.

"I am serious, child. A sacrifice must be made, and I can think of none better than this molester of young girls."

It was true he had done terrible things, yet I didn't want to be the one to kill him. I don't even like killing chickens or pigs. The thought of doing it to a human horrified me.

"Do it for all the times he hit you. Do it for all the times he told you that you were stupid."

I still stood there, frozen in hesitation as well as the cold.

"Do it for your sisters he soiled. Do it for the girls he will abuse in the future."

I felt anger swell up inside me, yet I couldn't get it to the blade.

Pith took a sudden gasp of air and I could see the spell had been broken. I didn't know if the spell wore off naturally or if Mother had released him, but he tilted his head up and said, "What the hell are you stupid bitches up to!" He tried to rise to his feet, but Mother grabbed him by the back of the neck and forced him to stay on his knees. He struggled, but could not escape her grasp. I had no idea she was so strong.

"Do it now!" Her eyes gleamed at me in the moonlight.

Mr. Pith struggled. "Let me go, you fucking hag!"

She held her grip, but I could see her arm was shaking. His eyes looked to me. "Did she tell you how old she is, Lorna? Do you know what she really is?"

"Do it now, before he kills us both!" Mother cried.

"I *am* going to kill you both if you don't let me go!"

I sprang forward and ran the blade across his throat like I had done before with many piglets. He did not squeal. He just stared at me with a shocked look on his face as Mother collected his streaming blood into the clay jar.

She put the lid on the jar when it was full, but Leonard Pith continued to bleed out onto the grass, his warm blood sending wisps of heat into the winter air like our breath.

When he was fully dead, Mother dragged him into the woodshed.

"We will deal with the body later. We have to make it to the obelisk before midnight."

I complained that I was cold and needed shoes and a proper coat to go anywhere. She put a finger to my forehead, and I felt warmth spread from there to my toes. I could feel the frozen ground melt under my feet.

I picked up the cloak and secured it around my shoulders, and we left through the garden gate.

We did not speak as we went, but I know this area well and as we drew closer I suddenly realised where we were going.

"The obelisk," I said. "You're talking about Cleopatra's Needle."

She smiled. "You know it?" she asked.

Of course I know it. It's hard to miss such a thing – a large stone monument alongside the Thames on the Victoria Embankment with all sorts of Egyptian hieroglyphics carved into it. It sits on a base of marble which puts it up higher and out of people's reach, and is guarded by two bronze sphinxes.

More than any other landmark in London, the Needle has always fascinated me. I have felt myself drawn to it. Sometimes when I'm handing out pamphlets for the parlour, I sit by the Needle to eat my lunch. There were times I would sneak out at night to stare at it and think my thoughts. I would climb up and try to touch the stone itself, but my arms are too short.

I told my mother this. "That makes perfect sense," she said. "It was calling to you."

When we reached the Needle, there was a drunken man sleeping at the base and Mother shooed him away. After he'd staggered off, she held her hand up and said an incantation. A fog swirled in, surrounding us and the obelisk, shielding us from anyone who might pass by at such a late hour.

She held the jar under her arm and reached out for my hand. "We have to get up to the obelisk itself," she said. I grabbed her hand, and she said another incantation in an ancient language, and we found ourselves floating off the ground! The cloak slipped from my shoulders as I rose, but the warmth Mother had given me still radiated through my body, and now the night air and the mist felt deliciously cool against my skin.

When we had floated past the pedestal and reached the Needle itself, I reached out my hand and finally touched the surface I had been gazing at for years. I traced the outline of the hieroglyphs and it felt like the stone was humming under my hand, as though there was power pulsing just beneath its surface.

Mother took the lid off the jar and let it fall to the ground. She began to pour the blood onto the white stone as we floated all around it.

"Now, Lorna, say these words: 'Awh, 'iilhat almawt aleazimat taftah biir alnufus alkhasat bik wadaena nakhdim qutuha.'" Oddly, I knew exactly how to pronounce the strange language and did not have to have the words repeated to me. We chanted and circled until she had spilt all the blood from the jar.

The stone started to glow a faint green colour. Mother dropped the empty clay jar, and I heard it crash on the pavement below. She touched the stone with her free hand and I did the same.

A great wave of energy passed through from the stone to my hand and radiated through my whole body.

"Yes!" Mother yelled in ecstasy. I could manage nothing more than a gasp. Our hair floated above our heads and sparkled with light like lightning bugs. I had never felt so much joy in my life.

"Pull in the power, Lorna! Let it fill you!"

I couldn't have stopped it if I'd tried, but why would I want to? I felt strong and vibrant. I felt the magic surging through me, like the beating of my heart, but deeper. I felt like I could do anything.

When we had our fill, the Needle slowly faded back to its weathered stone white, and we gently floated back down to earth.

I could see Mother in the moonlight. She looked younger and more radiant. The grey streaks that had formed in her hair were gone, and it was now as red as mine.

As we walked back home, she told me all would be different now. We were 'charged' and magic would come easy.

"We also opened the Spirit Gate and lifted the veil between worlds. We will have no trouble talking to the dead now."

So in addition to being a witch, Mother tells me I will be a genuine medium, not a pretend one. I hope I can use this ability to help people, and not just take their money.

FROM THE JOURNAL OF BRAM STOKER, 3RD OF MARCH 1884

10:10 p.m.

Henry threw a party at the Lyceum tonight to celebrate the success of our new production of *Macbeth*.

Ellen brought her latest suitor to the party and to my surprise it was Brent Blackwood, one of the White Worm operatives who had accompanied me to Finland. He strikes me as a fine enough chap, but one wonders if the Worms have planted him as a spy. It all seems like too much of a coincidence. And, to be honest, he is a good ten years younger than she is and that gives one pause as well.

Perhaps I am just being overly suspicious. After all, Ellen is an attractive woman and has had many suitors. She did meet him through me, as Mr. Blackwood has paid a visit or two to the theatre to fill me in on the Dr. Mueller matter. And he is an avid theatre buff, so attraction to an actress of her calibre is not out of the question.

Still, the White Worms have a way of insinuating themselves into my life and have planted people to spy on me in the past. They even went so far as to replace Noel's nanny on our American trip, though I admit I am grateful that she kept my son safe during our ordeal in the wilderness.

I dare not say anything to Ellen as it would spoil her happiness, and I must admit Florence is in better spirits when Ellen is occupied with a new beau. Any discussion with Florence of this matter is out of the question, of course; she may see it as jealousy on my part, and I wish not to stir up that hornet's nest.

At the party, Blackwood and I again speculated about whether Dr. Mueller really died in the fire at his lab. They did not recover a body so they do not know for sure, but it has been a year now and he has not reappeared.

"He is a clever one, though," Blackwood said. "I wouldn't put it past him to fake the whole thing so he could continue his mad experiments unhindered."

We were tucked away backstage in the prop room, but Ellen managed to track us down.

"Here you are, Brent," she said. "What are you two talking about, hidden away like a couple of schoolgirls?"

Blackwood glanced over to me.

"You may as well tell her," I said. "She is on the monster-hunting team, as it were."

"I most certainly am," she said, locking her arm in his. "Is that what we are talking about? Monsters? Did Bram tell you about the time Oscar and I saved him at Stonehenge?"

"I'm sure Oscar remembers it differently," I said.

"Well, I at least helped find you," she said.

I told her that Mr. Blackwell and I were discussing our pursuit of Dr. Mueller in Finland.

She said Florence had related the story to her and how dreadful it all must have been, just as Florence poked her head into the prop room.

"I hope you don't mind that I told her, Bram," Florence said as she joined us in the room. She had a flute of champagne in her hand. "We are all one big family here in the theatre, after all." She said this with a rather obvious sarcastic tone that put my guard up, but I suppose it's progress that she and Ellen were talking with one another again.

Blackwood added, "Mueller was the last of the Black Bishop's cohorts yet to be dealt with. Well, except for the vampire Carolyn le Fey, who disappeared in America."

"Oh, no, she is quite dead," Florence said. I could tell she had had too much to drink as she swayed a bit as she said this. "I dispatched her myself, in the desert. I assumed it was in Miss Chase's report as it was in the journal she stole from me."

Blackwood was staring at her in astonished admiration. "No, at least not in the report I read," he said.

Florence downed the rest of her champagne, then for some reason stared at Ellen as she said, "I pushed a stake through her tiny, bitter heart. She exploded like a popped tick."

Ellen's eyes grew wide at this, and she drew closer to Blackwood.

Florence continued gazing at Ellen and added, "I was covered in her blood and I had to wash it off in the river. Oscar was there. He will tell you how disgusting it all was." She lifted her glass to her lips again and, finding it empty, emitted an annoyed, "Hmmph," and let it fall to the floor. She jumped a bit at the crash, then giggled.

"Who knew theatre life would be so...exciting," she said. She stumbled, and I caught her, steadying her.

"I think it is time we said our goodbyes," I said, escorting Florence from the room past Ellen's amused smirk.

I asked Florence if she was all right as it is not like her to drink so much, especially in public.

"It's a celebration, Bram, I'm celebrating." She pulled away and shook off my hand from around her arm. "I am quite capable of walking on my own."

We passed through the partygoers on the stage, and she grabbed another flute of champagne. I thought it best not to wrestle it out of her hand in front of everyone, but this point was moot as she downed it in a gulp and returned the empty glass to the tray.

Before I could retrieve her, Henry came between us.

"Bram, may I have a word, in my office?" I thought I was about to be scolded about my wife's inebriation and gave her a worried glance as I followed him up the theatre aisle.

We climbed the stairs to his office and shut the door behind us.

"So, this Blackwood person, what do we think?"

"Seems like an upstanding young man," I said. "He was very helpful in Finland."

"That's what worries me," Henry said. "He's a White Worm operative. They continue to spy on us, even after we have helped them so many times. It's possible they planted him here, and he's not interested in Ellen at all."

I agreed that was a possibility I had considered myself.

"And thanks to their ineptitude, Mueller died before he could help me find a cure for my vampirism."

I assured him that Mueller had no intent of helping him and was just after my cursed blood for his own nefarious purposes.

"Perhaps," he agreed. "Still, I don't like them sticking their noses into our business."

I promised to keep an eye on Blackwood and made my way back downstairs.

Florence was chatting up Philip Pengrove, one of the more handsome actors in the troupe, and she was standing a little too close to him for my liking.

"And in some native tribes, wives are allowed, even encouraged, to sleep with other men in the village," she told him.

I merely had to shoot him a look of disapproval and he scampered off.

I told Florence once again it was time to leave, but she told me she was staying, then lurched forward and was sick all over my shoes.

This put a sudden hush to the party as everyone stopped to look on.

A stagehand was immediately at my feet with a rag to clean off my shoes, which made the embarrassment even worse.

"You are right, we should go," she said.

As I finish writing this, I can't help but worry. Things had been going so well since we rekindled our love in America. Now she is back to being unhappy. I shall talk to her about it in the morning when more sober heads will prevail.

FROM THE DIARY OF FLORENCE STOKER, 4TH OF MARCH 1884

I awoke this morning with a terrible headache. Bram did not chastise me for drinking too much at last night's party, but I could tell what he was thinking by the stern look he gave me when he brought me the cold compress for my head.

"Is Mummy sick?" Noel asked, crawling into bed with me.

I told him I was just a bit under the weather and sent him off to eat breakfast.

"I am quite embarrassed about last night," I told Bram. He was mixing me up a tincture of opium and putting it in my tea. "I am sorry I drank too much. You can go ahead and say, 'I told you so.'"

"I shall say nothing of the sort," he said. "I have occasionally drunk too much myself and am not in any position to lecture you."

"Did I say or do anything stupid?" I asked hesitantly.

"Aside from throwing a few glasses to the ground, being sick on my shoes or having a lengthy conversation with Philip on the sexual practices of Native American women, I can't think of anything."

"Not *so* bad then."

He handed me the tea and sat on the bed.

"What brought all this on?" Bram asked. "I mean, you haven't been yourself for days. Is the melancholy back?"

I sighed and sipped my tea, pondering my answer.

"A malaise, I suppose, but more of a long-burning frustration," I said. "I feel I have no purpose in life, that I am just going through the motions of living. I do what is expected of me and it brings me no joy."

He told me he often feels the same way, but refocusing on his duties usually snaps him out of it.

"That's just it," I said. "I have no duties. We have a maid, so I do no housework. We have a nanny for Noel. And, when you are in the middle of a production, I barely see hide nor hair of you for weeks at a time. I seldom have a chance to even perform my wifely duties. There must be something I can do at the theatre, even if it isn't acting."

He promised me he would look for where I could be useful, perhaps as an assistant to the seamstress or as an understudy. "All the understudy parts are covered at the moment," he said. "But you never know when one will get ill or leave the company."

So that's where I am, a seamstress's assistant or an understudy's understudy. This helps my frustration not one iota.

To make matters worse, I get to watch Ellen chew scenery in a leading role while she carries on multiple romantic conquests. I know this is none of my business and should not bother me – indeed, I should be happy she has moved on to new men and is not pining away for Bram. And yet, it is irritating to me. *She* is irritating to me.

Down deep, I know the feeling stems from jealousy. Furthermore, I know that is irrational. Bram and I have resolved our problems and are more in love than ever. I trust him implicitly. Why can I forgive Bram for their affair, but not her?

FROM THE DIARY OF LORNA BOW, DATE UNKNOWN

Today, Mother told me the story of my great-great-grandmother, 'The Witch of Endor', and how the very man she tried to help betrayed her. I know there must be some more 'great-greats' in there, since it was so long ago, but Mother says our magic gives us long lives.

It must be an important story because it is in the Bible. She told me not to believe what was written there, and this is the real story. But imagine having one of your relatives mentioned in the Bible!

This is the story she told me.

King Saul, the first king of Israel, outlawed all forms of magic and witchcraft. This included séances or any attempt to contact the dead. Saul did not kill the séance 'mediums', but Grandmother (I'm just going to call her Grandmother without all the great-greats) faced death by stoning if they caught her trying to contact the dead.

There was a war going on with the Philistines. Saul's family, soldiers and followers were being slaughtered. He could not hope to defeat the Philistine forces, because they'd cut him off from the northern tribes who might have helped him, and he was outnumbered.

As death stared him in the face, Saul prayed desperately to God for help, but no help came. God, it seemed, had abandoned him.

Saul was desperate and turned to the old ways. He asked his servants to find him someone who could speak with the dead. More specifically, one particular dead person: the prophet Samuel.

The search can't have been easy, since Saul had supposedly expelled all the mediums from Israel. But Saul's servants found Grandmother living in a cave at Endor.

Saul, of course, could not be seen with a medium, so he put on a disguise.

The journey was difficult and dangerous, but he took the risk with two of his soldiers, also in disguise. When he met Grandmother, he immediately asked her to consult a spirit. He had no time to lose, since the Philistines would attack at dawn.

Grandmother was reluctant. She was no fool. She saw through Saul's disguise immediately and knew he was the king who had ordered the expulsion of all 'witches' like herself.

But Saul insisted, guaranteeing her safety, so she finally agreed to help.

She summoned the spirit of Samuel from the beyond – or from Sheol, the Israelite land of the dead.

Saul did not exactly get what he was expecting from the spirit of Samuel. Through Grandmother, Samuel told Saul that God had turned away from him, that the Philistines would triumph. Saul's army, including Saul's three sons, would die at the hands of his enemies.

Deep in his heart Saul knew she was speaking the horrifying truth: he would die, his family and soldiers would be destroyed, and Israel would come under the heel of the Philistines.

Saul collapsed on the floor of the cave, unable to move.

Grandmother took pity on the man who had persecuted and exiled all the mediums like herself. She gave him and his soldiers (who had not eaten in several days) fresh-baked bread and succulent calf meat. (Succulent is a new word I just learned, which means 'delicious'.) Strengthened, Saul went out to meet his fate.

"Kill the witch," he said to his soldiers as he left. The soldiers drew their swords, but Grandmother was too powerful for them. She summoned the power of the wind and concentrated it with enough force to snap the men's necks. They fell down dead.

"She did as her king ordered," Mother told me. "She took pity on him and fed him, and he repaid her kindness with death. The lesson here is to take the word of no man."

Grandmother went on to work for the Philistines, assuring their victory. Then, even they turned on her, afraid of her magic.

Grandmother left the desert and went as far north as she could, finding sanctuary with the Celts. There, she found new magic, new spells, and she protected our line of powerful witches.

"This combination of Egyptian and Celtic magic has made us the

most powerful of all witches, and it is a power whose time has come!"
Mother said.

This power now lives in me. It's a big responsibility, but an exciting
feeling all the same.

REPORT FROM WHITE WORM SOCIETY DIRECTOR ERROL HAMMOND TO HER MAJESTY QUEEN VICTORIA

Date: 12 March 1884

Subject: Empire Experiencing Unusual Increase in Supernatural Activity

Your Majesty:

This is the monthly briefing on supernatural threats to the British Empire. Through reports from our agents across the globe, we know that there has been a sixty per cent increase in ghost sightings and a ten per cent increase in possessions.

While these types of supernatural intrusions are mostly harmless, the sharp rise in their number is a concern. It indicates that the veil between worlds is thin, or perhaps completely open, as happened ten years ago when spiritualism was on the rise in America and made its way to our shores.

Our Spirit Division suspects this increase is tied to a possible opening of the 'Spirit Gate', a supernatural barrier that keeps the Land of the Dead separate from our world.

Opening this Gate not only has the potential to increase ghostly activity, it has been known to intensify the unearthly power of witches, necromancers and clairvoyants. We believe someone opened the Gate on purpose for nefarious ends.

I will personally continue to investigate and research a way to close the Gate for good.

Until then, we remain on high alert, a status we have not needed to activate since the vampire uprising of 1881. All branch offices have been notified and are redoubling their vigilance as we continue to protect the Empire from all supernatural threats.

Sincerely,

Errol Hammond

Director, White Worm Society

FROM THE DIARY OF LORNA BOW, 29TH OF MARCH 1884

I understand now how much of my life has been a preparation for the path I have been set upon. My mother meant for my uncle to train me in performing fake séances to prepare me for the real thing once I received my power. Yet those fake sessions did little to ready me for what really channelling a spirit would feel like.

Yes, we are back in the séance business, though with no trickery this time.

"The dead are drawn to those they knew in life, so there is no trouble locating people's loved ones," Mother said. "Most are confused as to what has happened to them, and we can help them move on. We are doing good work, never forget that."

Uncle Leonard often said we were doing good work for the living, giving them some hope. He wasn't wrong there; most left happier than when they came in.

"There are usually a few spirits surrounding us. The most they can typically do is invade our dreams or spark a memory. Now that the Spirit Gate is open, more ghosts than ever are crossing over, and they're making themselves more obvious, even to those who don't have your gifts."

I remembered dreaming of a friend of mine who died of the flu in the boarding school. She came to me in the dream to tell me she was fine, and happy to know me when she was alive. I thought it only a dream, but it made me feel better nonetheless.

Mother told me we have to be careful when dealing with spirits. Most are harmless, but some are malevolent. "There are evil spirits who have been in the land of mist too long. They are fearful to move on because they know only hell awaits them. These spirits are always looking for a way to return to the living world and sometimes they succeed in a possession."

She could see I was becoming nervous at this, and added, "That is why you are never to attempt to channel a spirit without me nearby. I will be able to cast away these demonic types."

My first real clients came in today. In the old days we would refer to the people that sit at the table as 'marks', but mother says we should think of them as clients now.

Mr. and Mrs. Crenshaw are a wealthy couple who recently lost their daughter. I was nervous, doubting that I would be able to contact a real spirit, despite Mother's assurance that we had dropped the veil between worlds and it would be easy for me with my new powers. Mother didn't even allow Nell to wait in the spirit cabinet in case we needed her to make a ghostly appearance.

The Crenshaws and I sat at the round table in the darkened room. Mother joined us to complete the circle. I felt relieved knowing she was there and could help should something go wrong.

Mrs. Crenshaw was dressed in black with a black veil, still grieving the death of their daughter. Her husband was in a black suit with a yellow rose in his lapel. Previously I would have taken note of the flower; it is obviously something precious to his daughter and I would 'channel' the spirit to mention something about missing her walks through the rose garden and smelling the yellow roses. It is such details that would impress the gullible.

However, today I did not have to use such tricks.

"Please, clear your minds," I said. This was the standard way to open the fake séances. I wasn't sure if it was a requirement for the real thing, but old habits die hard.

I closed my eyes and cleared my own mind as Mother had taught me. Then I opened them and looked into the darkness. Mother had told me to relax my vision and wait for shimmers of light that would be spirits drawn to the couple.

To my surprise, the shimmers came straight away. Both the Crenshaws had cobwebs of light dancing around them, some faint and some strong. The colours were mostly white with a rainbow hue around the edges.

"Focus on the brightest light," Mother had told me. "Those are the recently dead and the dead that have the strongest emotional connection to the living."

I focused on the brightest thread, and the others dropped away. I instinctively drew in a large breath and this brought the thread to me and into me.

I felt it spread through my body, then to my head. An image of a young girl passed ever so briefly before my eyes. Then there was a sharp pain throughout my body. Mother had warned me of it, yet it took me by surprise and I let out a gasp.

The girl was me and wasn't me. She was inside and outside my body. With an effort, I relaxed, and the pain melted away and I gave my body to her to use.

"Mother! Father!" she said through me. I felt the voice passing over my lips, but the words were not mine and the voice did not sound like my own, or even the fake voices I am used to putting on.

"It is me, Cecily!"

Mrs. Crenshaw cried, "We are here!"

Mr. Crenshaw seemed unmoved, as if he suspected I was tricking him.

"I miss you ever so much," the girl said. "Where am I? Where are you?"

"Most of the time they don't know they have passed on," Mother whispered. "It is best to be honest with her in these matters."

Mrs. Crenshaw stared at Mother, tears in her eyes. "I can't," she said. "How can I tell my girl something like that?"

Mother squeezed Mrs. Crenshaw's hand. "I know it's hard, but it's worse for her to linger here, in confusion. Peace is what she needs from you now."

They looked at each other for a long moment, then Mrs. Crenshaw turned to me. Heartbreak and love mingled on her face.

"Cecily, darling," she said. "Your father and I miss you so much. I wish we could take you home, sweet girl. But you have…passed on."

The spirit was growing agitated. I could feel my heart pounding as though a small fist was flailing inside my chest, and my feet were twitching as though they wanted to run from the room.

"What does that mean?" the voice in my mouth asked in a timid whine.

Mrs. Crenshaw sobbed, though her husband sat stony-faced. "How do we know it is really her?" he asked.

"Ask her something only she would know," Mother said.

Mr. Crenshaw sighed. "All right. *Cecily*," he said, in a mocking tone of voice. "What is my pet name for you?"

"Bunny," the girl said through me. "I am your Bunny! You say it's because I hear everything."

Through no doing of my own, my arms flew up to the sides of my head, the palms of my hand facing forward and wiggling like bunny ears. She almost slipped away then, but I quickly rejoined my hands with the others', reconnecting the circle.

Mr. Crenshaw stared at me and his eyes filled with tears, "Yes," he whispered. "You are my Bunny."

"What is it like where you are, darling?" Mrs. Crenshaw asked.

"Mostly I can't see anything but grey," Cecily said. "Sometimes I can see you and Father. Sometimes I can hear you, but it makes me sad because you are always cross with each other."

"We are just sad you are gone," her father said. "We shouldn't be taking that out on each other." He looked to his wife as he said this, and she nodded and squeezed his hand.

"You fought today about my necklace," Cecily said.

"It is all I have to remember you by and I have lost it," her mother said. She was crying and went for her handkerchief to dry her tears, but Mother warned her not to break the circle.

"Don't cry, Mummy. It isn't lost. I put it in my stocking in the top drawer to keep it safe. The stockings with the rose pattern on them."

Cecily seemed distracted by something. She had turned her attention away from the table and I almost lost our connection.

"There is a door here, it came out of the mist," she said, coming back to me and the table. "That door wasn't here before."

Mother whispered, "Tell her to open it and go through it. It is the door to heaven, and she is ready to go."

"No," the woman cried. "I want to tell her so many things!"

"It is time, Mrs. Crenshaw," Mother said. "If she doesn't go now, she could be trapped in there forever. You don't want that."

"Open the door, Bunny," Mr. Crenshaw said.

There was a pause, then Cecily said, "Aunt Edna is at the door telling me to come through."

"Oh, Edna died when Cecily was very young," Mrs. Crenshaw said. "I am surprised she remembers her."

"Go through the door, Bunny," Mr. Crenshaw coaxed. "That's where you should be now."

I could feel Cecily's apprehension, like a butterfly in my stomach. "Will I see you and Mummy again?"

"Yes, you will see us in heaven soon. Go with Aunt Edna and she will look after you until then."

"All right."

"We love you, sweet girl," Mrs. Crenshaw cried, just as I felt Cecily's spirit suddenly torn away from me. There was an instant of pain, as if someone had plucked a hair from my head. I was once again myself and alone in my body.

Mother and I discreetly left the table as the Crenshaws held each other and wept at this second loss of their daughter. After a while they stood, their expressions strangely peaceful. They thanked me for allowing them the opportunity to say goodbye. They tipped me very well.

Later that day, a Mr. Pryce came to see me. He was the bloke that caused me to get nicked and he was there to apologise. It seems he had sent the couple in himself, hoping to test me once again. I guess I passed this time, because he asked to sit in on the next one so he could take notes and such.

Mother agreed, telling me it would be good for business to get the spiritualists on our side.

So, I guess I am a full-fledged medium now.

REPORT FROM AGENT BRENT BLACKWOOD

Date: 8 April 1884
Subject: The witch Endora and Lorna Bow

I was assigned to investigate reports that the witch Endora had been spotted in London. She has not been seen here since the White Worms trapped her in the Realm over a decade ago. This action was taken because her practice of necromancy was causing increased levels of spirit activity throughout England. The final straw came when she raised a mummy in the British Museum and used it to steal valuable artefacts. (See the report on the Mummy Rampage of 1874.)

Following leads obtained through contacts with the local spiritualist community, I tracked my suspect to a local séance parlour, and believe that the proprietress of this establishment is, in fact, Endora. She matches the description and sketches I have seen of Endora in the Society's archives, and our observations of her business further support our suspicion that she is the witch.

She has recently taken over management of the parlour, which had been the property of one Leonard Pith, who has apparently vanished. (This is, by all accounts, no great loss; the man was a known charlatan and worse.)

Surprisingly, Endora has retained the services of several girls who had worked for Pith. One, Lorna Bow, is the primary medium of the establishment, and she is unusually gifted. While under Pith's management, the parlour was patently fraudulent. With Endora at the helm we believe they are actually communicating with the dead.

Agent Chase attended a séance, and Lorna successfully communicated with one of her dead relatives. In this case it was her mother, who had only passed away last spring.

Chase said it was astounding, and the spirit knew things no one but her mother would know. As she was undercover and had claimed to be there to speak with a deceased fiancé, it would have been difficult for charlatans to gather information on her mother. Chase is quite convinced Lorna Bow is a true medium.

For this reason, I believe Lorna is Endora's daughter, the child the White Worm Society was unable to locate after trapping Endora in the Realm. We know that spirit communication is a talent that is prevalent in Endora's bloodline.

We have been observing the parlour for several weeks now and it is very popular with the upper classes. We even saw lords and ladies attend séances and come out chattering excitedly about what they had seen.

It is not known how Endora escaped banishment in the Realm. How shall we proceed? Should we bring her in for questioning?

RESPONSE FROM DIRECTOR HAMMOND

Date: 8 April 1884
Subject: The witch Endora and Lorna Bow

Agent Blackwood,

We should continue observing from a distance for now. I am afraid Endora has gained favour with some powerful people and as such we cannot make a move without offending them. Perhaps séances are all she is up to now and she has put her evil ways behind her. Even if she is picking the pockets of the rich and famous, it is not our concern at the moment. Should demons appear in Clerkenwell, we will know who is responsible.

I have a team researching ways to close the Spirit Gate, which will minimise the harm she can perpetuate.

Leave Cora Chase on the case and you, Mr. Blackwood, are to return to headquarters to be reassigned.

ARTICLE FOR THE *WOMAN'S GAZETTE*, 12TH OF APRIL 1884

Spirits Are Active on Merlin Street
by E.B. Farber

With spiritualism all the rage these days, it is hard to separate the impostors from the genuine.

We might see it as harmless fun, but according to Dr. Wesley Pryce, an expert in these matters and head of the Physical Society, communication with the dead is nothing to be trifled with and can be quite dangerous.

He has investigated many séance parlours and warns they are frequently run by fraudsters who wish to fleece patrons of their hard-earned shillings.

However, there is one establishment he believes to be genuine. Endora Bow is the proprietress, with her daughter, Lorna, acting as the medium.

"In all my years investigating these claims," said Pryce, "I have never seen a medium with the ability to contact the dead with a nearly one hundred per cent success rate."

This reporter has witnessed firsthand this girl's remarkable abilities. She was able to connect with my recently dead uncle. It was astonishing to hear my uncle's booming voice coming from such a tiny girl. Still, I thought it could be some sort of trickery; after all, mimicry is a talent many actors have, and this girl could have such a talent. With that in mind, as a test I asked a question only my uncle and I knew the answer to: what was inscribed on the pocket watch he gave me for my eighteenth birthday? When he answered the question accurately, I was convinced Lorna was channelling his spirit.

Furthermore, the young lady helped my uncle find peace and move on to heaven, something for which I will forever be grateful.

I say to you all with recently passed loved ones, book a sitting now. Madam Bow informed me the best success is with the recently departed, as many move on soon from the veil between worlds into paradise.

A small donation is appreciated, but not necessary. Sitting dates and times are limited.

Send enquiries to:
Endora Bow, 32 Merlin Street, Clerkenwell.

FROM THE JOURNAL OF BRAM STOKER, 1ST OF MAY 1884

1:00 a.m.

Another vision from my demonic powers shook me tonight. It happens so rarely these days that it is a shock when it does, especially from touching a seemingly benign object, as happened tonight.

I have just returned from the Athenaeum Club, where Willie was hosting Oscar's bachelor party.

The room was filled to capacity with Oscar's friends, both old and new.

Oscar's newfound fame has filled his social calendar with an entourage of fans. They hang on his every word and laugh at even his least droll jokes.

Willie is as concerned as I am that these sycophants may just be using him and that Oscar doesn't seem to notice or care.

After a meal of oysters and beef Wellington, and after all the toasts to Oscar's lost bachelorhood, Henry, Oscar and I escaped to the club's library for brandy and cigars. Several of his new friends tried to follow us, but Oscar shooed them back into the dining hall and closed the large library doors.

It was there that Oscar told us of Constance's father.

He told us that Mr. Lloyd had been a member of the White Worms and had disappeared while on an expedition into the Realm. The Worms must have thought he met his untimely end, for when he failed to return, the world was told he had died of a heart attack in Paris. "What the Worms don't know is that he kept a detailed diary of his journeys."

It is from twenty years ago, and Oscar told us it was written in a type of shorthand, one he could read. It contained reports of the many lands of the Realm, some we are familiar with and some we are not.

"Most importantly," Oscar said, "it has a map to an entrance in Cardiff. It might be an entrance the Worms are unaware of as he never turned in this diary."

He handed the book to Henry, who began thumbing through it with great interest as he still thinks a trip into the Realm may help him find a cure for his vampirism.

"I wasn't sure if I should hand this over to the White Worms or not," Oscar said. "They may want to shut the entrance at the very least, as there is no way of knowing what may come out of there."

"Indeed," Henry said. "Yet, as they have forbidden any further trips into the Realm, this might be my only way to continue my research into ridding the world of vampirism. What do you think, Bram?"

He handed me the journal, but before I could give him my thoughts on the matter, a jolt of what felt like electricity shot from my hand into my brain. My sixth sense was activated, as it sometimes is when I touch something that has been in contact with the supernatural. A blinding green light blurred my vision for a second, and then I found myself transported to a land of mist. I at once knew it was a memory from Horace Lloyd, Constance's father. I was seeing through his eyes, feeling what he felt – intense fear and desperation.

He was lost in this mist and had been for some time. He was dying of thirst and hunger and stumbling along with great effort. All around him was only a grey fog. Even the ground beneath his feet was obscured and felt as though it wasn't totally solid, like he was walking on marsh lands.

From the fog there were sounds of people moaning. *Is this heaven or hell*, he thought as he ploughed on into the void. Something whooshed by overhead and he looked up to see the horrifying face of a man, contorted in agony. The face screamed at him, a moan of despair and anger. Gazing upon it, Mr. Lloyd screamed as well, out of fear and out of empathy, for he could feel the torment of this lost soul.

And as he felt it, I could feel it too.

"Bram!" I heard Oscar yell over my own screams as he shook me out of my trance.

The library doors were open and people were pouring in to see what the scream was about.

"It's all right," Oscar said, stepping between me and the onlookers. "He just saw a mouse."

This seemed to be a logical explanation, and they returned to the dining room.

Henry had taken the book out of my hand, and that had probably been the thing to bring me back to the real world. I sat down in a big leather chair to catch my breath.

Henry placed a snifter of brandy in my hand.

I told them what I had seen and felt through Mr. Lloyd's eyes. "He thought he was in the land of the dead."

Oscar pointed out that as horrible as that place was, at least he had found his way out at some point. "He wrote about it in the journal. But he never turned it over to the White Worms. Why?"

I said there was nothing in the vision to indicate why, but I could understand that this is something he might not want the Worms to know about. Proof of an afterlife and a way to get there is something I might hesitate to entrust to the White Worms.

"Do you think this is where he disappeared?" Henry asked.

"Maybe so," Oscar pondered. "But you'd think he wouldn't want to go back there after finding his way out."

Henry, Oscar and I all agreed to keep the journal to ourselves for the time being. The journal had been undiscovered for twenty years. It could go on being undiscovered a little longer.

FROM THE JOURNAL OF DR. VICTOR MUELLER, 4TH OF MAY 1884

Against my better judgement, I have returned to England. I have done so under an assumed identity, having changed my appearance and name. I now have black hair and have purchased a home in the English countryside as Hans Delbruck, an Austrian citizen.

I think I have sufficiently convinced those troublesome White Worms that Victor Mueller is dead. Still, I would not have returned, but for the fact I need three things to continue my experiments: electricity, an ample supply of fresh bodies, and more of Stoker's blood. All of these are available in abundance in London.

The home that I have purchased includes thirty acres of land, so I am far from any neighbours or villagers, yet it is only a short journey into London. It also has a working windmill, which I am converting into a generator. I do not know why I hadn't thought of using wind power before, but it should provide a reliable source of electricity in this windy climate. I have purchased a supplemental kerosene generator, as well as chemicals and laboratory equipment, to set up my new lab.

I have also hired the services of a Mr. Pendergast, a worker at the London morgue. For a small fee, he delivers me fresh, unclaimed corpses, which the underclass of London are happy to keep supplying me.

I have very little of Stoker's blood left and fear the quantity will not be sufficient to continue my experiments much longer. I shall soon need to turn my attentions towards acquiring more.

The best news is that I have managed to rescue Charlotte from that brute, Risto. I left him at the bottom of a cliff and hope he is dead. Even if he lives, he has no way to find me here.

Charlotte continues to exhibit traits of a wild animal. Despite her feral condition, I have taught her some basic skills. However, she must remain locked in a cage for her own protection. She is calm today. I have given her picture books and they seem to entertain her.

I am exploring treatments for her. I have tried to balance her humours, but that has been a dead end.

Risto eventually learned to think rationally and to talk, but he remembers nothing of his past life. It was as if he were a newborn, a blank slate. Where did his old personality and memories go?

Could it be Charlotte simply lacks a soul? Has my Charlotte's very essence gone on to the afterlife – if there is one – and simply no longer resides in this reanimated corpse?

I have met with a friend at the London Physical Society, Dr. Wesley Pryce. I have been a benefactor of his work for some time now, so he will not reveal my identity to the authorities. He was eager to discuss spiritual matters. Namely, this: if spirits exist, can one be put back into a body? Despite my scepticism, he assures me spirits can possess the living temporarily, so why not permanently, in a body that is void of a soul?

Even if one of his mediums cannot contact my Charlotte, we could at least capture a spirit in a new body for study. It could answer so many questions about death and the afterlife. We could return worthy souls to the living world in the bodies of criminals destined for the gallows. This could be the breakthrough I have been looking for all these years. This is how we could cheat death once and for all time.

Dr. Pryce told me of a new medium now working in London. "She is the real thing," he said. "One of the most powerful mediums I have ever seen. Her mother, I am told, is a witch of some sort, a necromancer."

He then explained necromancers could raise the dead, which again I found to be straining credibility.

How much of the spiritualist movement is mere hopeful fantasy? Was I falling into the same trap, hoping an afterlife was possible without proof of such?

I asked if he could arrange a meeting with the girl and her mother for some sort of demonstration, and he said he could.

I write this looking at Charlotte in her cage and finding myself full of hope that she will once again return to me.

FROM THE DIARY OF OSCAR WILDE, 7TH OF MAY 1884

Dear yours truly,

The town is buzzing like a kicked beehive. This time, it is not about me, if you can believe it. It is over the latest spiritualist giving séances to the rich and famous.

Had I not had brushes with the supernatural myself, I would be one to dismiss it all as the work of charlatans, as I know many mediums are frauds who wish only to prey upon the grieving. However, I have it on good authority from Mr. Blackwood of the White Worms that this girl may be the real thing, and that would mean some sort of afterlife exists.

Constance informs me she met this very medium once in Hyde Park. Though she liked the girl and took an interest in her, she assumed she was a street urchin trying to rope her into fortune-telling shenanigans. She was very pleased to hear the girl is honest and making a decent living.

This has awakened in both of us an interest in all things spiritual. This morning we met for breakfast and began discussing the afterlife and what was in her father's diary about a land of mist and lost souls.

"Maybe she could contact my father," Constance said, reading the article in the *Woman's Gazette*. "That is, if he is in fact dead."

"Or maybe even if he is just a visitor to the afterlife," I said, not really taking it seriously.

"Oh, should we, Oscar? Should we go in for a sitting?"

"I don't see why not. It could be a fun evening out if nothing else. Shall I see if the Stokers and Henry Irving would like to go?"

"Certainly. The more the merrier," she said, turning to the next article in her magazine.

I admit I have become rather excited at the prospect of going. I have many dead relatives it would be nice to talk to again, and a few it would not.

I am especially hopeful that I might communicate with my poor sisters, Emily and Mary, who burned to death in a fire. I so wish I could tell them I love them and miss them. My half brother Henry, whom I barely knew, left me a nice sum of money when he died, and I would like to thank him for that as it came at a most destitute time. My father, on the other hand, could just stay in hell, which I'm sure is where he ended up.

Then there is Derrick. Could I talk to him once more? I am sure he is quite cross with me for killing him, but he would be the first to say it was in self-defence. At least the human version of him would say so. Since he was a vampire at the time, one hardly knows what he would think.

As I look at my ageing body in the mirror, my thoughts turn to mortality, and I find myself wondering what it would be like if I had let him turn me into a vampire. I honestly don't know where I found the strength to stop him.

FROM THE JOURNAL OF DR. VICTOR MUELLER, 16TH OF MAY 1884

I am trying to maintain my scientific detachment, but I cannot help it: my heart is full of hope that my beloved Charlotte and I will be reunited!

I investigated the necromancer Dr. Pryce told me about. I still have connections with the Order of the Golden Dawn and they tell me Endora is indeed a powerful witch and her daughter a gifted medium. While the witch is not part of the Order, they have a common enemy in the White Worms.

I witnessed firsthand a reading by the young lady, Lorna, as she channelled a spirit under the scrutiny of Dr. Pryce.

After the demonstration, I approached Endora to arrange my own séance, with a special request. A hundred pounds convinced her I was most serious.

"Could a spirit be put into a body?" I asked. "Not into the medium herself, but into a different body?"

The idea intrigued her. "It would require powerful magic," she said, "but possession has been demonstrated in the past. A weak-minded person as host would be necessary, as most would resist such a transfer."

I took the risk of confiding in her about my work with reanimation and said I had empty vessels we could use to try the procedure.

"If Lorna can channel the spirit, I can transfer it," she assured me. "But are you sure you want to play with life and death in such a way? The magic is unpredictable. Evil spirits will surely learn of this and wish to take advantage."

I assured her I am first and foremost a scientist and understand the risks of pushing nature to its boundaries.

She agreed to come to my laboratory in the country next week and try to make a connection.

Is it possible we can resurrect my Charlotte to her former self?

I am trembling at the thought of being the first man to conquer death!

FROM THE JOURNAL OF BRAM STOKER, 20TH OF MAY 1884

12:45 p.m.

What is the matter with me? I dislike the supernatural and how all things connected to it stalk me. Why then did I agree to go to a séance with Oscar and Constance? All I did was open myself up to evil forces once again.

To be fair, I thought it would be nice for Florence to get to know Constance, as she hasn't many women friends. And I must admit I thought it would be the typical charlatan theatrics and not an actual channelling of the dead.

In any event, Florence, Henry and I all went along on what should have been a merry evening with Oscar and Constance. We were all curious, especially since this particular medium, Lorna Bow, is the talk of the town. Thanks to Oscar's and Henry's celebrity status, we had no trouble getting a sitting despite the fact that she is booked months out.

We met the proprietor, the medium's mother, Endora Bow. She is a striking woman with flame-red hair. Upon shaking her hand, I should have known we were not in for a regular evening's entertainment. I wouldn't say she triggered my sixth sense as such, but there was something off about her. I felt a spark when I shook her hand, which at the time I attributed to static electricity, but my hand continued to feel the effect of the zap as I sat down at the big round table with the rest of my party. It seems she felt it too, as she looked at me oddly, though she said nothing about it.

She instructed us to all hold hands and to not break the circle. To clear our minds and keep scepticism out. Lorna entered the room through a set of black curtains and took her place at the table, holding my hand on the right and Oscar's on the left. Her mother remained standing behind her.

Florence was on my right, and Henry on hers, and then Constance and Oscar completed the circle. Florence and Constance were grinning at each other like a couple of schoolgirls in anticipation of the night's proceedings.

A single lantern in the centre of the table provided the only light, leaving the rest of the room in shadows.

"Let us begin," Lorna said, closing her eyes. Her eyelids immediately sprang back open, and she had a shocked look on her face. I'd say she had seen a ghost if that was not something she should be used to by now.

She muttered, "My goodness," and gazed around the room again with a look of surprise, perhaps even fear.

"What is it, Lorna?" her mother asked.

"There are many spirits here. I mean, more than I have ever seen before," she said. "Too many, I can't focus."

"Close your eyes and concentrate on one of the living at a time," her mother instructed. "Find their personal spirits and leave the others in the shadows."

Lorna closed her eyes and took a deep breath. It was then I could see what she was talking about. Wisps of green light wove around her, though I knew I was the only one who could see it. She turned her head slightly towards Oscar and a faint green light enveloped him. Then it shot back to Lorna and disappeared into her body.

Her eyes opened, and a wide smile spread across her face.

"Oscar! It's me, my love!"

The voice coming out of her mouth wasn't her own, but that of a man. If she was faking this, she was truly a gifted mimic.

A startled Oscar seemed to recognise the voice straight away. "Derrick?"

"Yes! Oh, how I've wanted to talk to you. I have haunted you, but you did not feel my presence."

He shifted in his chair uncomfortably. "I see. Well, it is wonderful to talk to you once again…old friend."

"I forgive you, Oscar, if you can forgive me," Derrick said.

"I do," Oscar said, with a bit of sadness in his voice.

"I now understand how horrible it would have been to turn you into a creature like me."

Constance was looking quite confused, and whispered to Oscar, "Who is this person?"

Oscar didn't answer her and continued his awkward conversation with his spirit 'friend'. "Not a day goes by when I wished I didn't have to…send you away," he said. "If only there had been another way."

Lorna smiled slightly. "'Send me away'. Yes, I suppose that's what we should call it, here among polite company."

Lorna turned to look at us one by one. "And who do we have here? I recognise Henry Irving, of course. And the Stokers. I remember them from one of Wotton's tiresome parties."

Oscar didn't break our hand circle but used his eyes to dart and point. "The other lady at the table is my fiancée, Constance Lloyd."

Lorna refocused on Constance, and her eyes hardened. "Fiancée? Good luck with that, my dear."

"Oscar, who is this?" Constance asked, this time not in a whisper.

Fortunately for Oscar, he didn't have time to answer as Lorna's eyes rolled back and she gasped loudly. I could see the green spirit that possessed her being whisked away and another filling her up.

"You murdered me," a woman's voice cried. "You monster! You creature from hell!" She was most definitely looking at Henry.

Other green wisps swirled around Lorna, dodging in and out of her like a swarm of fireflies.

"Vampire!" a male voice with a Scottish brogue yelled.

Then a younger male with a Cockney accent said, "How dare you walk the earth when you put us in 'ere!"

A horrified Henry shouted, "I am sorry, so sorry, I can only say I have changed my ways. I no longer kill to live!"

A concerned Endora put her hands on her daughter's shoulders and said, "Push them out, child, concentrate on someone more worthy around this table."

The spirits scattered out of Lorna, and she looked at Constance. Henry was in tears. I had never seen him cry unless acting called for it, and I saw Florence squeeze his hand.

A new green light filled Lorna, and this was brighter with supernatural energy than the rest. She turned from Constance to Florence.

"You stupid bitch!" This voice was a woman's, deep and familiar. "I could have made you so much more than a mere woman. I could have given you real power!"

"Le Fey!" Florence gasped, pulling her hands from mine and Henry's. This must have broken the connection, for le Fey was thrown out of Lorna with great force, knocking Lorna over in her chair in the process. Her mother was behind her and stopped her from hitting the floor.

"Enough!" Endora yelled. "This sitting is over. Who are you people? Why are you surrounded by so many evil spirits? And you," she said, glaring at Henry. "A vampire? At my table? How dare you disturb the forces in this house with your depravity?"

We all just sat there dumbfounded, for she was right: we had brought these evil spirits with us. Henry looked ashamed and muttered an apology.

Endora was gently tapping Lorna's cheeks, reviving her from the ordeal.

"What happened?" Lorna asked, taking some deep breaths and coming fully around.

"Get out!" Endora screamed at us.

We started to get up, most of us visibly shaken by the events, when Lorna said, "Wait." She sat up straight and looked up at me. "Mr. Stoker, who is the Black Bishop?" Her eyes rolled back in her head again, and Endora shook her.

"No, no more spirits tonight!"

Lorna's eyes sprang back open, and she once again looked up at me. "You are in danger, Mr. Stoker. Great danger. He haunts you!"

"Out!" Endora commanded again.

We made our apologies and left.

"Who is Derrick?" Constance asked on the way out.

"Just someone I used to know," Oscar said. "He was turned into a vampire. He tried to do the same to me, and I had no choice but to kill him. I don't wish to talk of it further tonight."

Florence was shaking, as was I, on the carriage ride home.

Must we always be haunted by the supernatural? We both have done so much to push the past out of our heads, only to have it come rushing back in. I was a fool to stir up old spirits like that. It is something I will never do again.

FROM THE DIARY OF OSCAR WILDE, 22ND OF MAY 1884

Dear yours truly,

With my wedding barely a week away, I am lost in a dizzying flurry of details. Constance and her mother are dealing with the more frilly bridal things – dress fittings, floral arrangements and the like. However, the duties normally taken on by the father of the bride have fallen to me as Constance's father is dead – or at the very least trapped in the Realm – and her grandfather is not well. And of course, I feel bound by both personal belief and public image to ensure that every detail of the event lives up to my Aesthetic ideals.

I designed Constance's engagement ring myself, and after much searching have also found the perfect wedding ring – at first glance, it is a simple and elegant gold band, but it is actually two interlocking rings, one inscribed with our wedding date and the other with our names.

My bride also firmly believes that the principles of Aesthetics should be evident in our nuptials. Constance has worked closely with her favourite dressmaker to create a stunning gown in saffron satin. It is lovely, and I am not the only one to say so: the dressmaker is displaying it in her shop to admiring crowds.

The press is beside themselves, and the papers have been breathlessly reporting any detail of the event they can dig up. Of course, I have been carefully managing what information is released and when. We must save some surprises for the big day!

The search for a vicar to perform the ceremony was no simple task since I've done my best to avoid setting foot in a church and Constance has done the same. It seems my past run-in with the Bishop of Salisbury – in which I erroneously accused him of being a vampire – has put me in the Church's bad books. Honestly, diary, it was a mistake anybody could make! But in the end, we succeeded in booking St. James's

Church for the joyous event. A reception at Lancaster Gate will follow the wedding, with a beautiful cake adorned with jasmine and lily of the valley. All in all, I feel it will set the standard for Aesthetic weddings for years to come.

There was one less-traditional duty which also fell to me. Constance expressed concern that the rift between Florence and Ellen was making it difficult to assemble a seating chart. (It doesn't help that six of Constance's cousins are her bridesmaids and none of the families get along).

Therefore, I have taken it upon myself to bring these two closer together, if only temporarily for the sake of the wedding. As a good friend of both women (their closest male friend, surely) I felt I was uniquely suited to play peacemaker.

I invited them both to my London flat for tea. Neither had been to my little hideaway before. It is a modest three-room flat I keep for when I want to avoid my adoring fans or the company of Willie and Mother. The landlady is very discreet and protects my privacy. I will give it up after the wedding, of course, and shall miss my little oasis in the city.

Florence arrived first and was surprised to find that Constance was not there.

"Why, Mr. Wilde, you mean we are unchaperoned?" she asked. She was teasing; we have known each other far too long to concern ourselves with such niceties.

"Not exactly," I said. "Another guest will arrive soon."

She looked at me suspiciously but asked no questions as I fussed about the teapot.

We had but moments to wait before the second knock upon the door. When I showed Ellen into the sitting room, both women froze, staring at each other, before regaining their composure.

"Why, Florence, how lovely to see you," Ellen said with little warmth.

"The pleasure is mine," Florence replied with similar frostiness.

I ushered them to their seats and as I poured the tea and offered sandwiches and cakes, I broached the purpose of our meeting.

"My dear friends," I said, "I have known you both too long and too well to be anything but direct. We all know what has caused the rift between the two of you, so I shall not bring it up. I only ask, can you not leave your grievances in the past and be friends, or at least friendly?"

Ellen, at first, could not let go of her chilly politeness. "I don't know what you mean, Oscar. I have no grievance against Florence," she said. But even with all her acting skills, she could not keep up the pretence. Her expression softened, and she looked Florence in the eye. "None that are rational, anyway. Florence, I...I have resented you. I loved Bram – there, I've said it – but he chose you. I cannot honestly say that I regret my feelings, but I am sorry for the pain they caused you. It was a time of high emotion, and Bram felt he couldn't confide in you for your own protection. He never would have turned to me otherwise. He loves you, and I've accepted that."

Florence said nothing for a moment, her expression inscrutable. Then, to my astonishment and Ellen's, she took Ellen's hands in her own.

"Thank you, Ellen," she said. "I think I understand now what you and Bram had together. After our ordeal on the American frontier, I can see how danger and anxiety can draw two people together. Besides, I have forgiven Bram. Why should I not forgive you as well?"

And with that, the two women fell into a tearful embrace.

"Oh, I am so glad to see you two getting along," I said. "Life is too short to let past indiscretions hinder future happiness."

"Oscar," Ellen said, dabbing her eyes with her handkerchief, "I think this occasion calls for something a little stronger than tea."

I brought out my best bottle of cognac to flavour our Darjeeling. After that, the party grew much jollier.

"You know, Ellen," Florence said after finishing her first cup, "men have so much and women so little. We must stick together for our own welfare. Good female companionship is hard to come by and we share common interests in acting, as well as killing vampires."

Ellen agreed, and they clinked teacups, laughing.

"Besides," Florence continued, "I do not like myself full of envy."

I agreed it is the worst of the seven deadly sins and one should aim higher and shoot for lust or gluttony.

Florence said, "If we were French, little affairs would be as normal as a Saturday night bath. Alas, we are not French and so I prefer to keep my husband to myself. Still, we are an overly pious people. It does not serve us well. We often fall from grace because we put too much stock in it."

"As Oscar is fond of saying," Ellen said as she refilled her teacup with more cognac, "'Men always want to be a woman's first love, and women like to be a man's last romance.'"

Florence, emboldened by drink, then asked me if I were ready for marriage, and if I was indeed happy with my decision.

"I can't think of a better match for me," I told them. "We are equals in art and intellect. It will be a good partnership on many levels."

They both thought that I sounded unromantic. (Imagine, calling me unromantic!) I assured them that my love for Constance is deep and true and that I would not give up my bachelorhood for just any woman. I added some paeans to her beauty for good measure.

"Should I read a poem at the wedding, Oscar?" Ellen asked. "Or perhaps Act 2, Scene 2 from *Romeo & Juliet*?"

I told her the ceremony would be short as Constance's grandfather is ill and we don't want him to be kept sitting for so long, but I appreciated the offer.

As they left, Florence kissed me on the cheek. "I am so very happy for you and Constance. A man is not complete until he is married, then he is finished," she said, quoting yours truly.

FROM THE JOURNAL OF BRAM STOKER, 23RD OF MAY 1884

6:15 p.m.

Poor Willie Wilde. I feel like I haven't been a very good friend to him of late. I hardly have any time available for socialising these days, what with work and family life. When I do find myself with a free evening, it inevitably coincides with a full moon, when Willie is, of course, indisposed. It must be difficult maintaining a social life when one is a werewolf.

Today Oscar sent me an urgent note asking me to come to Lady Wilde's home immediately. I rushed over to find Dr. Seward attending a bedridden Willie, and a fretting Lady Wilde and Oscar at his bedside.

Willie, apparently in an attempt to find a cure for his lycanthropy, had drunk a bottle of colloidal silver.

"Normally it isn't toxic," Dr. Seward told us. "In fact, I give it for all sorts of maladies and my patients have never had an adverse reaction. But given his…condition, the effects are more detrimental. It is like he swallowed thousands of microscopic silver bullets."

Dr. Seward paused to write something in his notebook, then said, "It makes one wonder if humans could drink colloidal silver to protect themselves from vampires and other supernatural creatures who are repelled by silver."

He gave Willie a sedative to help with his discomfort, told Lady Wilde to send for him if Willie's condition worsened, and took his leave. Between this and his work with Henry, he has quite a thriving side practice, tending to the supernatural creatures of London.

Once Willie was resting comfortably, Oscar took me aside and told me he fears Willie wasn't trying to cure himself but may have been attempting to end it all.

"He has been miserable, poor chap," Oscar said. "The change is extremely painful, and he becomes more morose as each full moon approaches. He worries he may harm someone, despite the precautions he takes. He did get loose once, you recall, and the memory haunts him."

I thought back to the time we hunted a werewolf in Ireland and the moments when I channelled the werewolf's memories of a brutal attack, and I feel I can understand Willie's apprehension. It must be terrifying to feel one's self-control slip away like that. I often lament my own supernatural curse, but it is nothing compared to what Willie must go through. My visions can be disconcerting and they often bring trouble to my doorstep, but they are not painful and, on the whole, they have proven useful when I channel them properly.

I have resolved to be a better friend to Willie and to the Wilde family. I will take shifts watching him on a full moon and relieve Oscar and his mother of some of the burden, and will make a better effort to socialise with Willie, for he and I have more in common than most. It is hard to explain to others how this unnatural power feels, how it corrupts and strips away our humanity. I hope I can help him make peace with his plight.

FROM THE DIARY OF LORNA BOW, 25TH OF MAY 1884

Dear diary,

Communicating with the dead is strange enough, but today's session was weirder than anything I have attempted before, and scary too. It was odd right from the start, as we did the séance outside of the parlour, which I have never done before.

We took a carriage all the way out into the country, to a large estate owned by Dr. Mueller. He attended one of our recent séances. He must have liked what he saw because Mother says he is paying us ten times the going rate to try to channel his wife. I did not know why we had to come all the way out here to do this, but when someone offers you that much money, a trip out to the country doesn't seem too much to ask.

Mother was concerned that a great deal of time has passed since the wife's death, that the spirit may have moved on and that Dr. Mueller would be very disappointed if we couldn't contact her. She warned him of this, but still, he insisted we try.

"Failure is possible in all experiments," he said. He has a German accent, but his English is very good. He is handsome for an older gentleman and seems to be a nice man, although you can't always tell, can you?

He took us to a building next to a windmill on the property. He told us he had converted it into a laboratory where he does research to help the sick.

In this laboratory, he had all sorts of science equipment and what he referred to as 'specimens' in all sizes of glass jars. And by specimens I mean body parts...human body parts. Hands, arms, feet, brains, eyeballs and the like. I should have been frightened at the sight of it all, but I wasn't. Mother was there, and I knew she could protect us if this was a maniac's lair we were walking into.

"Before we attempt a transfer, perhaps we could try to contact Charlotte to see if the soul is even available for the procedure," he said.

I did not know what he meant by transfer but did not ask questions.

He took us into a smaller, windowless room with only a round table and three chairs. The table had a single kerosene lamp in the centre, which he lit and turned down low. "I hope this is sufficient for the channelling."

Mother said it was, and we all sat down at the table and held hands to form our circle. I was glad Mother was holding my hand, as I can draw energy from her if I need it to make my channelling stronger.

Though I knew we were there to contact his wife, I asked him to say out loud who he wished to speak to and told him to picture her when he said her name.

"Charlotte," he said. We all concentrated, but to no avail. If Charlotte has not moved on, she is at the very least not lingering around her husband. I could feel spirits being drawn to him, but none of them were her. These were dark shadows, spirits who had been offered the doorway to leave and chose not to go. They had a feeling of dread about them and they circled but stayed just out of my vision so I could not see them clearly.

I would have to ask for help from the other side. There are what Mother calls 'spirit guides', those who are willing to help us find souls. She says it's because they long for any connection to the living they can get, and helping us is a fair trade for a momentary glimpse into the living world.

We have our trusted regulars, Mr. Shaw, Miss Bentley and Mr. Thomas. They seem to hover around us all the time in hopes of making a connection and being useful.

"I will attempt to find us a guide," I said. "Mr. Shaw? Miss Bentley? Mr. Thomas? Anyone available to help find a lost spirit?"

Then, in an instant, one of the circling shadows swooshed in and entered me with such force it rocked me back in my chair. Only Mother's hand kept me from falling over to the floor.

When spirits enter me, I grow smaller. I feel myself get pushed down as they look out my eyes and use my ears and voice. But I had never felt anything like this! I was pushed so far down I thought I would disappear. This spirit not only had control of my eyes, ears and mouth, it filled my entire body, pushing me out of the muscles in my arms and legs.

Mother saw immediately that there was something wrong. She squeezed my hand and shouted, "Get out, spirit, you are not welcome here!"

I felt a laugh come up from my belly and out my mouth and it...she spoke. "I often go where I am not welcome." Her voice was smooth yet powerful. I remembered that voice and that presence – though it was much stronger now – from a séance a few days ago. I did not like it.

"Who are you?" Mother asked.

"I am Carolyn le Fey," she said, grinning and turning her head – I could hardly call it mine anymore – to look directly at Dr. Mueller. "We meet again, good doctor."

Dr. Mueller looked terrified and pulled his hand out of the circle. This did nothing to weaken her, as it often does during a séance.

"Yes, I see you remember me. I believe the Black Bishop made me give you a pint of my blood." She glanced at Mother. "My vampire blood."

Mother squeezed my hand even tighter and began chanting an incantation. I could feel her trying to push le Fey out of me.

"No!" le Fey yelled as a shot of energy passed from my hand to Mother's, forcing her to let go and throwing her out of her chair.

"I think this young body will do just fine," she said. She ran her hands over my breasts. I felt her starting to control my legs as she began to stand. Suddenly, another spirit moved in and grabbed her and I fell back into my chair.

"No, no!" she screamed, and this other spirit forced himself in and her out. This one felt lighter. He did not try to control anything but my voice, and I slumped as I felt myself filling up my own body once again. We shared my body, but I was once again in control of myself.

"I am so sorry about Miss le Fey," the voice said. It was a male voice, friendly and calm.

Mother returned to her chair and retook my hand. "Who are we speaking to now?"

Before he could answer, Dr. Mueller said, "Richard? Richard Wilkins?"

"Yes," he said, turning to Dr. Mueller. "It's me, Victor. Reverend

Wilkins." He said it jovially, as if he was happy to see his old friend, though I wondered why Dr. Mueller still had a look of dread on his face.

Mother too was concerned and asked the doctor, "Who is this spirit to you?"

"A former colleague of mine," he said. "A very dangerous person."

Dr. Mueller turned back to me and Mr. Wilkins. "I should have known if anyone would haunt me it would be you."

"I bear you no ill will," Wilkins said through me. "The things I did, however misguided, were to help all of mankind. Tell me, how can I help you now? Why are you interested in the spirit realm?"

Dr. Mueller still seemed wary, but said, "I wish to locate my deceased wife, Charlotte. Is this something you can do?"

"Yes, we all have that power here. Though she may not want to talk to you. The dead can be resentful of the living."

Dr. Mueller jumped to his feet. "Tell her I can bring her back! I have reanimated her body, and all she has to do is step into it." He pointed to Mother. "This necromancer can help her cross back over!"

"I will look for her, wait here," the spirit said, and I felt him slip out of me like a silk handkerchief being pulled out of a pocket.

I told the others he was gone. We waited for what felt like a good half an hour before I once again felt him slipping into my body.

"I am sorry, Victor," he said. "I am afraid she has moved on. She did so almost immediately after arriving here. The good ones often do."

Dr. Mueller hung his head down, and a low moan escaped him as his shoulders shook.

After a moment, he collected himself. "I know I should be pleased that my Charlotte's soul has gone on to heaven," he said, dabbing at his face with a handkerchief. "But it leaves me with nothing. I had hoped that we would be reunited, but everything has been taken from me again."

I could feel the spirit of Wilkins patiently giving Dr. Mueller a moment to grieve, but eventually, he spoke.

"Could you bring me back, Victor? Could you put me in a new body?"

"And why would I do that, after you almost destroyed the world?" Dr. Mueller said. He pushed his chair in and turned to leave the table, telling Mother that we should end the séance, which I was only too eager to do.

But before I could push Wilkins out, he spoke again. "I know I have done bad things, Victor, but I want to atone. Give me a second chance to show I am worthy of redemption," Wilkins pleaded. "I can't do that from the afterlife."

"We only get one life," Mueller said. "You made a mess of yours. I can't help you."

Wilkins rose up within me and shouted like a street preacher, "Think of it, Victor. Not only could you conquer death, but you could conquer hell itself! We could offer everyone a second chance to come to God and do good for all of humanity. You say you have lost everything, but you still have your life's work – that can be your second chance, as well as mine. Charlotte would want your work to continue. You have brought people back from the dead, now rescue us from purgatory!"

Mueller pulled his chair out and sat back down. I could feel Wilkins' anticipation; I could tell as well as he could that Mueller would give in.

Mueller thought for a moment and said, "Yes, I need to see if this can be done, for science if nothing else."

"Bring me back and I will be your greatest creation," Wilkins said. I felt Wilkins experience something I can only describe as joy, but there was something not right about it. Wilkins' joy held a tinge of hate and I became frightened.

"I have a body I can use," Mueller said. "A young man who would be a perfect specimen for such an experiment."

"Any body will do," Wilkins said. "I am your humble servant."

"It will take me a day to resurrect him." He asked Mother if we were willing to attempt the transfer tomorrow. She said we would.

"All right, let's try this," Dr. Mueller said. "We will contact you at the same time tomorrow for the attempt."

"I will be waiting," Wilkins said. He slipped back into the darkness and I was once again all to myself.

Mother asked Dr. Mueller if he really wanted to do this, as he seemed not very pleased to see Mr. Wilkins at first.

"If any soul has the fortitude to make a transfer back to the living world, it is Reverend Wilkins," Dr. Mueller said. "His fear of hell will make him a most willing subject."

As it was getting late, Dr. Mueller offered to let us stay the night. Mother agreed.

We had dinner with him. He has an excellent cook, and we dined on goose cooked in apples. The servants made up a bedroom for me and I turned in for the night as Mother and Dr. Mueller stayed up and talked about the 'experiment'.

As I write this, I wonder if it is the right thing to do. Are we really bringing someone back from the dead? It seems like magic even beyond Mother's power. Somehow it does not seem like something we should be doing. I have my doubts, but I will trust in Mother.

FROM THE DIARY OF FLORENCE STOKER, 26TH OF MAY 1884

I stopped in at the Lyceum today only to find the theatre in an uproar. Ellen had locked herself in her dressing room and was refusing to come out.

Seems she had a bit of a row with her make-up man. Ellen insisted she needed more wrinkles to play Lady Macbeth as the character is older than she; he disagreed, and this sent her into a rage.

This was merely the latest tribulation, for though the production debuted with great success, it has recently had a run of bad luck. Bram has come home with many stories of actors and actresses forgetting their lines, missing cues and the like. Their Banquo took ill and had to be replaced, and the new costumer seems unable to properly alter clothing as his jacket had one sleeve three inches longer than the other. One wonders if someone accidentally uttered the word 'Macbeth' in the theatre!

Henry is not happy. He cancelled a week of shows, ordered additional rehearsal and a restaging and fired their Macduff. This had put the entire cast and crew in a foul mood, which I'm sure contributed to the friction between Ellen and her make-up artist.

Bram suggested maybe a woman would have a better chance of getting Ellen to return to rehearsal, so it was time for me to put our rekindled friendship to the test. I knocked on her dressing room door and announced myself. To my surprise, she quickly opened the door and yanked me inside before closing and locking it again.

She had been crying and drinking. Tears had made little rivers of ruined make-up down her cheeks.

"Oh, Florrie," she cried. (She has never called me Florrie before, always Florence or Mrs. Stoker). "It is all going so badly. I cannot remember my lines. I'm losing my acting instinct!"

I pointed out this was understandable as it is quite a long play and there are many lines for Lady Macbeth.

She sat in her make-up chair and picked up a glass of Scotch. She looked at herself in the mirror, which I have to admit was not a pretty sight at the moment, and said, "I am old. I am an old trollop who never could really act. Once I had my youth and beauty to cover for my inadequacies, but now I do not have even that." She gulped down some Scotch and continued to stare at herself critically.

I took my handkerchief from my sleeve, turned her gently from the mirror and dried her tears. "Nonsense, Ellen. You are still a great beauty and an even better actress. Why, you are the most acclaimed actress in all of London."

She looked up at me, blinking.

"Am I?"

"You are probably the most famous actress in Europe and maybe even North America after our last tour."

"Oh, no, that's Lillie Langtry, surely," she said in a small voice.

"Lillie Langtry? Ha!" I said. "Why, I heard she just went off to Paris for acting lessons, something you do not need. Must I remind you of your rave reviews? Now, let's stop feeling sorry for ourselves. Wash your face and we shall go to Brown's Hotel for a nice tea."

"They're waiting for me to rehearse."

"They can rehearse some other scene. You need time to gather your composure, and they need time to remember who the star is around here."

This lifted her spirits. She fixed her face, and we went and had a lovely tea.

I must admit, even after our reconciliation at Oscar's flat, I am somewhat surprised at myself for helping her. There was a time when I would have used her lack of confidence against her, maybe even tried to steal the part from her. I am happy that I could rise above those baser instincts and be a friend to her when she needed one.

At tea she confided to me that she has been melancholy lately because she has grown apart from her children. They are off to boarding school in Switzerland and when they are home on holidays that home is with their father and his male 'companion'.

"They barely know me, and that is all my fault. I put career over them and now I feel it is coming to an end and so it wasn't worth it."

I pointed out that her career is far from over. Maybe she will have to start playing older characters, but she should look forward to the acting challenges those roles will bring. That set me to wondering what challenges were left in my own life.

"Why does it have to be so difficult for women to be true to themselves and still have a family?" I said. "I wish I could have my own career, for when Noel is grown, what will I have left to do?"

After that, the conversation drifted here and there and I found myself telling her about the séance Bram and I attended with Henry, Oscar and Constance.

"How ghastly," she said. "A shiver has just run down my spine. Imagine, actual spirits and some evil ones at that."

I asked her what she knew about Derrick, the spirit that had talked to Oscar.

"They were friends, he told me," she said. "Very special friends, I would imagine, as he was said to be a very beautiful young man. Oscar tried to find him when he became involved with the Black Bishop's vampires. When Derrick became one himself, a vampire I mean, he tried to turn Oscar as well, and Oscar was forced to kill him."

Poor Oscar, I thought. Then my thoughts turned to Constance. I have long had my suspicions about Oscar's...proclivities. Will they surface once he and Constance are married? Is his love for Constance enough? I did not say this to Ellen, but she seemed to sense it.

"I am quite fond of Constance," Ellen said. "I hope Oscar doesn't break her heart."

"Well, we will just have to see that he doesn't," I said, toasting with my cup of tea.

As we were preparing to leave, she thanked me and said I had put her into better spirits. She also said that she would talk to Henry about more roles for me, maybe even leading roles.

"If I have to lose roles to a younger woman, I would like it to be you."

FROM THE DIARY OF LORNA BOW, 26TH OF MAY 1884

I awoke this morning in a big feather bed in Dr. Mueller's house. A fire was burning in the fireplace and servants had set out a breakfast for me, croissants and hot chocolate. I could get used to being rich.

A maid drew me a bath, and I soaked for a while, thinking about what was about to happen. Could we really put a spirit into a new body? It shouldn't be as surprising to me as it is since I put them into my own body. Still, how will they stay in them?

I dressed and went out into the hall, where I saw Mother coming out of Dr. Mueller's room in a dressing gown. She didn't see me as she went to her own room.

Will I be calling Dr. Mueller 'Father' soon, or was it just a dalliance? None of my business, I guess, but shocking considering they barely know each other. Still, I could think of worse people for mother to bed down with. Dr. Mueller is kind and handsome and rich and smart.

While Mother dressed, I wandered through the big house. I lost count of the rooms but was happy to find a large, well-stocked library. A lot of the books are in German, but plenty were in English. Maybe I will learn German.

I am told Dr. Mueller owns an automobile. Won't that be something to see?

Later in the morning, Dr. Mueller called Mother and me to his lab. The windmill was spinning quite fast that day, as it was very blustery. In the main room, gears were turning high in the ceiling. Dr. Mueller has attached something he calls a 'dynamo' to it to generate electricity for the house and lab.

I was shocked to see a naked man lying on a table at the centre of the room. There wasn't a sheet on him or anything!

I'd say he was in his early thirties. He had blond hair and was very muscular. I tried not to look at his member, but I couldn't help it.

Mother caught me staring, and I thought she would tell me to stop, but she only smiled at me and whispered, "They usually aren't that big."

Dr. Mueller was busy removing wires from the man and he stirred on the table, occasionally moaning. The man had stitches on his left shoulder, and the arm there looked different enough from the right arm to tell me it had been taken from another body and sewn onto this one.

Dr. Mueller noticed me and covered the man's lower half with a sheet.

"He's alive?" Mother asked.

"Yes," Dr. Mueller said. "Resurrected just an hour ago. I've given him a mild sedative."

"Where did you get...the body?" I stammered. Visions of Dr. Mueller murdering people for his experiments went through my mind.

"He was a factory worker who died when his arm was ripped off in machinery. It was too mangled to reattach, but I found a suitable replacement. He should make an excellent specimen for our experiment."

To the side of the operating table was a round table for our sitting. In the centre of the table was a small cage with a white rat in it. I wasn't sure if this was part of the magic or not, but didn't like that it was on our table. I'm not fond of rats, even if they are safely locked away in cages.

"Are we ready?" Mother asked.

Dr. Mueller said we were, and we all sat down at the table and took each other's hands.

I went into my trance state and immediately saw Reverend Wilkins waiting for me. The scary woman spirit that tried to take me over was hanging around too. He gently pushed her away back into the shadows and slipped into me.

"Thank you all for this," Wilkins said through me. I could feel his anticipation for what was to come.

Mother got up from our round table and went over to the man

on the operating table. She placed her hand on his chest and held up her other hand towards me. She began mumbling something I could not hear, and I felt Mr. Wilkins slipping away from me, but not back into the shadows. This time I watched him as a misty light, fluttering towards mother and into her outstretched hand.

With a *snap* I could feel and hear, he left me and went fully into Mother, breaking my trance state in the process.

She looked up to the ceiling and started chanting her incantation louder and louder. She looked to be in great pain. Streaks of white appeared in her beautiful red hair and her skin began to wrinkle.

Then, in an instant, it was done. Mother dropped to her knees. "Lorna, bring me the rat."

I knew then it was to be a blood sacrifice to restore her vitality. Without hesitation, I opened the cage, grabbed the rat (with my bare hands!) and rushed it over to her.

She took it and crushed it between her hands until it burst open and spilt its blood through her clenched fingers. Dr. Mueller looked on, his mouth hanging open but his eyes shining with curiosity, as Mother's hair once again went back to red and her skin smoothed. I helped her to her feet.

We all turned to look at the man on the table with great anticipation. He took a deep breath and his eyes opened. He sat up and his sheet slipped to the floor. This time Dr. Mueller did not rush to cover him, but I did not care as I was eager to see if the reverend was truly in the body.

He smiled broadly and looked up and down his body and at his hands as he turned them in the air.

"It worked! It really worked!"

Dr. Mueller brought him a dressing gown and helped him slip it on.

"We did it, Victor, we actually did it!" He clasped Dr. Mueller by the shoulders, and both men laughed loudly.

He got off the table, and the two men danced around the room in joy. Mother and I joined them, for we were all elated and amazed at what we had just done.

Later we all sat down to a celebratory feast. There was a big ham and lots of bread and vegetables. And, best of all, many desserts! Cakes and puddings with all sorts of icings and sauces.

Yes, I could get used to being rich, I thought as I saw Dr. Mueller taking Mother's hand under the table.

Mother is right; we are doing good work, and it feels gratifying to do so.

FROM THE JOURNAL OF DR. VICTOR MUELLER, 27TH OF MAY 1884

I have made the greatest scientific breakthrough in history. My one regret is that it was not in time to return my beloved Charlotte to life. But I know she would want me to continue our life's work. It is all I have now.

I alone have conquered death!

I have successfully transferred a lost soul into one of my creations. I have rescued the Reverend Richard Wilkins from purgatory and placed his soul into a new, superior body.

He is grateful to have a second chance at life and a second chance at redemption.

I sent Endora and Lorna back to the house for a well-deserved rest. Wilkins admired his new body as he got dressed.

I asked him how he felt, if there was someone else in the body he had to contend with.

"I feel remarkable. I sense no one else in this…vessel. It is mine and mine alone." He made a fist and bent his arm to flex his bicep.

"I am so strong and vital. My sin of gluttony, I am ashamed to admit, ravaged my last body. I am grateful to have a fit body to start with in my rebirth."

He caressed his left arm with his right hand. "This arm is numb and cold."

I told him I had to replace it with a spare and it should come fully to life in time.

"My first success, Risto, I stitched together with parts from many different bodies."

He told me he was misguided in his past attempts to usher in a new age of the church by bringing monsters into the world, but his heart was in the right place.

"Think of how many souls we can save, Victor," he said, at his first dinner in his new body. "What will be our next steps?"

I told him I had enough of the Stoker Serum to bring back two, maybe three more. I told him I hope to one day synthesise the properties of Stoker's blood so we would no longer have to use it, but for now, getting more of it was our only option.

"We will have to replenish our supply then," he said. "You can leave that to me and my friends. That is, if you can bring a couple of them back for me. We will need them to help carry on our work."

Mr. Pendergast at the London morgue has come through again with more bodies.

Wilkins wishes to bring back a female, Miss le Fey. I have my reservations about this, knowing her reputation, and the way she tried to overpower Lorna two days ago, but Wilkins assures me that was the vampire in her and she will behave much better as a human. I agreed, since it will be interesting to experiment on a female, to see if there are any differences in the results.

He also wishes to bring back two others, Lord Wotton and Lord Sundry, who he says will be loyal to our cause and will help him in getting more of Stoker's blood for our work.

"They have a burning hate for Stoker and the White Worms, as I do," he said.

I told him of my dealings with the Worms and that they are most bothersome. And I mentioned what they had done to Endora, banishing her to the Realm and separating her from her child.

"They are monsters," he said. "If we were to join forces with Endora, we might be able to put an end to them once and for all."

REPORT FROM WHITE WORM SOCIETY AGENT CORA CHASE

Date: 27 May 1884
Subject: Endora Bow Investigation

My continued surveillance of the Bow séance parlor has uncovered some troubling events.

I saw Endora and Lorna Bow leave by private carriage on Sunday. It was a well-appointed carriage of gleaming mahogany with red velvet upholstered seats, indicating it was sent by someone of means.

I hired my own, less luxurious carriage and followed them, staying far enough behind to remain unobtrusive.

We ended up at a country estate in Bricket Wood, just outside of London.

There they were met by a man, a distinguished older gentleman with dark hair and rose-colored spectacles.

The man took them into a building adjacent to a windmill on the property.

The windows of the building were too high for me to see inside, and on the side of the building where I could remain hidden there were no windows at all. I secreted myself in nearby shrubbery and waited.

An hour or so later, Endora, Lorna and the man left the building through a side door and went up to the main house.

I took that opportunity to slip inside the building, where I found a laboratory stocked with beakers, chemicals and electrical equipment. It appears the windmill is being used to generate power, both to provide electrical lighting to the lab and to power this equipment.

To my horror, as I went deeper into the lab, I found human body parts stored in liquid-filled jars.

I also found papers and letters, and after only a moment of reading, I deduced this lab is owned by none other than Dr. Victor Mueller!

It appears he is up to his old tricks, resurrecting human bodies, but this time with a twist. According to his notes, he has hired the necromancer and her medium daughter to 'put a soul' into one of his creations. Is this possible? And, if so, what would be the point in such an endeavour?

Not knowing how much time I had before Mueller returned to the lab, I grabbed some of his notes and correspondence and made my exit.

I had sent my carriage away, not wishing it to attract attention, and so I walked to the nearby village where I arranged transport back to London.

I am awaiting instruction on how we should proceed.

MEMO FROM WHITE WORM SOCIETY DIRECTOR HAMMOND TO AGENT CORA CHASE

Date: 27 May 1884
Subject: Mueller Investigation Next Steps

Outstanding work, Agent Chase. We shall take it from here as we do not wish to delay your return to America. Please turn over all materials to headquarters before you leave. When you return to America, you will resume your duties with a rise in rank. Thank you for your service in this matter.

Order signed:
Director Errol Hammond

SOCIETY COLUMN FROM *LADY'S PICTORIAL MAGAZINE*, 29TH MAY 1884

By Lady Violet Greville, exclusive to *Lady's Pictorial*

The event that has long been anticipated among Londoners has finally arrived: the wedding of Mr. Oscar Wilde and Miss Constance Lloyd. Many wondered if the perpetually avant-garde Mr. Wilde would actually commit to something so conventional as marriage – especially after a planned April wedding was postponed. But we are happy to report that the ceremony took place on the 29th of May at St. James's Church in Sussex Gardens, and the young couple was radiant with joy.

The bride followed her retinue of six bridesmaids – all cousins, we have learned – down the aisle, beaming from beneath a pearl-embroidered veil of Indian silk gauze and a wreath of myrtle leaves. Her gown was of saffron-hued satin – the colour, we are told, that maidens wore on their wedding days in ancient Greece. In keeping with the tenets of Aestheticism, it was of simple but pleasing design, un-bustled, with a low-cut bodice, a Medici collar, a long train, and puffed sleeves. She carried a bouquet of lilies.

The groom, despite his reputation as a dandy, kept his attire simple as well. Wearing a traditional frock coat, he awaited his bride at the altar alongside his best man, his brother, William Wilde. He appeared serene, with none of the nerves that bridegrooms often exhibit, and gazed adoringly at his maiden fair as she walked down the aisle on the arm of her uncle. The couple exchanged their vows, and Mr. Wilde placed a ring on the new Mrs. Wilde's finger.

Following the ceremony was a brief reception at Lancaster Gate. A beautiful cake covered in jasmine and lily of the valley was served, and champagne flowed in abundance. Family and friends toasted the happy couple, including such luminaries as James Whistler, Henry Irving, Ellen Terry and Lillie Langtry.

Only one incident marred the day: an uninvited guest. This correspondent witnessed a tall, handsome blond man helping himself to glass after glass of champagne, yet he seemed to take no pleasure in the occasion. Indeed, he spent most of his time staring with apparent hostility at the groom, as well as another of the guests, a large, ginger-haired man whom we have identified as Bram Stoker, manager of the Lyceum Theatre and long-time friend of Mr. Wilde from his youth in Dublin.

Someone must have alerted William Wilde to the interloper's presence, for he soon appeared and, after a brief conversation, took the stranger by the elbow and escorted him from the venue. The only part of their exchange we overheard was Mr. Wilde saying, "Drinking more than one's fair share of champagne is my job."

By late afternoon, the happy couple was en route to Charing Cross Station to leave for their honeymoon in Paris. The bride by this time had changed into a dark mahogany travelling dress that perfectly set off her chestnut tresses. One positively envies the Parisians for playing host to the young couple's no doubt blissful first weeks of matrimony, but we Londoners need not despair; they will return to our welcoming arms soon enough.

FROM THE DIARY OF LORNA BOW, 31ST OF MAY 1884

Something remarkable happened to Mother and me today.

As we walked together in Dr. Mueller's garden, she said, "With every spirit, we bring to this earthly plane, I feel my power grow stronger."

I told her I was also feeling more…charged than usual. Not only can I contact spirits more easily, I feel as though I have other powers ready to burst forth. "I don't know how to explain it," I said. "But it's like I'm a horse in a stall, just waiting for the door to open so I can run free."

There was a ruckus coming from the kitchen and we returned to the house to see what it was about. One of the maids had fallen down the stairs and broken her leg. They had her laid out on the kitchen table, and people were in a panic trying to tend to her. The cook sent a footman to fetch Dr. Mueller from his lab.

The woman was screaming with pain, and I could see a bone sticking out of her leg! I would have certainly passed out if that were happening to me since I was almost fainting just at the sight of it.

Mother put her hand to the woman's forehead, and she suddenly stopped screaming. In fact, a look of calm came over her face and she started to breathe normally.

Mother has told me we can use our powers to heal people and animals, but it requires a life to 'balance the scales' as she calls it. I asked her if I should go to the barn and get a pig, but she told me she didn't need it.

Mother kept one hand on the woman's forehead and put one hand on her leg near the protruding bone. Mother closed her eyes and recited an incantation over and over again. All around were shocked to watch the bone pull itself back into the leg. The bleeding stopped and the gash in her leg closed up.

There were hushed mumblings among the staff until Dr. Mueller came in. When he learned what had happened, he reminded the servants that they were being paid well for their discretion and told them all to go back about their work. Mother said the healed maid should rest for the remainder of the day and she was permitted to return to her room.

As she was leaving, supported by a kitchen maid, she stopped in front of Mother. "Thank you, miss," she said, curtsying awkwardly.

Mother laid a hand lightly on her forearm and smiled. "Not at all," she said. "You rest now, your body has been through a great deal."

The two maids continued on their way, but even before they made it out of the kitchen, the injured woman was standing straighter and barely leaning on the other woman anymore.

Later, Mother came to my room. She reminded me it was my birthday. I had forgotten, as I did most years. She gave me a large, old book.

"These are the spells of our ancestors and their ancestors. Strong magic that we now have the power to do. That *you* have the power to do."

It was in some old language with an alphabet that looked like pictures. I couldn't read it, of course, but mother had a spell for that and cast it on me. When I looked at the writing, it leapt off the page into my mind and I could understand every word.

"There is no telling how powerful we can become if we continue to bring souls back to life. I think we get a part of their energy every time we do." She opened her clenched fist and sparks of green energy danced in her palm.

"Can you feel it?"

I nodded.

"I can do magic now without a blood sacrifice," she said. "With this new energy, there is no better time to start your training."

FROM THE JOURNAL OF BRAM STOKER, 2ND OF JUNE 1884

11:35 p.m.

For as many times as I've cursed my sixth sense and the visions it brings, today I curse its failure to manifest. Is it gone for good? Why didn't it activate today when I was attacked by something that was clearly supernatural in nature?

The girl medium had even warned me I was in danger from the Black Bishop, and I still suspected nothing! I assumed she spoke of a spirit and I had nothing to fear. But the horrible truth is that the fiend has returned from the dead and I almost let him kill me.

Why should I have suspected anything when a tall, fair-haired man appeared in the lobby of the theatre? He was well dressed and seemed friendly enough. He introduced himself as Mr. Salisbury and said he was a theatrical promoter and wished to discuss a possible tour of the continent for which he would pay our troupe handsomely.

I would have preferred him to make an appointment but felt I should hear him out, so I invited him in and took him upstairs to my office. It was our dark day, so I was alone in the theatre except for a few craftsmen working on scenery in the basement.

His nom de guerre of 'Mr. Salisbury' should have triggered something in my brain, since Wilkins was a vicar in Salisbury, but that dreadful experience is long past, so I thought nothing of it.

There was no tingling of my supernatural sense as he sat across from me at my desk, chattering away.

"We would like to start the tour in Paris and then Vienna, Prague, Berlin and St. Petersburg," he said, looking around my office. "Is Mr. Irving in to discuss the matter?"

I told him we did not expect Henry until the evening, but I am the one to speak with in matters like these and that I would evaluate the worthiness of the offer before bringing it to Mr. Irving.

Having concluded our discussion, we both stood, and I moved to show him out.

He reached into his jacket pocket, saying, "Here, let me leave you my calling card."

I held my hand out, and he put something in it that wasn't a card. A black bishop chess piece stared up at me from my open palm!

A wide, evil grin spread across his face as he tilted his head down slightly and stared into my eyes. It was his eyes that gave him away. There was something cold and dead about them now.

"Yes, Bram. It is I, Richard Wilkins. Dr. Mueller sends his regards."

I went for the pistol I keep in my centre desk drawer, but he shoved the desk towards me with substantial force, pinning me up against the wall. Though he was simply holding the desk with one hand, I could not budge it.

He had the strength of a vampire but wasn't triggering my sixth sense. Then Dr. Mueller's voice bounced around in my head. Hadn't he said his creatures retain vampire traits? Risto hadn't triggered my sense either.

"As you can see, Mr. Stoker, not even death can keep me from my mission. God and Dr. Mueller have granted me a second chance. This time you will not stop me! You laughed at me in that country church as you let the vampire rip my head off. I could return the favour – I have that much strength. But we need you alive. Once again, we need your cursed blood."

He leapt onto the desk and kicked me hard in the face, almost knocking me unconscious, then jumped down off the desk and shoved it away. He grabbed me by my lapels and yanked me to my feet. "You will come with me to help us with our work, or I will send you and your loved ones to hell!"

The office door was flung open, and he turned to see Ellen standing there with a pistol.

"Drop him," she ordered. He instead threw me across the room, crashing me into a bookcase.

Ellen did not hesitate. She shot him twice, hitting his left arm and the upper right part of his chest. He flinched with each shot, but they did not drop him.

He made a move as if to lunge at Ellen, but she held her ground, sighting down the pistol. "The next one will be through your head," she said.

He obviously didn't want to take his chances. His only exit not blocked by a gun was my office window, and he crashed through the glass and onto the street, two stories below.

Ellen ran to the window. "Oh drat, he is halfway down the street already." She returned to me and helped me to my feet. "Vampire?"

"No, something else. Something worse," I said. "He is the Black Bishop in a reanimated corpse."

She stared at me for a moment but remained remarkably unperturbed.

"Nothing is ever ordinary around you, Bram, is it?"

I set my office back to rights. There was a little blood on the floor where he had been standing, and also some odd, greenish fluid that must be a by-product of Mueller's work.

I have seen Mueller's success with reanimation of corpses, of course, but the mystery remains: how did the Black Bishop come to be in one of these creations? He was most definitely dead the last time I saw him. Had Dr. Mueller retrieved his head and transplanted his brain into this new body? He could have kept it on ice, like his wife's corpse, until he had need of it. But why?

I have contacted the White Worms, and they have sent Mr. Blackwood to watch the house and other agents to guard Ellen and the theatre. They are also investigating this new development. They seem just as astounded as I am.

As I write this, Florence is beside herself with worry. I have given her a small pistol to carry with her at all times, as Ellen already does.

I will also talk to Oscar when he returns from his honeymoon. The Bishop will likely be after him too, and he needs to be warned. Together we can figure out what our next steps should be.

We have killed this bastard once, and we can do it again.

FROM THE DIARY OF LORNA BOW, 3RD OF JUNE 1884

We returned to London yesterday. It is good to be home with the girls again. They were happy to see us and learn about our new line of work.

Mother called me to the garden this morning to begin my training. Molly asked if she could watch and Mother said she could but had to remain quiet.

"Before the selfish gods took over Greece and Rome, before the trinity god conquered both of them, the gods of the north and south shared their power with humans," Mother said. "That power still flows through our bloodline and lets us wield the forces of nature."

She pointed to a grass snake in the flower bed. "The snake does not slither; it *is* the slither. The bird does not fly; it *is* flight. We can harness their essence. Their power is our power."

She told me to hold my left palm over the snake and hold my right palm towards a coiled rope by the door. "Close your eyes," she ordered. "Feel for the snake in the air between you and the creature."

I did what she said.

"Repeat what I say: 'Calla benty moroto.'"

I did and remembered reading that in the book Mother had given me. I had not known what the words meant, but knew it was a spell to connect life to inanimate objects.

I kept repeating the phrase, but nothing happened.

"Just concentrate now," she said, interrupting my incantation.

"I don't know what I am supposed to do," I said.

"Do you feel the warmth of the sun on your palm? The air on your fingers?"

"I do."

"There is no distance between you and the snake. You are connected by the sunlight, by the wind. Grab the snake's slither."

I concentrated harder than ever, and as I stood there, I felt the scales of the snake in my mind! It was as though I was connected to the snake, to the rope, to the air around me and the earth under my feet. I felt the slithering motion of the snake moving through the grass. I felt the slither passing through one hand to the other.

"Now make the snake and rope one!"

I did. The life force of the snake, its breath, its heartbeat, were dancing on my fingertips and I was pushing them to the rope. I twisted my right hand, mimicking the slither and side-to-side movement of the snake.

"Open your eyes."

I did and saw the rope was slithering through the grass. I commanded the rope to wrap itself around Molly's leg, and it did.

She let out a shriek, shook it off her leg and ran back into the house. This broke my concentration, and the rope flopped back down to the ground.

Mother pulled me into a hug. "You did it. I was twice your age before I moved objects. With training, you can do this without the snake. You will make its power your own. It will be just like when you learned to tie your shoe and now you don't even have to think about it any longer."

I wanted to try again, but the snake had slithered off, so I grabbed my spell book and flipped through it, looking for another one we could try. "I want to do this one to control the weather," I said. She took the book from my hands.

"Remember, Lorna, these spells can be dangerous if used without care. Summoning clouds might seem harmless until you are struck by lightning or flood your house. We will learn all these in due time, my girl."

Mother has given me another book, this one translated into English. It has the secret history of the witches of the north and of the south. The history of both sides of my family, the Egyptian necromancers and the Celtic witches, as well as the Land of the Dead, that both sides draw magical energy from.

Mother says the Land of the Dead is a place the living can visit and she will take me there someday. It all sounds so very mysterious and wonderful. I cannot believe how magical my life has become.

FROM THE JOURNAL OF DR. VICTOR MUELLER, 4TH OF JUNE 1884

Reverend Wilkins foolishly put our entire endeavour into jeopardy by attacking Stoker. He apologised for letting his anger get the best of him, saying he had only gone to retrieve Stoker for his curious blood when one of Stoker's employees shot him.

Now we have lost our element of surprise, at least if we keep Wilkins in this body. I am not sure if Endora and I could put him into a new body and it would be very risky to try.

He has suffered two bullet wounds, one to the upper right chest just below the clavicle, and one into his left arm. The bullet to the chest has already healed itself; however, the other wound concerns me. The replacement arm I had sewn on is not healing and, in fact, is necrotising rapidly and I fear I will have to amputate.

I've administered more of our precious supply of Stoker Serum, hoping that it will reverse the damage. And now we wait.

"We will need to bring back the others, as many as we can, with the Serum you have left," he said. "My former colleagues will have no trouble bringing Stoker in, and then we will have an endless supply of his blood."

So now I am preparing three new bodies, the last in my icehouse. It is all we can bring back without more Stoker Serum. I truly wish Mr. Stoker would join us willingly. If we could only convince him of the importance of our work. But Wilkins tells me Stoker will not be persuaded, and that he is a selfish man who thinks only of himself.

I have discussed the new resurrections with Endora, and she has agreed to continue to help us.

My sweet Endora. I feel tremendous guilt that I have found a new love, but Charlotte would not want me to be alone now that she has moved on.

Meanwhile, I don't know what to do with the mindless creature made from her body. It continues to show signs of learning, and may even be capable of speech one day like Risto was. I think about terminating her, but when I go to do it, my hand and heart waver. I will arrange to have her sent to a convent to live out her remaining years.

FROM THE DIARY OF LORNA BOW, 9TH OF JUNE 1884

Mother gave me money so I could do some much-needed shopping. I desperately need new clothes, especially if I am going to move up in society. My clothes are out of fashion and no longer fit.

However, a strange thing happened as I walked down Carnaby Street.

Passers-by crowded the street, and interspersed in the crowd I could see spirits. They stood out against the warm-bodied shoppers. Slightly transparent with a greyish tint, like they were made of smoke and soot.

Most were dressed in rags, and old-fashioned rags at that. They sat in doorways and alleys as they had in life, begging for food they could no longer eat. It was horrifying, not in the way most would be afraid of ghosts, but in their pain and poverty.

They were drawn to me as if they knew I could see them. They surrounded me, crying and begging. I could feel their hunger for food and love. It was overwhelming, and I pushed my way through them as if I were walking through fog, and took refuge in a shop.

Even then, they pressed their faces up to the glass. I could see some had died from the pox and others had been beaten to death or trampled by horses. Still others were covered with ice and snow.

One look at them and I knew their stories. There was Will, who died in 1649 after being beaten by robbers who took his shoes. Beth, who died on New Year's Eve 1799 in a workhouse after eating tainted stew. They just wanted someone to know they once existed and witness how they had died.

"May I help you?" the shopkeeper asked me. I was happy to talk to the living and hoped that would send the ghosts away. I turned to the counter to look at his selection of gloves and hats and gasped as I saw a ghost hanging from a noose behind him. A despondent spirit who took his own life when his shop had failed and he could no longer feed his children.

I regained my composure and purchased a pair of gloves. I exited the shop back into my crowd of the dead.

"I hear you," I said. A live woman passing gave me a quick glance, thinking I was talking to her, but continued on.

"I hear you. I see you. I am here to help you move on to the next world," I said, as I had so many times in my séances. There were so many of them I wasn't sure there would be a door they could go through, but it was all I could think of to say.

I ducked down an alley, out of the bustle of passers-by, and the spirits followed. Composing myself, I focused on one of them, Beth. I looked her in the eye and said, "I'm sorry about what happened to you. You never had a chance in life. But you don't have to stay here. You can move on. You should move on. There's nobody here you know anymore. It's all right. Do you think you're ready to go now?"

She still seemed frightened and sad, but she nodded. Suddenly a shining door appeared beside her. It swung open and emitted a blue light. With one last look at me, Beth turned and went through the door.

I moved on to the next spirit. And the next. It went quicker than I expected. Most of them just needed some encouragement and off they went.

When they were all through, I sat for a bit. I was spent. Then a shopkeeper came out to the alley and shooed me off. I made my way back to the parlour and the safety of Mother and the girls. I threw my arms around Molly and she tried to shrug me off, but I just held on tighter than ever, so happy to feel a live person who had no death story yet.

"Oy, what's got into you?" she asked, finally pushing me away.

I told her about the ghosts on the street and she said she would have been terrified as well. "I ain't never seen a ghost except for fake ones coming out of the spirit closet. I hope I never do."

I wondered if the ghosts are always there and we just can't see them. Was I seeing into the Land of the Dead that Mother talked about, or was it spilling into our world? How terrible to be dead and still have to walk the earth watching people laughing and eating and living.

There were so many dead, and so many were poor. I only saw a few upper-class ladies and gentlemen. Perhaps they go on to the next world straight away. Just like in life, the rich get more choices and better treatment just for who they are.

Would Dr. Mueller be bringing back any of those poor people? I thought not.

LETTER FROM DR. WESLEY PRYCE TO DR. VICTOR MUELLER, 10TH OF JUNE 1884

Dear Victor,

I had an interesting visitor today enquiring about your activities. It was none other than Errol Hammond, the director of the White Worm Society. It seems he not only knows you are back in England but also knows something of what you are doing.

While I thought this to be of concern, it soon became apparent he doesn't wish to stop your experiments and may even want you to continue unhindered.

He arrived unannounced to my office at the Physical Society with two of his agents. He asked to speak with me and I obliged, despite the fact the Physical Society and the White Worms have often been at odds, what with them wanting to suppress magical knowledge and us wanting to further man's understanding of such matters.

His men waited outside the office, and he shut the door behind him.

He told me bluntly that he knows not only that you are living in England under an assumed identity, but that you have been attempting to reunite souls with reanimated bodies.

I, at first, pretended to not know what he was talking about, wishing to protect you and your important work. It was for naught, as he has been tailing me for some time and knew all the dates and times of our meetings.

He then told me not to worry and that the White Worms would continue to observe from a distance. That, in fact, your work does not totally fall under the jurisdiction of the White Worms, and powerful people are becoming interested in your experiments and the scientific breakthroughs they might bring.

He asked me questions about your methods, most of which I could not answer.

Then he asked me the question I am sure gets to the heart of his visit.

"Could he bring my son back to life?"

I said I didn't know the details of your work but that in theory you could, assuming a proper body could be acquired and that his son's soul hasn't moved on.

He seemed very pleased at this answer and requested that I arrange a meeting with you.

Victor, I hope I did not speak out of turn about matters I know only tangentially. I only wished to make Director Hammond an ally in our cause. I think if we can give him hope, even if temporarily, it could go a long way to getting the White Worms out of our affairs.

If you wish to not raise his hopes or do not want to meet with him, it will go no further. However, if you think you could do what he wants, please let me know a date and time that works for a meeting.

Sincerely,

Dr. Wesley Pryce

FROM THE DIARY OF LORNA BOW, 12TH OF JUNE 1884

Mother and I are staying at Dr. Mueller's estate again tonight. He wants me to guide more spirits into resurrected bodies. The thought of it both frightens and thrills me. It is a power that I never could have dreamed of wielding when I was a child at the orphanage or Leonard Pith's tool for fleecing the gullible.

Mother tells me our abilities have been passed down through generations of women in our family. Surely we would not have this power if we were not supposed to use it.

And yet, something happened tonight that made me question the people we've allied ourselves with.

Reverend Wilkins is still living here at the estate. Truth be told, he wears on my nerves a bit; over dinner, he kept prattling on about religion and philosophy and how poor people are poor because they've turned away from God or some such. (I doubt he's ever even met a poor person, let alone been one himself, so I don't know why he thinks he's such an expert.) So as soon as I finished my last spoonful of custard with blackberry sauce, I excused myself and slipped from the dining room.

Dr. Mueller has said I'm welcome to read anything in his library, but I was too restless to settle with a book, so I wandered outside. The sun was sinking towards the horizon, but the evening breeze was warm and the air felt refreshing after the stuffiness of the dining room. There's a small pond at one end of the grounds where I like to sit and read or just think, and I decided to head there to watch the sunset.

I was passing the laboratory building when I heard a loud crash. I wheeled around, looking for the source. It could only have come from inside the building, which should have been empty. I looked back towards the house – surely nobody could have got from there to the lab without passing me on the way.

I knew there were bodies in there, slowly thawing in preparation for receiving new souls. It wasn't possible that a spirit could have inhabited one of those bodies early – was it?

Once the thought occurred to me, I could not shake it. What if by resurrecting Reverend Wilkins we'd opened the door for other spirits to come through at will? How would we stop any spirit from taking control of any dead body – or any live one? How would we even know what spirits had crossed over?

I shook my head, forcing myself to get control of my racing thoughts. It was no use jumping to the worst conclusions without proof. I had to see what was happening in the lab.

The door was locked, of course, but there's a window that I know is usually left unlatched, and some crates piled up outside that some of the doctor's equipment had arrived in. I pulled a crate beneath the window and used it to boost myself up and through. I lowered myself into the lab and crept as quietly as I could to the back, where the bodies would be.

The setting sun provided enough light to see that they were still on their tables, and still lifeless. Perhaps some creature had got in and caused the noise? But I could see nothing amiss, no shattered glass or overturned table.

Then I heard it again – a distinct clattering this time, as though someone was throwing something about. It was coming from behind a door that I had not really paid attention to before, assuming it led to a storeroom or perhaps a water closet.

Could somebody have broken into the lab? I considered running back to the house to alert Dr. Mueller, but something pressed me forward. I walked past the thawing bodies with barely a glance at them, and approached the door, slowly, quietly. I threw the switch to the electrical lights for this part of the lab, hoping the illumination would make me braver.

I pulled the door open with a jerk. A small hallway led to another door with a window in it. On I went.

As I approached, I could see that the setting sun and the light spilling from the lab behind me faintly illuminated the room beyond. Another loud clatter made me jump, but I pressed on.

I reached the windowed door. The room held a large cage, and something was moving about in the shadows at the back of it. Ah, I thought, this room must hold some animal for the doctor's experiments. I pressed my face to the glass, curious what it could be.

The creature suddenly rushed forward, slamming into the bars of its cage, and I jumped back, gasping. It was a woman!

She was thin and wild-eyed. Her golden hair hung in her face as she reached through the bars, grasping for some means of escape. Her dress looked like it had once been fine, but now it hung, loose and ragged, from her body.

A metal dish lay upended on the floor of her cage, spilt food beneath it. This, then, was the crash I had heard earlier.

She saw me through the window, and her arms strained through the bars again, trying fruitlessly to reach me. She snarled and moaned. The only words I could make out were 'Victor' and 'out'.

This must be Charlotte, Mueller's wife, whose soul had moved on. Trying to put her spirit into her body had started everything.

Why would he keep her here like this? He had said his creations were mindless without a spirit to inhabit them, but she seemed like a person to me.

I hesitated at the door. Should I free her? I tried the door, but it was locked, and I'm ashamed to say I was relieved. I hated to see her in a cage, but she frightened me as well.

She seemed well fed and had water and what looked to be a comfortable bed. Her clothes were worn but clean. The chamber pot looked like it had been emptied recently. She had toys and picture books. Besides the bars, it could have been any little girl's bedroom.

She lost interest in me. She sat on her bed and started to look through a picture book.

In the end, I simply backed away, and went back to the lab, shutting the door behind me. I turned out the lights and returned out the window the way I had come.

By this time, the sun had nearly set, and I returned to the house. I slipped in and immediately ran into Dr. Mueller.

"Were you out watching the sunset?" he asked. "It's a lovely night for it."

I just stared at him for a moment. How could he be so pleasant and warm when he had a woman caged not a hundred yards away? I should have confronted him then, but cowardice stopped me. If he wanted us to know about her, he would have told us. What would he do if he knew I know his secret?

So I just agreed it was a lovely night, excused myself and fled for my room. My comfortable room, in this lovely home, with my gracious host, who has a woman in a cage. What kind of man does that? And is he someone we should be helping?

FROM THE DIARY OF OSCAR WILDE, 14TH OF JUNE 1884

Dear yours truly,

I returned from a blissful honeymoon in Paris to a message from Stoker asking to see me at my earliest convenience on an urgent matter. Some things never change. Nothing will burst one's romantic bubble like an overwrought note from a large, ginger Irishman.

With a sigh, I sent word for him to meet me today at my London writing retreat. I warned him to be sure that nobody followed him as few know of this place and I would like to keep it that way. (I shall be giving it up soon, of course, but I have a lease and one hates to break a contract.)

When he arrived, he was in a terrible state. He was even more rumpled than usual and looked as though he hadn't slept for days.

When he told me what had happened, I could understand why.

Somehow, beyond all understanding, the Black Bishop has returned from the dead! He appeared to Stoker in a new, younger guise, but soon revealed himself for who he is, and tried to abduct Bram.

When he described the Black Bishop's new body, my blood ran cold. I think he was at the wedding – a tall blond-haired man whom neither Constance nor I recognised. I took him to be a wedding crasher – invitations were highly coveted, so it wouldn't have been surprising – and had Willie discreetly ask him to leave, which he did without making a scene. Now I wonder whether he had actually been there to kill me, for he must hate me almost as much as he hates Bram.

It seems that the madman whom Bram hunted in Finland has brought him back, and once again they need Stoker's accursed blood for their nefarious schemes. The first time it was to open the gates of hell, so I'm sure any use they have for it now isn't good.

"My blood is how he resurrects his creatures," Bram said sadly.

Before Bram could fret too much about this thought, I said, "It doesn't really matter what they want your blood for. He won't get any more of it. We all will make sure of that. You have me, and your vampire Henry, and Willie, Ellen and Florrie. All seasoned monster hunters and protectors of all things Bram."

That seemed to bolster his spirits, and we sat down to two cups of strong tea and some biscuits.

I did not let him see my own fear. Now that I am a married man, I have more than myself to worry about. Constance could easily get caught in the crossfire should that madman come for me. I could not live with myself should that happen.

How the Black Bishop must be gloating now, having cheated death. And imagine being able to trade your old body for a new one. There could be a market for that. But then, that is something Derrick would have said, and seeking eternal youth did not end well for him.

REPORT FROM WHITE WORM SOCIETY AGENT CORA CHASE

Date: 16 June 1884
Subject: Endora Bow Investigation

Director Hammond has ordered me back to America and with a raise in rank to boot. Why then do I feel something is not right? He pulled me off my surveillance of the Bow séance parlor and I see that no one else has been assigned to take over. Why? They appear to be dabbling in genuine occult rituals and are mixed up in what is happening at the Mueller country estate. Should we not be trying to stop it?

I generally find that following my instincts serves me well, so I have delayed my passage back to America and paid a visit to Mr. Stoker this morning at his home. To my surprise, I found Mr. Blackwood there guarding it. Apparently, the Stokers are under round-the-clock protection.

I was shocked to learn from Mr. Blackwood that a man of inhuman strength had attacked Mr. Stoker in his office. Further, this man let slip that he is in league with Mueller. With what we know of Mueller's activities, the logical deduction is that the attacker is an evil spirit put into one of Mueller's creations, and they are after Mr. Stoker's blood to continue their ghastly experiments.

Mr. Blackwood questioned my business with the Stokers, but I told him it was purely a social visit as I am leaving soon for America and wished to say goodbye.

I was not sure this ruse would work, as neither of the Stokers consider me a friend, and I would not have been surprised if they had refused me entry. However, Mr. Stoker met me at the door and let me in, even welcoming me cordially. We left Mr. Blackwood on the front stoop to his guarding duties.

Mrs. Stoker took one look at me and scowled. "What are you doing here?"

"Let's all go to my study," Bram said. "We can't afford to turn down any potential ally in these times."

With the doors closed behind us, I told them of the director's odd behaviour and my orders to leave England.

"If they know where Mueller is, why not take him into custody?" Mr. Stoker asked. "And they should have every agent and police officer looking for Wilkins. The Black Bishop almost destroyed the world, and now he is back. You'd think it would be a top priority to arrest him."

Mrs. Stoker sat down, her face pale.

"His son," she said. "Mrs. Hammond is a member of my bridge club. Her son died, and she is quite distraught, as one can imagine. Mr. Hammond might see some hope in Dr. Mueller's work."

I told them that if this is true, we might not be able to trust any of the White Worms.

"You are a White Worm," Mrs. Stoker rightfully pointed out.

"Yes, but one that Director Hammond wants out of the way. I assure you, my mission is still ridding the world of supernatural evil, not bending it to suit the director's purpose," I said. I then asked them if they trusted Mr. Blackwood.

"He seems like an upright young man," Mr. Stoker said. "He proved very competent in Finland. I get the feeling that he dislikes Hammond, but I cannot be sure where his loyalties lie."

We all agreed we were now on our own and should act accordingly.

I told them I fear that the Black Bishop may attempt to kidnap Stoker again, and with the White Worms standing down he might just succeed.

I also promised that I would remain secretly in England to investigate Director Hammond further, as we have no proof yet that Mueller has turned him.

"In the meantime," Mr. Stoker said to his wife, "I think we and Noel should stay at the theater under Henry's watch. He will be your best protection from these monsters Mueller created."

A small shuffling sound from the hallway caught my ear, and as I was standing near the study door, I opened it quickly. Mr. Blackwood was there, eavesdropping.

"What is the meaning of this?" Mr. Stoker cried.

"Sorry to invade your private conversation," Blackwood said. "But I've been feeling of late that there is something odd going on, and Miss Chase's visit piqued my curiosity. I too have had my suspicions about Hammond. We spent months tracking down Mueller, only to let him walk around a free man. What I am saying is, I am at your service, Mr. Stoker. Let's get you and your family safely to the Lyceum."

And that is where things stand. Our two priorities now are protecting the Stokers and learning what we can about Hammond's plans.

FROM THE JOURNAL OF DR. VICTOR MUELLER, 16TH OF JUNE 1984

I am officially out of Stoker Serum after resurrecting three more of Reverend Wilkins' cohorts.

We have successfully reanimated the body of a woman, which Miss le Fey now inhabits. She seems pleased with the new body, a raven-haired beauty. The body in the former life was that of a dance hall girl who took her own life by slitting her wrists.

We have also brought back Lords Wotton and Sundry, as we have deemed them worthy.

Both men are elated to have young, robust bodies. Wotton inhabits a stevedore who drowned in the Thames.

Sundry is in an older man, but not as old as he was at death. The forty-year-old man was a blacksmith who died from carbon monoxide poisoning.

None of these three will be recognisable to Stoker and should be able to get close enough to abduct him.

The success of these resurrections indicates that the process works best on those who have drowned or been asphyxiated. This type of death leaves a corpse in excellent condition, and it takes very little of the Serum to bring it back. I have noted this for future experiments.

REPORT FROM WHITE WORM SOCIETY AGENT CORA CHASE

Date: 24 June 1884
Subject: Investigation into the Spirit Gate

I have decided that the most profitable area of focus for me right now is attempting to close the Spirit Gate. Until we manage to cut off the supply of souls to Dr. Mueller, we continue to fight a losing battle. Dead bodies are sadly easy to come by in London, and as far as we know there is no limit to how many times he can resurrect his companions, so not even killing our enemies guarantees us a victory. And with the White Worms seemingly uninterested in moving against Mueller and Wilkins, defeating them by force seems an impossible task.

I know that Mr. Wilde's mother is a noted scholar of the supernatural, so I asked him to introduce us. She warmly welcomed me into her home and we had an interesting discussion about souls and the afterlife.

"I have heard of the Spirit Gate, of course," she said. "But it has not been a particular area of study for me, so my knowledge is not extensive. You are welcome to look through my books. I'll help you."

We spent two days paging through stacks of dusty tomes, to no avail. We found several mentions of the Gate, but not how to open or close it.

The one true lead I found was in a footnote of a brief description of the Gate. It directed me to the book *Portals to the Afterlife*, which might have just what I'm looking for. Lady Wilde does not own the book, which is quite rare. But, undaunted, she sent letters to some of her fellow collectors and tracked down a copy in a library in Scarborough. So I am on a train to the north of England, with a letter of introduction to the occult librarian there. I do not know if my quest will be successful, but it is the only thing I can think of to try at the moment.

FROM THE DIARY OF LORNA BOW, 26TH OF JUNE 1884

I am trying hard to settle into what I guess is my new life. We have moved into Dr. Mueller's country estate for the time being. It is nice living here with fresh air and servants to wait on us hand and foot, but I miss the girls at the parlour. Mother says we will move back to London soon. Dr. Mueller is setting up a new lab there for better access to electricity, chemicals, and other things he will need. By 'other things' I assume she means bodies.

Contacting spirits and moving them into new bodies is exhausting. I did three yesterday and both Mother and I were spent for the day.

We brought back two gentlemen, actual lords, friends of Dr. Mueller and Reverend Wilkins.

And we brought back her! That one who tried to take over my body. I was glad to hand her over to Mother for the transfer. Something about her spirit just sets me on edge. Every second I was in contact with it, I could feel her malice and hatred. It was like a vicious dog inside me, straining to break free. But it is done. Although she claims her old body was more beautiful, I think she's just boasting; this new one was a lovely dancer in life. In any case, she seems happy to have it.

Once safely in their new bodies, the three of them thanked me and Mother profusely (a new word I learned today). They laughed and danced around the room with Reverend Wilkins like kids on Christmas morning. I suppose they are happy to be out of that boring place, happier still to not be dragged down to hell.

When the four of them sat down with us for dinner, they stuffed their faces like they had been starving. I guess I would too if I hadn't eaten anything in years.

Mother and Dr. Mueller joined them in toasts, drinking more wine than even Mr. Pith used to drink.

It was then they started to talk about Mr. Stoker. I remember him. He and his wife and friends attended a séance once, and it turns out he has something to do with the serum Dr. Mueller uses to resurrect the bodies.

I was shocked to hear Reverend Wilkins talk about kidnapping him. Suddenly I remembered that spirit warning Mr. Stoker about…about what? It was hard to recall that part. It was about black something? A black bishop?

I looked at Reverend Wilkins, smiling and talking to Miss le Fey. Are they the danger that I sensed around Mr. Stoker during the séance? Could Wilkins be the Black Bishop? Even if he's not, he's definitely going to do something bad to Mr. Stoker.

It was like a veil had been lifted from my eyes, for when I looked at all their smiling faces now I saw them for what they were: corpses inhabited by evil spirits. They smiled at me, but their eyes were dead somehow. Their pupils were bigger, darker. The light was out. Their grins seemed mean and threatening, not warm and happy.

I said I was exhausted and asked to be excused. Retreating upstairs to my room, I lay down on that big feather bed. I could still hear them downstairs, laughing and talking about how they were going to change the world.

What have I done? What did Mother have me do? She had made me kill Mr. Pith. He might have deserved it, but she seemed to take great joy in it, didn't she? Are we evil now?

I fell asleep and dreamt I was back in the big library at Mrs. Roberts' boarding school. I was warm and cosy in the big chair by the fireplace, reading *Black Beauty*.

FROM THE JOURNAL OF DR. VICTOR MUELLER, 2ND OF JULY 1884

Our work continues. We have acquired more Stoker blood and from a most unlikely source. Errol Hammond, the Director of the White Worms, has joined our cause. He cares not about my goal of advancing science, nor Wilkins' efforts to save souls. His goal is more personal: he wants us to resurrect his son and in exchange, he will keep the White Worms out of our affairs.

He has provided us with a pint of Stoker's blood. Stoker, it seems, had donated it, hoping it would lead to a cure for Henry Irving's vampirism.

This will easily allow me to bring back five to ten more souls. So while Stoker is out of our reach momentarily, we shall still be able to grow our ranks.

We have resurrected Messrs. Dripp and Leech. They were servants to Lord Wotton, who suggested we bring them back to do the brutish work they did in life. We have put them in the bodies of two strapping young sailors who drowned last week. It seems many captains don't report such deaths and leave the poor wretches to the sea. As luck would have it, three washed up onshore and were brought to the morgue, where they easily found their way to me for a few shillings.

Lorna contacted a third soul for us, a Mr. Coal. Astonishingly, he turned down the offer of a new life. He said he wished to repent for his crimes, to be punished for killing his beloved 'Lucy'. Reverend Wilkins told him he was hardly responsible for the horrible deeds he had done as a vampire and pleaded with him to return, but he refused. It never occurred to me that someone would turn down a chance at redemption.

Still, we have enough of a team now to handle Stoker. At some point, I will also need more vampire blood, but I still have many pints donated by the Order of the Golden Dawn, and I'm sure the White Worms have a supply that Director Hammond could share with me. For now, we must focus on the scarcer resource of Stoker blood.

Meanwhile, we have put Dripp and Leech in charge of procuring more bodies and have taken to robbing fresh graves and funeral homes.

While I am hesitant to rob morticians, we are going to need an ample supply of cadavers to continue our activities. It will provide a better class of subject than the criminals and lower-class bodies available through my acquaintance at the London morgue; however, stealing bodies is bound to draw unwanted attention from the police.

Reverend Wilkins says I am not to worry, and that he will figure out that end of the process. I do have enough to be getting on with, so I will take that advice.

FROM THE DIARY OF OSCAR WILDE, 10TH OF JULY 1884

Dear yours truly,

Bram and I have sent the women out of London for their protection, as we continue to investigate Dr. Mueller and company.

We went to see Inspector Abberline, an acquaintance of Captain Burton's. We filled him in on the activities of Mueller and the recently resurrected Reverend Wilkins. As we explained it, he had that look on his face I have seen all too many times before: a combination of scepticism and amusement, as if we were both mad and trying to convince him the sky is red.

Despite Burton explaining in a letter that our story was true, Abberline laughed at us in front of the other constables.

He then invited us into his office, where his attitude changed as he shut the door.

"I apologise," he said. "I can't let on that I believe you, though I assure you I do."

He had helped mop up the rest of the vampire nests in London after we dispatched the Black Bishop, so he was aware of the supernatural.

"We know where Mueller and Wilkins are," Bram explained. "It should be a simple matter to go there and arrest them."

Abberline had us sit down and explained it would not be as easy as all that.

"We have already looked into the matter. Mueller is going by the name Hans Delbruck and I have no proof he isn't who he says he is. He has all the necessary papers and people to vouch for him. I have no grounds on which to arrest him."

"Wilkins tried to kidnap me," Bram protested, "Surely, that is an arrestable offence."

"I believe you, but he is being protected by people well above my station," Abberline said. "Rumour has it even the Queen herself is curious about contacting the afterlife and reuniting loved ones, though I hope that is not true. If we had more, something that would have to be dealt with, perhaps we could do something."

"Like what?" I asked.

"Where is he getting these bodies? Grave robbing, murder? Either would look bad even to those protecting Mueller."

I asked him if he could spare a detective or two to help with the legwork.

"Truth be told," he said, lowering his voice, "I am not sure who I could trust even among my men. Mueller has deep pockets and connected friends."

I told him how disappointed I was in him. Bram and I left in a huff. It looks like it is up to us to save the British Empire once again.

FROM THE DIARY OF FLORENCE STOKER, 10TH OF JULY 1884

How on earth is one supposed to live a normal life when one's enemies won't stay dead?

Yesterday, worrying about our safety, Bram sent Noel, Ellen, Constance and me to Canterbury to stay with Captain Burton and his wife. Accompanying us is Mr. Blackwood, who will remain by our side as a bodyguard. I should think that Captain Burton is quite capable of protecting us, but Bram insisted Mr. Blackwood come along to help.

Bram, Henry and Oscar are going to root out Dr. Mueller and the Black Bishop and put an end to them once and for all. Burton has put them in touch with friends at Scotland Yard. They have no love for the White Worms, who now appear to be compromised, and will provide assistance if Bram can gather evidence of illegal activities.

Once here, we felt safe enough. We assumed our enemies didn't know we had left London, and we had armed protection around the clock. In addition, Ellen and I both carry small pistols should we need to take matters into our own hands.

We foolishly felt safe enough to take tea at a charming teahouse on Whitehall Road.

Constance had popped into a bookstore next to the teahouse, accompanied by Mr. Blackwood, while Noel, Ellen and I found us a table. I did look around the room for suspicious characters but felt silly as I did not really know what to look for.

Noel was a bit fussy, as he often is in public, but a tea cake quieted him down.

A woman with a French accent said, "He is adorable!" as she sat down alone at the table next to ours.

I thanked her, and she asked his age. I told her he is four.

"Oh, they are such fun at that age."

She ordered her tea, took out a travel guide and began studying it.

The woman had stylishly arranged black hair and was well dressed, obviously upper class. It is unusual to see a woman travelling alone, but I know it is done.

Constance and Mr. Blackwood joined us. Constance had a large pile of books she awkwardly stored under our table.

Mr. Blackwood sat next to Ellen, who immediately took his hand. He pulled it back – he was on duty, after all – but Ellen just reclaimed it.

"I am so glad you are here to protect us, Brent," she said. She then told us he knows karate and told us how he saved Bram's life in Finland.

"I hardly did anything, I'm afraid," he said. "They kidnapped him right from under us."

"But you killed all those reanimated corpses that attacked you."

"Yes, indeed, but we failed to stop Mueller and now he and his monsters are terrifying England," he said. He paused and took a deep breath. "Shall we order?"

I was glad he changed the subject, as I didn't think it was an appropriate subject at tea or in front of Noel. He understands more than one would think for a four-year-old.

The talk turned to the theatre, and we all had a lovely tea, but I should know by now not to get too comfortable.

The woman at the next table paid her bill and left. I then noticed she had left her travel book on her table.

I retrieved it and rushed out to catch her. She had just opened the door to her carriage.

"Mademoiselle, you forgot your book."

"Oh, thank you so much. I would have been so lost without it. It's my first time in England."

As she took the book with her right hand, something glinted in her left. I saw too late it was a hypodermic needle. She hugged me tightly and pushed it into my stomach. I tried to scream in pain, but it came out as a little yelp. The shock of it confused me, and then a warm sensation spread from the needle to my head.

My legs gave out and she held me up, then lifted me and shoved me into the carriage. She was incredibly strong and I could not fight her. She set me on the bench, got in and shut the door.

My shaky right hand went up my left sleeve, where I keep my

Derringer strapped to my left wrist. I could barely work my fingers and had trouble retrieving it.

"We meet again, Florrie."

I could see my reflection in her cold, black pupils. "Le Fey," I whispered. It was all I could manage as my mouth went numb from the sedative.

"Yes, I have returned. This time you won't have a team of horses to trample me." She tapped on the ceiling of the carriage to signal her driver and we started to move. "I offered you eternal life, and you killed me. I might have a second chance, but you will not if your husband doesn't help us."

"Stop!" I heard Mr. Blackwood yell. He was standing in the carriage's path.

My fingers found the barrel of the gun and managed to get it into my palm.

"Run him over!" she yelled to her driver, and he snapped his reins to speed up his horses.

I pulled the trigger of my unaimed gun. My thought was just to scare her or the driver to make them stop, but the bullet went into her side.

She didn't even react to the bullet, just grabbed my wrist and tried to wrestle the gun from my hand. My second shot went off, putting a bullet under her chin. It came out at an angle through her cheek, turning her beautiful face into a gory mess.

She shrieked and put her hand up to her wound to stanch the blood, but there was none, only greenish pus. She yelled something at me, but her words were garbled.

I was sure I was only moments away from death when I heard another gunshot. Mr. Blackwood had fired at the driver — I could not see whether he had hit his mark — and was still in front of the carriage, aiming for a second shot. The horses pulled to the left to go around him, but a lamp post was in their way, which brought them to a grinding halt.

Le Fey flung the carriage door open, jumped out and fled down an alley. I heard a thump outside as the driver jumped down from his seat and took off in the opposite direction. Mr. Blackwood checked on me and I told him I was uninjured and to get the woman. "She's one of Mueller's monsters," I said.

He ran after her. I heard a shot come from the alley.

Mr. Blackwood returned moments later and told me she was dead.

"She turned on me and I had no choice but to shoot her in the head," he said. "It's the only way to kill those things."

I started to laugh, which I could tell Mr. Blackwood found confusing. "It was le Fey," I told him. "This is the second time she died trying to kill me, and hopefully the last."

He helped me out of the carriage and had to hold me up as I fought sleep.

"Her body…it decomposed before my eyes," he said. "She looks like a corpse that has been dead for weeks, not minutes."

A crowd was gathering in all the commotion, and Ellen and Constance came rushing out. Constance was holding Noel, who was trying to squirm his way free.

"Mummy, are you hurt?"

I told him I was fine, just sleepy. I remember little else until I woke up in my bed in the Burton cottage.

Captain Burton was standing guard over me with a rifle.

"Ah, good, you're awake. I've smoothed things over with the local constables. All I can say is it's a jolly good thing those monsters decompose so quickly – the coppers thought the body had been there for weeks, so nobody knows you or Blackwood had anything to do with it. Anyway, it's not safe here now they know where you are. We will need to move you to another location. And I will join Bram and the others in bringing in Mueller and Wilkins."

"You will do no such thing," his wife said, entering the room. "You have pneumonia and the doctor said you are to stay in bed."

"Nonsense, it is but a chest cold. I am ready to fight!" Before he could continue, he succumbed to a coughing fit.

She took the rifle from him and escorted him back to their bedroom.

I've discussed things with Mr. Blackwood and the others. We are tired of running away and hiding and have decided to return to London.

"We aren't safe anywhere," Ellen said. "As you can see, Brent, we are quite capable of protecting ourselves and we are better off sticking together and taking the fight to them."

Even Constance, who is new to the monster-fighting business, agreed. She said she would feel better if she could keep an eye on Oscar.

We leave for London in the morning.

REPORT FROM WHITE WORM SOCIETY AGENT CORA CHASE

Date: 15 July 1884
Subject: Investigation into the Spirit Gate

I am on a train back to London, no further along in my quest to close the Spirit Gate. I found the book I sought, and while it did discuss the magic that bound the Gate closed, it did not include any instructions for how to close it once it was opened.

The occult librarian, Mr. Selby, was most helpful. He has encyclopedic knowledge of his collection and was able to point me to more volumes that might have the information I need, but it seems this is a subject that scholars either have not studied extensively, or they are reluctant to put their findings down in print for some reason. Some of these old researchers are strangely superstitious for people who spend their lives delving into the supernatural.

If only the White Worm archives were open to me. Alas, I dare not show my face at headquarters. I shall have to find another way.

FROM THE DIARY OF OSCAR WILDE, 18TH OF JULY 1884

Dear yours truly,

I haven't saved Stoker's life in some time now, and it appears I have got out of the habit. To be fair, I nearly died today, so saving myself was frontmost on my mind.

I don't know what it is about me that on one hand elicits such adoration from people of impeccable judgement, and on the other creates enemies who vehemently hate me, so much that not even death can keep them from trying to kill me!

I thought the Black Bishop's return would be the summit of my worries. It never occurred to me that he would bring back other ne'er-do-wells to torment us. There is le Fey, whom Florrie so heroically killed on the American frontier. She came back and tried to kill Florrie, only to be killed herself a second time. Some people never learn.

Then I find that my nemesis, Lord Basil Wotton, slithered out of hell to put an end to me! That vile creature who turned Derrick into a vampire. That wretched thing who helped the Black Bishop almost end the world.

He did not like me one bit before, so it is a safe bet that he fully loathes me after I killed him in Salisbury. If you recall, dear diary, I cleverly spat a silver cross down his throat and set him ablaze from the inside out.

One thing I have noted about the evil people I have met is they all seem to have one-track minds, and Wotton is a locomotive headed right for poor Oscar tied to the tracks.

All of us – Constance, Ellen and the Stokers – are living at the Lyceum Theatre at present. This is so we all will be under the protection of Henry Irving. It seems these creations of Mueller's are no match for our vampire and are keeping their distance while we are under his roof.

Despite my pleas, I cannot persuade Mother and Willie to join us here and they remain at home. Willie assures me he can protect them and will open the doors for no one. Miss Chase has kindly asked one of her Pinkerton detective friends to watch over the house covertly, for which I am very grateful.

Henry has closed down all performances of *Macbeth*, telling the press that several members of the cast have come down with typhoid.

All of us, including the women, have armed ourselves with pistols, and we men are standing guard around the clock. Ellen's gentleman friend is also guarding us, having been sacked by the White Worms.

We were plotting our next moves to battle Mueller when he had the gall to show up at our door this afternoon. I had never met the bad doctor, but immediately knew it must be him as he was met on the theatre steps with the barrel of Mr. Blackwood's gun.

He was flanked by two burly men. One was a dark, swarthy man I did not recognise, though I knew anyone could be in that body. I could tell he wasn't all human. Something about the eyes and an unnatural tint to the skin.

The other I remembered from my wedding reception: the tall blond man who I now knew to be the Black Bishop.

"Mr. Stoker, may I have a word?" Mueller said.

"No, I don't care what you have to say," Bram said. "Except maybe why we shouldn't shoot you dead right now." He told me to get Ellen to wake Henry, who was fast asleep in his coffin in the tunnel under the theatre.

"No need to wake your vampire, Mr. Stoker," Mueller said. "I am here to propose a truce. We promise no further threats to you and your loved ones if you would willingly give us a pint or two of your blood. I fear you do not see the big picture here. With your help, we can cure all diseases, give those who deserve it everlasting life, and for those who do not, perhaps a second chance at redemption."

"And who decides who deserves everlasting life? You are not God," Bram said. "And playing one will lead to nothing but disaster, as Mary Shelley could tell you."

"This isn't a fairy tale, Mr. Stoker. Join us and we will conquer death once and for all," Mueller said.

Wilkins stepped forward and added, "Think of it, Bram. We could all be around for Judgement Day. A thousand years from now, we can welcome our saviour back and bring to him multitudes of saved souls."

Same old Wilkins.

"You failed at this madness once, Wilkins. You will do it again," Bram said.

Henry appeared in the doorway with us. Although he would be weakened out in the sunlight, he provided added protection at our backs.

"I bear you no ill will, Bram. I did, but I now see the light," Wilkins said, taking a few steps towards us with outstretched hands. "A pint of your blood is all we ask, to show you what we can do. To show the good of it."

"One of your monsters tried to abduct my wife!" Bram shouted.

"That was unfortunate," Mueller said. "Miss le Fey acted entirely on her own. Obviously, she should not have been brought back. We will be more careful whom we choose in the future."

"The answer is no," Bram said. He took a step forward with his pistol. "Now feck off, the lot of you. I have spoken to Scotland Yard and I think they would like to have a word with you about missing bodies."

"I am sorry you feel that way, Mr. Stoker," Mueller said. "I hoped I wouldn't have to resort to this." He held up his hand as a signal and Wilkins pulled a pistol and shot Henry!

Bram and Mr. Blackwood returned fire, but Mueller and the creatures scattered. Mueller took refuge behind a large concrete pavement planter while his goons moved on Bram's location. They might not have been vampires, but they were extremely fast.

Bram and Mr. Blackwood took cover behind the theatre's large outdoor pillars.

Bram managed to shoot the swarthy one in the stomach, but it barely flinched and continued its assault, grabbing Bram's wrist and twisting the pistol out of his hand.

Wilkins then punched Bram hard to the jaw, and he went slack. Wilkins hoisted him up and put him over his shoulder like a sack of flour and simply walked down the steps.

Mr. Blackwood gave chase but did not dare shoot for fear of hitting Bram.

I took cover just inside the doorway and tended to Henry. A sizzling sound told me the bullet was silver, but it had not hit him in the heart; if it had, he would have exploded into dust, being an older vampire. The younger ones burst into blood and guts like a tick.

I tried to help him to his feet just as the other creature jumped me and pulled me off. I thought he was there to finish off Henry, but he turned his attention to me.

"We meet again, my dear Oscar," he said, holding both my wrists.

"Oh? We've met before?" I asked, struggling to free myself from his clutches.

"It's me, Lord Wotton."

I was stunned. I stopped struggling and just stared at him in his new, younger, fitter body.

"What, nothing to say, Oscar? You usually can't shut up. Well, say something witty now, just before I snap your fat neck."

"Let...him...go," we heard a voice say. It was Henry, who was weak but on his feet.

Wotton released one of my wrists in an attempt to retrieve a pistol from his trouser pocket. I took that moment to pull my silver cross. Not the best move on my part as Henry, in his weakened state, recoiled at the sight of it.

Wotton laughed and put his pistol back in his pocket. "That won't work on me this time, Wilde. I'm not a vampire." His free hand went around my throat.

I flipped my cross around. You see, it has a pointed end I sharpened myself for close vampire-to-human combat. I plunged it into his eye and he let out a horrible shriek, not unlike Mother seeing a mouse.

An out-of-breath Mr. Blackwood re-entered the lobby and pulled Wotton away from me. As Blackwood tried to aim his pistol at Wotton's head, Wotton grabbed my arm and, with superhuman strength, flung me at Blackwood, sending us both crashing into a wall. Wotton ran off before Mr. Blackwood could recover his balance and get off a shot.

We tended to Henry again, getting him to his feet once more. Mr. Blackwood was astounded as the silver bullet pushed its way out of Henry's flesh and clinked on the ground. I am sure he knows Henry is a vampire but hadn't witnessed this sort of thing yet.

"I lost them," Mr. Blackwood said. "Mueller had a carriage waiting, and they took Mr. Stoker away."

"The sun will be down soon and I will retrieve him," Henry said.

"How will you track them?" Mr. Blackwood asked.

"I can smell them," Henry said. His voice was close to a snarl, and his eyes were wild like an animal's, dilated pupils surrounded by red veins.

FROM THE JOURNAL OF DR. VICTOR MUELLER, 18TH OF JULY 1884

We now have an ample supply of Stoker's blood. I have taken four pints from our captive and Wilkins is already eager to bleed him again, though I dare not take more for fear of killing him. I told Wilkins we must wait at least four days, possibly more.

We have locked Stoker up in a guest room in the main house. He is chained, but that is just a precaution, for he is not going anywhere in his current state.

He said something odd over and over as we put him to bed, "Like a thousand silver bullets," and he would laugh as he said this.

I put his blood on ice and had it shipped to my new lab in London. There I will have a better generator and more room to work. Its location is also a secret, which is very important if we are to continue our work. Though Director Hammond has neutralised the threat from the White Worms, we know not whether more official law enforcement agencies are aware of our activities.

Today was our first successful resurrection of a soul for a second time. Miss le Fey, whose own stupidity led to her second demise, was again transferred into a new body.

The potential of this is fascinating. One could be brought back forever and truly become immortal. If I didn't feel like a god before, I do now. Charlotte would have been so proud to see our work reach its full potential.

Things did not go smoothly with the transfer, however. Lorna initially refused to act as a medium for le Fey, telling us channelling such an evil spirit was painful.

"Her anger burns me," Lorna said. It took some convincing from Endora before she would even attempt it.

Our second setback came in the choice of vessel. There was talk of using the feral Charlotte, but I could not bear for someone like le Fey to inhabit my wife's former body. It would have also meant killing her and that I will not do. Even if she isn't my Charlotte, she is a human being.

It didn't help that the only female body we could procure was that of a fourteen-year-old girl. I did suggest putting her into a male body, but Wilkins objected on religious grounds.

Channelling le Fey again was traumatic enough for Lorna; seeing a girl close to her own age on the slab was almost more than she could bear.

Reverend Wilkins promised he would keep le Fey in check and that he would work hard to reform her and make her worthy of yet another return.

Le Fey was relieved to return to the land of the living, but was not as happy with this body as the last one.

Upon waking, she felt her body under the sheet. When she touched her small breasts she shrieked, "Am I a man?" Then her hands reached down further to confirm she was once again a female.

She jumped up from the table and ran to the mirror in the corner of the room. "It's a child!" she screamed. "A weak child!"

Wilkins wrapped her in a robe and chastised her for being so ungrateful. He told her the body would mature and grow. This seemed to calm her a bit.

To be honest, I am not sure that's true. Does the natural maturation process continue? Or does the vampire blood used in the procedure arrest the body as is? I do not have enough data yet to say. But as the deed was done, I thought it best not to share these thoughts. I will have to find an excuse to regularly examine Miss le Fey in her new body, to gather data on this fascinating new experiment.

Le Fey continued to pout before the mirror. "She's not pretty. Look, she has buck teeth!" She was overreacting, of course, as the body, while no great beauty, has a pleasant face and features.

Wilkins pointed out that if she hadn't botched the abduction of Mrs. Stoker, she would still be in the first body we had given her.

Lorna took all this in and said to me, "I told you, something's not right with her. She doesn't even appreciate what we did for her... twice!"

Le Fey turned and hissed at Lorna like an animal and then laughed as a frightened Lorna took refuge behind her mother.

"That will be enough, Carolyn," Reverend Wilkins scolded. "We have a mission for you, one that your current body might serve you well for. Complete this mission and perhaps we can get you a new body in the future."

As for this new mission, it may be a way for us to secure Stoker Serum now and for the future. Stoker might not be the only one with the special blood we need.

FROM THE DIARY OF LORNA BOW, 19TH OF JULY 1884

I am growing ever more concerned about the people we are resurrecting. Every day I bring back a new lord or lady. Where are the common people who deserve redemption?

Mother loves bringing people back because it increases our magical power. I don't think she is thinking clearly, blinded by the magic. But today I brought up my concerns to her and she told me she has a bigger plan. Reverend Wilkins and Dr. Mueller are merely a means to an end. She is well aware of their evil ways but is buying time.

"We need the White Worm Society destroyed," she told me. "With them out of the way and our new power, no one can stand against us, not even Mueller and Wilkins."

I came right out and asked her if she loved Dr. Mueller (because I know they are having relations).

She said, "No, I don't. When you are an adult, you will realise woman have carnal needs just like men. He is merely a dalliance. Someone to spend the cold nights with. When I have what I want, women will never have to bow down before men again."

She asked me to trust her and to go along with what I am doing for a while longer.

I said I would. I too want to help bring change to the world. I just wish we didn't have to work with Reverend Wilkins and Dr. Mueller to achieve it.

FROM THE JOURNAL OF BRAM STOKER, 19TH OF JULY 1884

11:35 a.m.

The cruelty and ruthlessness of our enemies know no bounds.

Mueller's monsters kidnapped me yesterday, right from the theatre in broad daylight. They have become emboldened by the White Worm director's defection to their cause and their protection by upper-class members of Parliament they have bribed with the thoughts of bringing loved ones back to life.

I was taken by carriage to Mueller's laboratory in the country. There, they drained me of many pints of blood, to the point where I passed out. I awoke hours later in a dark bedroom chained to the iron frame of a bed by my ankle.

A servant came into the room and gave me a sandwich and a glass of milk, which I ate ravenously as I plotted my escape. When the servant had exited, I saw there was a man left guarding the door. He took the opportunity to peek inside at me and re-introduce himself.

"Good evening, Mr. Stoker," he said, in a thick Eastern European accent. "You might not remember me. I am Mr. Dripp. It is so nice to see you again." The sarcasm was not lost in his accent. "This time I will not be so easy to kill. It is me has the, how you say, upper hand."

I did not recall killing Dripp, but then I killed so many vampires it is all a blur. I did try to burn him to death, but he had escaped that fate.

There was a tapping at the window that startled us both, and we turned to see Henry there. "Invite me in, Bram."

"He can't do that. He doesn't own this house!" Dripp said, laughing.

"I beg to differ. Since you kidnapped me, this is my new home, even though it is against my will," I said. "Please come in, Henry."

There was a sudden burst of shattering glass and a gust of wind, and in the blink of an eye Dripp's head hit the ground and rolled under the bed. It seems he was not so hard to kill as he thought. His body dropped to reveal Henry standing behind him. "Mr. Blackwood said taking the heads off of them is the fastest way."

He broke my chain and helped me to my feet. I still felt weak from the blood loss, but he held me up as we headed out into the hallway and down the stairs. It occurred to me then we should have left through the window, for there were three men downstairs waiting for us. They were already on guard from hearing the crash upstairs.

They had guns, and I assumed they had silver bullets, as Wilkins would anticipate a rescue by Henry.

"Stay right where you are," a burly man ordered. "I know how to kill a vampire as I was one myself once." The accent was familiar, as Dripp's had been. I assumed this was Dripp's cohort, Mr. Leech.

We froze on the stairs. Henry let me go and I steadied myself on the banister and took a step down to be in front of Henry.

"If you shoot me, Leech," I warned, "Wilkins won't like it. He needs my blood."

"Shoot Stoker in the leg," Leech told the other two men. "When he drops, shoot the other one, aim for the heart."

Before the word 'heart' reached my ears or a shot could be fired, Henry had leapt over me, landed at Leech's feet and ripped the gun out of his hand. Actually, he ripped his hand off at the wrist with the gun still firmly in his palm.

The others fired several bullets at Henry, but they all went wide. In a blur of motion and violence, he made quick work of the other two.

When it was over, in mere seconds, all three were headless. There was some blood, but not as much as one would think. Henry tried feeding on one body that was still oozing blood from its neck, but then spat it out. It appears their Stoker Serum blood was not to his liking. He turned to me, and I could see the hunger in his eyes. I don't know if it was the effort of travelling here or the violence he had inflicted on my captors, but he looked fierce, savage – like a predator out for prey.

I had not seen him in such a feral state before, and it was troubling. I was in fear of him despite the fact he had just rescued me. There was no humanity left in him. He was panting and foaming at the mouth like a rabid dog.

"Too bad Mueller isn't here," he growled, wiping the blood from his lips with his sleeve.

It was I who had to help him now. He seemed disoriented and frozen in a confused state.

"We should go, Henry," I said, calmly taking his elbow and turning him towards the door. As I walked him outside he snarled and growled and I was again in fear for my life as I thought he might, in his agitation, turn on me.

We had just stepped outside when Wilkins, in his new tall body, pounced on Henry. There was a bit of a struggle, but Henry eventually got the upper hand, literally, as he pulled off Wilkins' left arm and dropped it at his feet.

Wilkins let out a horrible scream. His shoulder dripped blood but did not gush as one would expect when an arm is ripped from a body.

The arm, still alive and seemingly with a mind of its own, was wriggling away, the fingers pulling it along. It was as if it wanted to be free of Wilkins.

A shot rang out, and a bullet just missed Henry's head and chipped off the masonry of the house behind us. We could see another shadowy figure running towards us.

The danger seemed to snap Henry out of his crazed state. "Quick, on my back," he said. I hopped on and we sped away. This is my least favourite mode of travel, but needs must. We made it all the way back to London in less than half an hour. There were times I feared I could not hang on or that going so fast I wouldn't be able to catch my breath.

When we returned to the theatre, everyone was relieved to see me. "Get Henry some blood, please, quickly," I said, and after one look at him, Ellen rushed to comply. Once he had fed, I told them all that I could remember of my ordeal.

"So now they have enough of your blood to make – what do you think? – dozens more monsters?" Oscar asked. I nodded, discouraged. Even more forces for Wilkins to use against us. This has to stop. And if I have to kill Mueller and his witch to do it, I will!

FROM THE DIARY OF FLORENCE STOKER, 20TH OF JULY 1884

I am already consumed with worry about the forces arrayed against us, but this week my fears were realised; Dr. Mueller and his minions took Bram. Henry rescued him within a day, but they then resorted to something even worse than that.

Bram was sleeping in his office upstairs, still weakened from the massive amount of blood that Mueller took from him. Henry was also asleep in his coffin; the events of the previous day had taken a toll on him as well. The rest of us were restless and anxious, milling about the theatre and trying to come up with any plan to defeat our monstrous enemies.

I carry my pistol at all times, but perhaps it gives me more courage than it should, for when I heard the child crying at the theatre's side door I was brave enough to open it.

She couldn't have been older than thirteen, dressed in an expensive blue dress and clutching a porcelain doll. She was not the typical ragamuffin one sees in the theatre alley, scrounging for scraps of food.

Ellen came to the door to look out with me. "Oh, poor thing," Ellen said. "Are you lost?"

"Yes," the girl cried. "I was shopping with my father and I lost him in the crowd."

We brought her in, and Constance joined us to tend to the lost child.

"Where did you last see him?" Constance asked, bending down to dry the child's tears with her handkerchief. "Do you remember what shop you were near?"

"It was a cigar shop, I think."

Noel wandered over to us to see what the fuss was about. He asked why she was crying and we explained she was lost and needed help to find her father.

We heard a man's voice calling down the alley, "Julia! Julia!" He seemed quite frantic.

"Father!" she squealed with recognition. Like a fool, I swung the door open and saw a well-dressed man running towards me. I kept my hand on my pistol out of instinct, but the little girl suddenly grabbed my wrist.

In an instant, she had twisted the gun away and had it in her own small hand. "Back," she commanded, waving the gun at Ellen and Constance.

Sensing something was wrong, Oscar came running to us, only to have the girl take a shot over his head, stopping him in his tracks.

"I said back!"

The man from the alley pushed his way inside and grabbed Noel, who started kicking and screaming. He was terrified, reaching for me, but I dared not move with the girl pointing a gun at me. The man was holding him so roughly I was afraid he would break Noel's neck.

"Careful with the boy," the girl said. "We need him."

Ellen swooned as if she were about to faint. "Oh, heavens," she cried, putting the back of her hand to her forehead, overacting a bit to be sure, but it was effective. She fainted right into the man, momentarily throwing him off balance and causing all eyes to turn to her.

Constance took that moment to punch the little girl square in the face, very hard as we could hear her nose break.

I grabbed the gun in her hand and managed to point it to the ceiling as she pulled the trigger. The girl was incredibly strong – clearly one of Mueller's creatures! We wrestled with the gun and it went off multiple times into the air.

Ellen and Oscar began attacking the man holding Noel, who was screaming and squirming even harder. The intruder was forced to drop him to contend with Oscar's and Ellen's pummelling.

Noel ran to me for protection, but Constance and I were still struggling with the girl, so I yelled at him to run and hide, which he did without a second order.

To our shock, and I'm sure the monsters', a shot rang out and the man, the reanimated thing, took a bullet to the forehead. It was Mr. Blackwood, with a rifle, running to join us.

The girl hissed at us and ran out the door into the alley. I recognised that hiss. That feral sound devoid of any humanity. It was le Fey, and she had almost taken Noel.

They terrorised my sweet boy tonight, and he clung to me until he fell asleep in my arms. As I write this, Constance is applying ice to her hand, swollen and painful from its encounter with le Fey's face. We are all shaken and more fearful than ever.

FROM THE DIARY OF OSCAR WILDE, 20TH OF JULY 1884

Dear yours truly,

With that monster maker Mueller hunting Bram and Noel, I have taken it upon myself to find them a better hiding place. Under the cover of darkness and in disguise, I have moved them to my secret flat. There is concern the monster will find them here, as le Fey did manage to find Florence in Canterbury, but Mr. Blackwood thinks she received that information from the White Worm director, who has gone over to their side. Mr. Blackwood assures us that relocating to a new safe house (as Miss Chase would call it) is the best course of action.

So Bram, Florence, Noel and Mr. Blackwood will hide away here and Constance, Ellen and I will remain under Henry's protection at the theatre.

"You are sure no one knows of this place?" Bram asked, as he lit the gas wall lamps.

"Well, Florence and Ellen have been here, but other than that, not a soul," I told them. "Just the landlady, and I pay her handsomely to keep my secret. Not even Constance knows of this place."

It was then I noticed Florence giving me a scolding look. "Constance doesn't know? You told me you were going to get rid of it after the wedding."

I marshalled all my dignity. "Florence Stoker, I do not like what you are insinuating. I am still in my honeymoonial bliss and have not had a moment to spare to think about disposing of the flat. In the meantime, this is merely my little writing apartment where I can go when I need privacy and anonymity. Using this as a paramour flat has not even occurred to me."

"Thank you, Oscar," Bram said, saving me from further interrogation. "We will not intrude here any longer than we need to."

We decided we must get word to Agent Chase. With her help, we will gather evidence and take it to Scotland Yard. Inspector Abberline says that with sufficient proof of nefarious activity, he can plead the case to a high enough authority that even Mueller's well-placed friends won't be able to protect him any longer. And the Stoker and Wilde names still hold some sway with the Crown after we saved England from the Black Bishop's dastardly plan.

I told little Noel a bedtime story, then said my goodbyes and returned to Constance and the others at the theatre, where we all turned in for some much-needed sleep. Well, except for Henry, who is pacing up and down the theatre halls on the lookout for trouble.

Until tomorrow, good night, dear diary.

FROM THE JOURNAL OF DR. VICTOR MUELLER, 28TH OF JULY 1884

I have relocated to my new London laboratory. I have purchased the entire cellar of the Grosvenor Art Gallery. The gallery above is the perfect disguise for our activities below. It has a secret entrance off Grosvenor Mews, and best of all the building has its own power station.

It even has an entrance to the sewer system, so Wilkins and his men can move about the city undetected.

The timing of the new laboratory couldn't be more fortuitous. Now that Stoker's vampire invaded the country house, we never know when he might return to cause more mayhem. His rescue of Stoker created more work for me, as he killed Mr. Dripp and Mr. Leech and detached Reverend Wilkins' arm in the process.

We have put Mr. Dripp into a new body, that of a sturdy foundry worker. Mr. Leech isn't as lucky. We are short on bodies at the moment and he will have to wait.

I recommended we find a new one for Wilkins, but he likes the one he has, so I have sewn on a new arm and administered more of the Stoker Serum. It seems to have worked as the arm has regained life and is a better fit than the old one.

Lord Wotton has had his eye poked out in an altercation with Wilde. I replaced it and with an infusion of Stoker Serum, the new eye has become fully functional. It seems my discovery has no limits. Imagine, I have the power to replace missing limbs and revive dead organs.

And with our fresh supply of Stoker's blood, I have enough of the Serum to bring back dozens of souls, which Wilkins claims he can deliver. He has a plan.

REPORT FROM WHITE WORM SOCIETY AGENT CORA CHASE

Date: 31 July 1884
Subject: Director Hammond

Disguised as an overnight cleaning woman, I infiltrated the White Worm headquarters and Director Hammond's office. As I have feared, he is under the thumb of Dr. Mueller and Reverend Wilkins. I found correspondence confirming Mueller has promised to bring back Hammond's son, something Mrs. Stoker had already suspected.

I was collecting evidence when I heard voices down the hall. As it was well after midnight I thought my activities would go undisturbed, but then I found myself trapped in the office looking for a place to hide, as I was sure one of the voices was that of Director Hammond.

I crammed myself into a small coat closet just as the office door swung open.

Looking through the keyhole, I could see he was with the necromancer Endora, and another man who was fair-haired and tall. From Stoker's previous description, I assumed him to be Wilkins.

"What makes you think I plan to have the Spirit Gate closed?" Hammond asked. He lit the gas lamp on the wall and offered the other two a seat.

"The White Worms did it before," Endora said. "But I warn you, closing it would mean we could not bring back your son."

"And to be fair," the other man said, "we wouldn't want you getting the idea to close it after we bring your son back."

"You keep telling me you are going to bring Andrew back, but you have yet to make good on your promise," Hammond said. "I have given you the White Worm Society's stores of vampire blood, kept my agents at bay, and still I don't have my son. So you can understand why

I might be hesitant to keep the Gate open. We are getting reports from all over the Empire that ghostly activities have risen. The Queen has expressed concern. Endora is right, I can and will attempt to close the Gate if I don't see my son again."

"We are having trouble locating his spirit," Endora said. "That can happen when one dies in a Realm world. But Lorna tells me he is there and has not yet passed on."

The others slid their chairs back and stood.

"You have my word as a Christian and a gentleman," Wilkins said. "We will bring him back. We've just had a bit of trouble acquiring what we need, but that has been taken care of. Rest assured, we will contact you in a few days to come pick out a new body for your son."

I heard Hammond stand, and he said, "Good. I'll be waiting."

"So the Gate stays open?" Endora asked.

"Yes, yes, of course. For now."

The other two said their goodbyes and left. Hammond remained at his desk. Through the keyhole, I watched him retrieve a file from his desk and examine its contents. After a few minutes of reading, he returned it to a box on his desk marked *To be refiled*. He left, closing the door behind him.

I left my hiding spot and examined the folder he had been reading. Its label read, *Spirit Gate*. I took the folder and made my escape.

The folder contains valuable information on how to enter the spirit world through the Realm and close it from the inside. I must study this carefully and formulate a plan to close the Gate and cut off their supply of souls for good.

FROM THE JOURNAL OF DR. VICTOR MUELLER

A day of shock and grief. I have killed my children.

I had returned to the country house to see to the closing. Most of the servants have moved on to other employment. Only the butler remains, overseeing the packing of the furniture for storage. Endora and Lorna had returned to London.

I arranged for the mother superior of a nearby convent to collect Charlotte. For this, I was going to make a large donation to the order and pay a monthly stipend for Charlotte's care.

I went to the windmill, where her room is. The last of the equipment was packed up, ready to be delivered to the new London laboratory. It was getting dark, and I lit a kerosene lamp. She was standing at the bars of her cage, waiting for me as I entered. She backed away after seeing the flame from the lamp, as she is fearful of fire, so I put it down on a nearby table.

I told her we were going on a trip and she would no longer have to live in a cage. Then I heard someone approaching behind me. I turned around and there was Risto, alive and well. Last I had seen him was at the bottom of a ravine after I had pushed him over a cliff to save Charlotte.

"Hello, Father," he said, with an evil grin across his face. He had the eyes of a madman and a large axe in his hand. "Happy to see me?"

So great was my shock that all I managed to say was, "How?"

"How did I find you, Father? After I climbed my way out of that gorge you pushed me into, I went back to your lab. I dug through the rubble, looking for any clue to where you had gone. I found a strongbox buried in the ruins, with letters from your solicitor, detailing the purchase of this property."

I had no idea he could read. One of the many surprising things I would learn that night.

Charlotte was jumping up and down with glee in her cage. Then she spoke! "Risto! You save me!"

"Yes, my dear," he said, taking slow steps towards me. "You should be with your own kind, not this monster." He pointed the axe at me. "Open the cage. She isn't an animal!"

I complied, knowing his strength is such that he could easily split me in half with the axe.

She ran to him, and they embraced. I took that moment to take a few steps back towards the table with the lamp.

"These were also in the strongbox," he said, taking two rings from his pocket. They were our wedding bands, mine and Charlotte's. I'm not sure why I had forgotten them. He slipped a ring on his finger and the other onto Charlotte's. "We are man and wife now."

He noticed I was backing away.

"Stop!" Risto commanded. "We have not finished with you." He turned to me. "You will make us some children, so we can be a family."

Charlotte clapped and jumped with joy. She knew what he was talking about. She must have been more intelligent than I realised to know concepts like 'family'.

"I can't do that for you," I said, even though I knew I could.

"You will. You owe us a real life," he said, taking a step towards me and threatening me with the axe.

I took a few more steps back, bumping into the table. I knew I had but one chance for escape: I turned, grabbed the kerosene lamp and threw it at him with all my might.

It hit him, and he burst into flames. Charlotte rushed to help him, but within seconds the fire engulfed her as well. I dashed past them and out of the windmill, and made it to the house. I yelled for the butler to get water, but it was too little, too late. The windmill was now consumed in flames. In less than an hour, it was a pile of ashes.

I fell to my knees and wept. That body might not have held the soul of my Charlotte any longer, but while it lived, a part of her was still in this world. Now I have murdered that final remnant.

I have been so consumed with playing God that I lost everything that made my own life worth living. Risto was right; I am the monster.

What do I have left? I return to the London laboratory with a renewed vow that my work will be used for the good of all mankind. Their deaths will not be in vain.

FROM THE DIARY OF OSCAR WILDE, 2ND OF AUGUST 1884

Dear yours truly,

Today, for the second time in my life, I must dispose of a body. I am in the cellar of my mother's house, a six-foot-deep hole before me. I am covered in blood, dirt and tears as I write this, but my heart aches and writing is the surest way I know to cope with loss and grief.

They say killing gets easier the more you do it, but I don't think that's true. It grows tiresome like any repetitive task.

It began earlier today when I came to Mother's house to see to the safety of her and Willie. I've sent them off to the country to keep them out of the mitts of Wilkins and Mueller. Having heard about Bram's kidnapping, they have finally agreed to go. I would not put it past those villains to try to get to Bram through me and go through my family to get to yours truly.

I was closing up the house when a young man called to me from the pavement.

"Oscar!"

I did not know him, but as I am quite famous now, I am often recognised by those who are unknown to me.

He was well dressed, wearing a fashionable top hat and coat, and was no more than twenty-five. Very handsome, thin and tall. I would have remembered him had we met before and said as much to him.

"Oh, but we have met before, Oscar." There was a twinkle in his eye and a playful smile on his lips.

My heart raced as I assumed he was one of Mueller's monstrosities come to give me a thrashing, but there was nothing but love on his face.

He bounded up the steps and embraced me, whispering into my ear, "It's me, Oscar. It's Derrick."

My legs buckled, but he held me up. I dropped my walking stick and its large, brass handle hit me squarely on the foot, but I was in much too much shock to react to the pain.

He made sure I was on sure footing before releasing me. "Should we go inside and catch up?"

He said it so matter-of-factly, as if he were any old friend I happened to run into on a summer's day, that the suggestion actually seemed to make sense.

I picked up my cane, put the key in the lock and opened the door, and he whisked me inside. He kicked the door shut with his heel, grabbed me and kissed me fervently on the lips.

I broke away, still in shock.

"Yes, Oscar, Reverend Wilkins saved me from purgatory. He restored me to life." He stepped back so I could look at him better. "And while the body isn't as pleasant as my last one, it has its charms. I hope you approve."

I sat down on a bench in the foyer. I was shaking and having trouble catching my breath.

"What do you want?" I finally managed to ask, for I knew this was more than a social call.

"To start our life, Oscar." He sat down next to me and put his arm around me. "I finally got what I wanted, Oscar, everlasting life, and you can have it too. I forgive you for killing me when I was a vampire. I understand now why you did it. I mean, who wants to live forever *that* way? You can't eat gourmet food, you can't drink wine, and you can't dance in the sunshine. But this, Oscar, this is something different. You can use up one body and simply trade it in for a new one!"

"I'm married now," I said. "Happily. Any love-that-dare-not-speak-its-name is all in my past."

His face hardened a bit, but he did not seem particularly heartbroken. "I highly doubt that, but as you wish," he said. "Well, I am happy for you, Oscar. Can't you be happy for me? Can't you see how wonderful this miracle is? Think of it, I have a second chance at salvation. We can live our days over and over until Christ returns on Judgement Day."

"And how will that day go, Derrick? Mueller thinks he's God, and Wilkins is stealing bodies for his friends. Do you think God will look favourably on those who find a loophole in the death clause?"

He got off the bench and paced agitatedly in front of me. "Well, we will just have to cross that bridge when we come to it. Reverend Wilkins tells me that's a thousand years away. In the meantime, I don't know why you wouldn't want this for me, for you, for your loved ones. That new wife of yours, I bet she would want to live forever."

"She wouldn't," I said. "Not this way, I am sure of that."

He suddenly grabbed me by my necktie and yanked me to my feet. Like all of Mueller's minions, he was incredibly strong.

"Stop being such a wet blanket, Oscar." He was getting very angry now. "I won't let you ruin this for me as you did before! When I came to you as a vampire, it was out of love. I offered you immortality, and you repaid me with a stake to the heart!"

My pulse was racing, but I forced myself to remain outwardly calm. "Why are you really here?" I asked, this time with steel in my voice.

"I told you, Oscar, for you! And I was hoping you could speak to Stoker for us. We will need more of his blood."

There it was, the real reason Wilkins brought him back.

"My powers of persuasion are remarkable," I said. "But I prefer to use them for good rather than evil."

He lifted me off my feet and threw me into the wall above the bench, shattering the large mirror that hung there. I fell to the floor with shards of glass raining down onto my back.

"Wotton was right about you all along," he said, as he picked me up from the floor. "You are a vain, selfish person and I deserved better." This time he tossed me into the door. Luckily my shoulder took most of the blow, but once again I was on the floor.

I crawled to where my cane lay, hoping to get it and the sword it contained, but he kicked it away.

"You just stay down there and grovel at *my* feet for a change," he said. "You will help us or I will kill you, then kill your wife, mother and worthless brother!"

My hand was on top of a large shard of the broken mirror and I curled my fingers around it. The sharp edge cut into my palm.

He became quiet and calm again and knelt down to be more level with my face. He ran his fingers through my hair. "In time, Oscar, you will see how important our work is to all of mankind. You will enjoy having a new body. I should think you'd be happy to rid yourself of this fat bloated one you have treated so badly and get into something better. My God, Oscar, what happened to you?"

Anger surged inside me and in one quick motion, I took the shard of glass and plunged it into his ear, piercing his brain.

He fell back with a surprised look on his face. He tried to stem the blood with his hands and I jumped to my feet, watching in horror. The flow of blood gave way to spurting greenish pus.

I held his head in my lap as his life drained away, his eyes looking up to me. Oddly, they were Derrick's eyes, the ones I remembered. He was looking at me with a mixture of love and fury. As the light went out from them he was trying to speak, but the only word I could make out was 'sorry'. I don't know if he was talking about himself or me.

I had killed Derrick Pigeon for a second time.

I wrapped his body in the hall rug and dragged it to the cellar, where I have been digging his grave.

When I put my pen down I shall lower his body into the hole, as gently as I can, and cover him with dirt. I still have the hallway to clean up, and myself, so I can return to the theatre and my wife without looking like the murderer I am. That all seems impossible to me right now – I am so very tired and heartsick. But if I didn't know before, I know now that we are at war, and soldiers must perform their duties. Once more unto the breach, dear friends, once more.

POLICE REPORT FROM CONSTABLE STEWART FIFE, BROADSTAIRS

7 August 1884
Subject: The Wrecking of the *Jamaica Inn*

The following is the testimony of Vincent Watson, keeper of the North Foreland lighthouse. These events happened on the evening of the 30th of July 1884.

"It was midnight, and I went to refill the lamp with oil, as I do every night. It was then I saw the false light. I know that skyline like the back of me hand. From time to time I see campfires and the like on the shore. But this was something different. It was very bright, like the beacon of a lighthouse just a mile or two down the shore. I recognised it straight away as an attempt at wrecking.

"It was the perfect spot too. If a ship rounded the cape, it would see that light first. The lamp from the lighthouse would be barely visible through the fog until a ship goes another mile. Aye, I haven't seen a wrecking lamp in over thirty years, but it was clear what it was. I could see the lamps of a ship round'n the cape, headed right for the rocks.

"I ran to the foghorn and sounded it loud and clear, hoping it would get the ship to look my way. But it was too late. The ship crashed, I could tell that even in the dark as the lamps went out as she sank."

— Let the record show that the ship he witnessed was the *Jamaica Inn* out of Barbados. All on board are believed to have drowned. The odd thing is the ship's cargo, Jamaican rum, washed up onshore and was not recovered by the wreckers. Curiously, we have not found a single body. It seems the crew has vanished, perhaps washed out to sea.

REPORT FROM WHITE WORM SOCIETY AGENT CORA CHASE

Date: 8 August 1884
Subject: Dr. Mueller's Cadavers

Disguised as a working girl, I continue to investigate the activities of Dr. Mueller and Reverend Wilkins. Today my surveillance led me to a most ghastly discovery.

Mueller, Wilkins and the others have left his country estate and at least some of them have returned to London. Endora and her daughter Lorna are back in their séance parlor.

I have lost track of Dr. Mueller but picked up the trail of Reverend Wilkins. He is up to something and is very busy ordering his minions to perform tasks all over London.

I tracked him to a warehouse facility in Whitechapel, a large icehouse that is used for fish storage.

I saw him leave the icehouse and tailed him across town, where I lost him somewhere on Bond Street. This forced me to return to the cold storage warehouse to ascertain what function it serves.

I found an unguarded coal chute by the bins in the alley. The smell is almost unbearable, as old fish guts are piled up and rotting outside.

Once inside, I carefully made my way deeper into the building where it is extremely cold. I was not dressed properly for the climate and only had a few moments to look around at the risk of frostbite. It was mostly empty, at least of workers or guards.

It seems only one of Mueller's men remained behind to watch over the building, and he was staying in an office that had a stove. The office was on the upper level and overlooked the work floor. It was easy enough to stay out of his sight as I proceeded to the central part of the building where there were large fish hanging on hooks.

To my horror, when I got closer I could see it wasn't fish or slabs of beef hanging there, but human bodies dangling from the hooks by leather straps run across their chests and under their armpits. There were at least thirty by my quick count, mostly male. Apparently, Mueller and Wilkins are working hard on their plan. Where they acquired so many bodies is a mystery, but by the looks of the tattoos, most appear to be the remains of sailors.

Unfortunately, I did not keep as well out of sight as I had hoped. The guard yelled down from the upper level, "Hey, you, how did you get in here?"

I dashed for the cellar stairs, quickly made it to the coal chute door and scrambled up to escape down the alley.

To my surprise, the man had exited through an alley door and was hot on my heels. I made it to the street and disappeared into the crowd. I ducked down several alleys to make sure I gave him the slip.

I must tell Mr. Stoker and the others about this at once. If Mueller puts souls into all those bodies, there may be no stopping him.

FROM THE JOURNAL OF DR. VICTOR MUELLER, 9TH OF AUGUST 1884

We are back in business in a big way. Over the last three days, we have brought back twenty worthy souls, mostly upper-class men known to Reverend Wilkins and Lord Wotton.

Lorna and Endora are exhausted, as am I. We have depleted our supply of sailor bodies. It took much more Stoker Serum to bring these bodies back to the living. Perhaps it is because the sailors were wracked with scurvy and other ailments. I am carefully tracking this data for further analysis.

There also has been a setback with Wilkins' reattached arm and Wotton's new eye. They required second doses of Stoker Serum to keep them from going gangrenous. Perhaps Stoker's blood is thinning with age or affected by diet.

I have examined it under the microscope, and it appears to be different. There aren't as many unique corpuscles as before.

When we recapture Stoker, more experiments will have to be done. We will have to get him back soon; if all our new bodies require extra Serum, we will go through our supplies much more quickly than I had planned.

I still hope that Stoker's son possesses the unique blood properties and will be able to take over as a source as Stoker ages and becomes no longer useful. I shall also continue my attempts to synthesise his unique blood properties, as eventually both he and the child will die. Perhaps we could breed him again in the hopes of providing more donors.

We had to move fast in putting spirits into the new bodies, as an intruder infiltrated our storage facility. I assume she was working with Stoker, as what other reason could someone have for breaking into a warehouse that stinks of fish? We were forced to move them from long-term cold storage to the lab for fear Scotland Yard would be notified.

With Director Hammond's help, the support of several lords and our new army, we will put an end to the White Worm Society's meddling once and for all.

Their ancient order is so mired in the past they cannot see what the future holds! Eliminating them is what we must do to move forward.

I hope we can do it with little bloodshed. The director has turned many of the members to our cause and has sacked the rest.

I have put any remorse I felt at the loss of my two creations behind me as I dedicate my life to the good of the human race.

FROM THE DIARY OF LORNA BOW, 12TH OF AUGUST 1884

I am seething with anger! Reverend Wilkins has shown me his true colours. I was suspicious of him when we first met, but allowed myself to be convinced otherwise. Now there is no question: he is evil.

I was in Dr. Mueller's new laboratory. It is much bigger than his old one, with cold storage for bodies and human parts. It is located underneath a fancy art gallery and I like to sneak up there sometimes to look at the paintings and sculptures.

I was there today, wandering down a row of paintings, when I heard the voices of Wilkins and Dr. Mueller from around a corner. I saw them reflected in a window across the way. They were sitting on a bench in front of a painting. Not wanting to run into them – I see them quite enough as it is – I was about to turn around and tiptoe away when their topic of conversation caught my ear.

They were casually discussing who they would bring back from the dead next. Talking as if they were just ordinary businessmen planning a new shipment of goods.

Then they started talking about a failed attempt to kidnap the Stokers' son because he might have the same blood as his father. Dr. Mueller needs a steady supply of this blood for his resurrection serum.

They would do that? Kidnap a little boy?

Later, down in the lab, I asked Dr. Mueller about it, but he waved me off and told me to talk to Wilkins since he is the one in charge of that end of things. He said he wasn't sure if Noel's blood would work and thinks another kidnapping attempt isn't worth the risk to find out.

Then I remembered Charlotte in the cage in Dr. Mueller's lab in the country. I had told myself it was okay since she was a wild animal, but was she? She seemed able to communicate and liked to look at picture books.

I asked him where she was and he went all sad and said, "She died. There was a fire that destroyed the old lab and she didn't make it out." He went back to sewing up the chest of a corpse. (Funny how quickly you get used to these things.)

I ran out of the lab, crying for Charlotte. If she hadn't been in the cage, she would have been able to run out. It was his fault she was dead.

I wasn't looking as I rounded the corner for the stairs that lead outside and smacked right into Wilkins.

He scolded me to watch where I was going. I was already so angry, and that didn't help. "Did you really try to kidnap a child?" I asked, probably yelling it louder than I meant to.

He did not even try to deny it. "When it comes to doing God's work, the ends justify the means," he said. "In any event, it is no concern of yours."

"It is if you want me to keep talking to the dead for you!"

Then he slapped me hard across the face and called me a spoiled child.

"You will do what you are told," he said.

"And if I don't?" I said to him, most defiantly.

"We wouldn't want anything to happen to Molly and the other girls," he said. "If I am such a monster that I would kidnap a child and drain his blood, I wouldn't have any reservations about hurting them."

I ran up the stairs and out into the alley, still stinging from his slap and his words. He did not follow me, but I ran all the way back home.

Later, I told Mother what I'd overheard. To my surprise, she was not surprised. "I would have made sure the boy came to no harm," she said.

I felt as though someone had punched me in the stomach. "You knew? You knew they tried to take that boy?"

"I would have returned him to his mother when I have everything I need from Mueller and Wilkins."

I did not even bother telling her about Wilkins slapping me. I'm sure that would have angered her, but I don't want her anger for something so trivial when she can be so unfeeling for a child being taken from his mother.

FROM THE JOURNAL OF DR. VICTOR MUELLER, 13TH OF AUGUST 1884

All attempts to locate Andrew Hammond in the afterlife have failed. It seems he has moved on.

This was the one thing we needed for the director to rid us of the White Worms' interference.

But Reverend Wilkins has come up with a cunning plan. Since the soul would be in a new body, it would be quite simple for someone else's rescued spirit to pose as Andrew.

Lorna has been misbehaving lately and is reluctant to contact the dead for us, but Endora has persuaded her to continue helping us. Endora explained to her that we need to stop the White Worms and this is the best way to do that. Fortunately, the girl still wants to please her mother.

There are many spirits eager to return, and we found one that could pull it off. The spirit of a school chum of Andrew's who has only recently died agreed to pose as him in exchange for a new body and a second chance at life.

He knows Andrew's past well enough, has spent time with the family and assures us he can fool the director. He can explain away any slip-ups as the lingering effects of being dead.

Wilkins feels the director will be so happy to have his son back he probably wouldn't see through the ruse, adding that many fathers and sons know very little about one another.

So the deed has been done. Endora and Lorna have channelled him into one of my creations.

After a bit of coaching, we have sent him off for a joyous reunion with his father. As he is a man of honour, I am sure Director Hammond will keep his end of the bargain.

FROM THE JOURNAL OF CONSTANCE WILDE, 14TH OF AUGUST 1884

Everyone is in hiding, and I do not like it. Mueller's monsters are looking for any opportunity to grab Bram for the unique properties of his blood. As Oscar says, why must it always be blood with these supernatural creatures?

While Mueller is busy stuffing the upper-class dead into new bodies, I am worried about poor Lorna. She is a child, after all. She is intelligent for her age and has powers to contact the dead, but still a child.

This morning I went out for supplies and saw a girl I recognised from Lorna's séance parlour. She was busy picking the pockets of shoppers.

I managed to grab her, and she put up quite a fight for someone so small.

"How would you like to make a pound?" I said. She stopped struggling at once.

I took a pound from my purse and put it into her palm. "To earn this pound, you must simply tell Lorna to meet me tomorrow at noon in the café where I bought her lunch. She will know what I mean. This message is only for Lorna, mind."

With that, the girl scampered off.

The next day, Florence and I put on hats with veils to hide our faces and ventured out to the café. We weren't sure whether Lorna would show up, but happily, she did. We had chosen a secluded corner of the restaurant to protect her from being seen, though Lorna immediately said, "You needn't have picked such a dark spot for my sake, miss. Nobody I know would see me here. They're all too caught up in what they're doing to bother with something like going out for lunch."

"And what are they doing?" Florence immediately asked. I'd hoped to sidle into the subject more subtly, but she can be quite direct. I suppose it's the influence of all the time she spent in America.

Lorna seemed to hesitate, and I said, as gently as I could, "Lorna, we don't want to put you in an awkward position. But the people you're working with…they're dangerous. They've threatened our very lives. They tried to abduct Mrs. Stoker's child!"

Lorna looked desolate. "I heard about that," she said. "After it happened," she hastened to add. "I feel awful."

"We know it's not your fault, Lorna," Florence reassured her. "But you must see that we can't go on like this. We need to know what's happening, and how we can stop it."

After a few moments' hesitancy, Lorna confessed all. Apparently all the souls who are being returned are people who helped Wilkins in his scheme to rule the world. "But what makes them so special?" she asked. "Why should they get the bodies, and not the souls that had been born in them, whose lives had been cut short? Why is it always these fancy lords and such that Reverend Wilkins knows? What about some poor thing that never had a chance at a decent life in the first place? Shouldn't they get the first crack at a new start?"

I didn't think anyone should have this unnatural new lease on life, but felt it best not to take too hard a line at the moment. "Oh Lorna, you're so right," I said.

"Wilkins is an evil man," Florence added. "He tried to create an army of vampires just a few years ago. My husband, and Constance's, helped defeat him. If he's bringing these people back, it can't be for anything good or righteous."

"It is to hear him tell it," Lorna said. "He's always going on about 'redemption', and 'God's work'. Well, I'm not much of a churchgoer, truth be told, but I can't believe any god worth following would want Wilkins on his side."

"You're an exceptionally perceptive girl," I said, causing her to blush.

"What do I do now?" she asked plaintively. "I don't want any part of this anymore."

"You can stay with us," Florence immediately piped in.

"Or us," I agreed. "You can't go back there. It's too dangerous."

She brightened for a moment, then her face fell again. "No. Leaving is what would be dangerous. My mother has powers you can't even imagine. She would turn the city upside down looking for me."

Florence and I both fretted and tried to persuade her, but she would not change her mind.

"I'll try my best not to channel any more souls. Perhaps I can convince them that the people they're looking for have moved on. It might be hard to fool Mother, but I'll try," she said. "Besides, this way I can keep an eye on them and let you know what's going on."

"Do not put yourself in any unnecessary danger," Florence pleaded.

"Well," Lorna said, a sly smile on her lips, "I have powers too. Mother would not hurt me, and if anybody else were to try, they'd regret it."

I clasped her hands in mine. "That's the spirit!"

"If you have anything to report, or if you need our help, you need only send word. The trouble is, neither of us is staying in our homes right now, for safety reasons. We've moved into a flat on—"

But Lorna interrupted her. "It's best you don't tell me, Mrs. Stoker. I wouldn't tell, not on purpose, but my mother...."

We understood immediately. If her mother found out Lorna was working with us, she might be able to glean the information from her, by magic or by force.

Lorna thought a moment, then pulled the diary I had given her from her bag. "I've learned a spell that will help. If it works," she said, with a nervous laugh.

She opened the diary to a blank page, then had us all lay a hand on it. She closed her eyes and muttered an incantation that I didn't understand. The strangest feeling overtook me: a fluttering in the stomach, a light-headedness, and a sensation of weightlessness. It only lasted a few moments, then Lorna opened her eyes and pulled her hand away. She ripped the blank page from the journal and said, "Now, if either of you wants to send me a message, write it on this page, and it will appear on the blank page here. I can do the same in reverse to send word to you."

Florence looked sceptical, though I could tell she had experienced the same feeling I had when the magic coursed through us. "Could we test it?" she asked.

And we did. Lorna wrote, *Greetings*, in her thin, spidery hand on the blank page in her journal, and we watched as the word magically crawled onto the ripped-out page before us. I scrawled a quick *Hello* on our page and we watched it appear in the diary.

"How wonderful!" Florence whispered.

Lorna seemed almost as amazed as we were. "And useful. Just make sure you check it from time to time."

"Hourly, at least!" I exclaimed.

With that, she said she'd best be getting back before her mother started wondering where she was and took her leave. Florence and I remained for a while longer, discussing our new ally. I hope we can stop these people and their evil plot, and that Lorna does not get hurt in the process.

LETTER FROM ERROL HAMMOND TO ELEANOR HAMMOND, 15TH OF AUGUST 1884

My dearest Ellie,

I write to you with the most amazing news. You will find it difficult to believe, but everything I am about to tell you is true and you will want to be on the next train home as soon as you read this.

I have always taken pride in my work. Studying the supernatural and stopping it whenever it brings evil to our shores has been my duty and my privilege. However, I have at times run across situations where magic is not evil and, in fact, can be a force for good. I have discovered such a magic recently.

It is actually a combination of science and the supernatural. As hard as it may be to believe, this magical process can communicate with the dead and put them into new bodies.

I have authorised this use of magic and science to bring Andrew back to life!

He sits next to me eating lunch as I write this. His soul has been put into a new body, and that takes some getting used to, but he is his old self and very happy to be alive once again.

I know this all seems too good to be true, but it is! Come home at once and see for yourself. Our son is back and waiting for your return.

With much love and joy,

Errol

REPORT FROM WHITE WORM SOCIETY AGENT CORA CHASE

Date: 18 August 1884
Subject: White Worms Compromised

I do not know why I am writing this report. I have remained in England against orders and have been saving all my recent reports until such time as I felt enough confidence in my superiors to file them. Now I know that day will never come. Director Hammond has cleaned house, as it were, and now Reverend Wilkins and Dr. Mueller sit on the governing board of the White Worm Society. How he persuaded the rest of the board to go along with this, I do not know.

Mr. Blackwood has been dismissed. I assume I would be, too, if they knew where to find me.

With no official duties to perform, I took it upon myself to watch over headquarters. There I witnessed magical books being removed from the library. Some were taken away to who knows where, while others were actually burned in the alley. Many of these tomes are, I'm sure, irreplaceable.

All hopes of getting other agents to join us have been dashed. It is now up to me, Mr. Stoker and the others to enter the Realm and close the Spirit Gate once and for all.

FROM THE JOURNAL OF DR. VICTOR MUELLER, 18TH OF AUGUST 1884

We succeeded today in our plan to take over the White Worm Society, albeit with more bloodshed than I wanted.

I thought it would be simple enough to have the director place us on the governing board, but several board members objected and had to be killed by Wilkins and his men. Once again, I am wondering if the ends justify the means. I did not think the business of bringing people back to life would involve so much death.

Wilkins had these board members drowned and we are placing more of his friends into their bodies. That way there will be no murder investigations, and the governing board looks to be staffed with the old guard. Clever, really, but I think in time we could have persuaded them to join our cause. How many more have to die?

Wilkins has been spending most of his time in the Society's library. He is going through the collection, burning books that may aid others in closing the Spirit Gate, as well as books he finds to be the work of the devil.

There are shelves and shelves full of magical artefacts that I hope to study, some of immense power. I was inventorying the vault where they are stored when I spotted Miss le Fey retrieving an artefact for herself, a small vial with a dark red, almost black, liquid.

I asked her what she was taking. She grinned at me and said, "The last of the dragon's blood." She laughed in a deep, guttural voice, which was off-putting coming from the mouth of a child.

Before I could question her further, Wilkins stepped into the vault and confronted her.

"Where do you think you are going with that?" he asked. He tried to grab it from her hand, but she kicked him hard in the shins. Even with Wilkins' strength, it must have hurt because he backed away.

She hissed at him like a feral animal. "It's mine! I want to be a vampire again. I want the power. I want the desire for warm blood again!"

With that, she downed the flask.

"You have no right!" Wilkins shouted.

She laughed at him again, smashing the vial to the ground. She swooned and had to steady herself on one of the shelves. Then a look of confusion and pain came over her face. "It didn't hurt this way before," she said, holding her stomach and looking at Wilkins. "What's happening?"

He just stared at her and backed away as she staggered towards him, moaning, "Help me!"

She then, for the lack of a better term, exploded. Her blood and guts were everywhere, including on us.

Wilkins and I looked at each other, aghast.

"She said it was dragon's blood," I said. "Did she know it could do that to her?"

He shook his head.

"I've never seen it do anything like that. It should have turned her into a vampire." He pulled out his handkerchief and started to wipe the blood from his face, but soon realised he was going to need a much larger piece of cloth to remove the stains. As would I. He continued in a shaky voice. "We won't be bringing Miss le Fey back again."

I must admit, I was glad to hear it. I did not care for her, and persuading Lorna to put her into a third body would be a challenge, to say the least.

Wilkins mused that it was like she had been pierced through the heart by a stake or a silver bullet. It's true; I know from my research that new vampires explode in guts and gore, and old ones dissolve in a cloud of dust when killed.

I then remembered the latest batch of Stoker's blood. There was something about it. Something that made the Serum less effective. Could Stoker be polluting his blood with silver? It would explain why I now have to keep administering Stoker Serum to keep the bodies from going gangrenous. That clever bastard!

When we recapture Stoker, we will put him on a more appropriate diet.

FROM THE DIARY OF OSCAR WILDE, 19TH OF AUGUST 1884

Dear yours truly,

It seems we are honorary White Worm agents now, though apparently the White Worms as we knew them no longer exist. Miss Chase tells us they have been corrupted, and she needs our help. She has recruited Bram and me for a mission into the Realm.

The last time I was there, I did not care for it. Not one bit. We were chased out by four-armed beasts, and we all nearly lost our lives.

This time is different, I am told. Miss Chase says there are many worlds inside the Realm, and this one is relatively tame. However, it involves us going into the Land of the Dead and closing something called a 'Spirit Gate'. That doesn't sound tame to me, but I cannot let Bram go in there on his own. Who would save him should the need arise (as it inevitably will)? The whole thing sounds positively harrowing, but with Mr. Lloyd's journal we will at least know what to expect.

The fact we need to travel to Wales doesn't make the prospect any more appealing. It is a dreadful country that is nothing but rocks and thistles. Why does the battle against evil never take one to Paris?

Miss Chase promises us it will be a quick in and out. We enter the Land of the Dead, perform some ritual, and the Gate will be closed. That will cut off the spirits Wilkins is putting into Mueller's monsters. I must say, the idea that the next time I kill Wotton there will be no avenue for him to return does make me a bit more eager to go.

Still, I have a bad feeling in my bones about this and confided in Constance.

She is worried for our safety, but trusts Miss Chase and points out this might be the only chance we have to stop Wilkins.

"He doesn't know we know how to close the Gate," she said. "This gives us a significant advantage."

Constance, Florence and Ellen are thick as thieves these days and I worry they might be thinking of continuing the surveillance on Mueller and Wilkins on their own. I made Constance promise me she would stay hidden and leave the detective work to the professionals.

We will be back soon enough, hopefully with the Gate closed. Then it is only a matter of getting Scotland Yard on our side to round up the monsters.

I would like to write a book someday about how many times I have saved the world, but who would believe it?

FROM THE JOURNAL OF CONSTANCE LLOYD, 19TH OF AUGUST 1884

I am at once terrified and overjoyed. I had been feeling poorly and went to the doctor anticipating bad news only to be told I am expecting!

This is the same doctor who told me I may never be able to have children after that 'fall' down the stairs in my childhood. I have long told myself that it was an accident, but on this very day when the doctor told me the joyous news, the memory of what actually happened came flooding back into my mind, as clear as day. Imagine, a mother throwing her own daughter down the stairs on purpose. What sort of monster does that?

All these years the thought of her doing that to me was so painful I pushed it deep into the recesses of my mind. Only the thought of me holding my own child threw a light on it.

The doctor told me he is quite sure as I am a good month along already. I had noticed a slight weight gain but assumed it attributable to dining with Oscar. Still Oscar's fault, to be sure, but for a much better reason.

I told Oscar, and he is over the moon. He is already picking out baby names and passing out cigars.

"There is no way I can go on Miss Chase's mission into the Realm now," he exclaimed. "I cannot leave you in this condition. I cannot risk not coming back."

I told him I would be fine and that he should go. There is so much at stake. Furthermore, we want the world free of monsters when the baby is born. (Imagine, all some parents have to worry about when preparing for a baby is picking out a cot and decorating a nursery!)

He reluctantly agreed and confided in me he had been looking for an excuse to back out since he is becoming more and more fearful at the thought of entering the Land of the Dead.

"It sounds ghastly, doesn't it?" he asked. "But I must find the courage for you and the baby."

"And for Queen and country," I added.

According to Miss Chase, it is a very simple mission. Step into the Land of the Dead, find a temple, which thanks to my father's journal they have a map to, and perform a simple ritual. Three people are needed for the circle, and so three must go into the Realm.

"Yes," he said, "but I find these things never go as planned. You undertake a simple mission to rescue Stoker and find yourself in the belly of a giant serpent, or buried within a collapsed cave. Things like that are always happening when Bram's along."

In any event, he agreed it was best that he go.

But tonight we celebrate this great miracle.

REPORT FROM WHITE WORM SOCIETY AGENT CORA CHASE

Date: 22 August 1884
Subject: Mission into the Land of the Dead

Using Horace Lloyd's diary, we have found an entrance into the Realm that in turn will lead us into the Land of the Dead. This will be my first trip in and I am very excited to go, especially if it means we can thwart Mueller and Wilkins in the process.

We have outfitted ourselves with proper exploration attire: hiking boots, pith helmets and the like, as well as hiking packs on our backs with food, water and other supplies. We know not what we will face once we are inside.

I am told there are many worlds inside. Actually, I suppose 'inside' is not the proper term. Mr. Doyle tells me it is more like the hub of a wheel with each spoke leading to a different world, or even a different universe.

The entrance we used is near Cardiff, Wales. We made our way to the base of a remote cliff overlooking the Bristol Channel. There we found what looked like a shallow cave, but nearly concealed in the back was a small opening that led to a narrow passageway.

Mr. Wilde consulted his father-in-law's diary, which is written in shorthand he can decipher and was serving as our guidebook on this expedition. "There should be a crack in the rock wall— Ah, there it is," he said, indicating a small fissure. "He provides an incantation." And here Mr. Wilde recited the words that I will not transcribe here; until such time as we have restored the White Worm Society to trustworthy leadership, I shall not take the chance that this information falls into the wrong hands.

There was a low rumbling, and a section of the rock wall slid open.

I was half expecting to step directly into the Land of the Dead that Lorna Bow describes as a gray void. We instead walked into a sunny, warm world. It was a shock as we were leaving behind the damp world of Wales, where it was foggy.

Mr. Wilde consulted the diary again. "This is a world he calls 'Sunshire'. Apparently the sun never sets here, and it is semitropical."

"Any mentions of four-armed creatures or dinosaurs?" Mr. Stoker asked.

"No," Mr. Wilde said. "And in fact, he drew a smiling face by the entry." He showed us the page. "It's this skull and crossbones by this other entry that has me worried."

Mr. Stoker sighed. "I am certain that is the direction we need to go then."

And we did. As we walked through Sunshire, we noticed many birds, insects and animals. Many of them looked familiar – butterflies, rabbits and the like – but many did not. There was an animal about the size of a fox, but with lavender fur and a trunk like an aardvark. The largest lizard I've ever seen observed us from a sunny spot on a rock, then turned its head to call over its shoulder with a noise that sounded like a chicken's squawk.

We could hear the roar of ocean surf nearby and there was salt in the air like in Cardiff, but we seemed to be walking away from the shore.

"There is a village up ahead," Mr. Wilde said. "Lloyd notes the people are friendly to strangers."

As we rounded a hill, we could see a village spread out in the valley below us. There were hut-like structures. As we came closer, we saw the villagers going about their day's work. They seemed to be an agrarian culture, primitive by our standards. There were horse-drawn carts moving goods about, or should I say pony-drawn as the horses were quite small. The people, too, were short in stature, I would say no more than three feet tall. Other than their size, they looked like they could be from our world. Most of them had reddish hair on their heads. Their manner of dress would not be out of place in any English country town.

We cautiously entered the village and caused quite a stir in the population. They dropped what they were doing and came running up to us. We all tensed, worried we were about to be attacked. I even reached for my pistol, but they swarmed around us, smiling and chattering in some unknown language.

An older member of the village (I assume, for he had white hair and beard) pushed his way through the crowd and motioned to us to follow him, which we did.

He led us to a log-cabin-like structure that seemed out of place among the small huts and knocked on the door.

"Enter," we heard someone say in an English accent.

Inside there was a regular-sized human hunched over a desk strewn with books, journals and maps. He looked up, clearly surprised to see us. Surprised and annoyed.

"White Worm Society operatives, I presume? Here to rescue me? I assure you I need no rescuing."

"No, and no," I said. "We had no idea someone from our world was here. We are on a different mission."

"Mr. Lloyd?" Mr. Wilde exclaimed.

"Why, yes, I am."

I looked from him to Mr. Wilde incredulously. "Horace Lloyd?" I asked.

"Everyone thought you were dead," Mr. Stoker said.

"As you can see, I am fine. Now off you go. Attend to your mission, or whatever, I am a very busy man."

He turned back to his desk and his work.

"Mr. Lloyd," Wilde said, stepping toward the man. "I am Oscar Wilde. I am your daughter's husband. She has been crying over your death for years."

He turned back to us. "Constance?"

Wilde took a photograph from his jacket pocket, and handed it to Lloyd, who leant back against his desk for support as he gazed at it.

"Could you not find a way out of here?" Mr. Stoker asked. He seemed worried, as was I now that he put the idea in my head. I remember Mr. Doyle saying that not all entrances into the Realm were also exits. Could we be trapped here?

"No, no, the way in is the way out. I could leave at any time. But there is so much here to research. I have been very busy."

"So busy you could not come out to see your daughter?" Mr. Wilde asked. "How could you abandon Constance like this? You left her alone with a horrible mother." He shook the journal at Mr. Lloyd, and I feared he might strike the older man.

"I am very sorry about that," Lloyd replied, handing the photo back to Mr. Wilde. "But it couldn't be helped. I have important work to do here. I am on the verge of a breakthrough that will explain how the Realm functions."

"You've been in here over ten years!" Mr. Wilde shouted.

"I have? Well, one loses track of time here. It doesn't work the same way, you see."

"No, I don't see! My father was a terrible man, but at least he provided for us and was there to see us grow up."

"Oscar," Mr. Stoker said, "let's get back to the matter at hand." He turned back to Mr. Lloyd. "We are looking for a way into the Land of the Dead. Can you help us?"

"Why in the world would you want to go into that dreadful place?"

"We need to find a temple," I said.

"We need to save the world you left behind," Mr. Wilde said. Lloyd ignored the contempt in Wilde's voice.

"I wish you luck. It's one of the most baffling worlds in the Realm. Almost didn't find my way out. It's easy to lose all sense of direction in there."

"Is there a temple there?" Mr. Stoker asked.

"Yes, in fact it's the only structure I could find in that land."

"Could you take us there?" I asked.

He sighed, clearly feeling put upon. "I can. When I explored it, I tied a rope to a tree in this world so I could find my way back out. I tied the other end of the rope to a pillar in the temple. You can follow the rope in and safely get back out."

He took us to the entrance, which was a few miles away. There was his tree with a rope tied to it. It lay on the ground and went off through the grass into the mouth of a cave that I would say was four feet wide and six feet high. A cold wind wafted over us from the cave. It smelled like rot and decay.

"Are you sure you want to go in there? It is a strange and frightening place, even by Realm standards. It befuddles one's senses. You cannot see the ground beneath your feet. There is no left, or right, or forward, or backward. You see hallucinations and ghastly apparitions. The dead are drawn to the living like moths to flame."

He handed us wads of cotton. "If you hear voices, then put these in your ears and don't listen to them. Never listen to them. The natives tell me you could be trapped in there forever if you do."

"I must say, I am having second thoughts about this," Mr. Wilde said.

"What do these spirits look like?" Mr. Stoker asked.

"First they appear as a ghostly mist, then they come into view and look as they did in life. I only saw people I knew in there," Mr. Lloyd said. "People who had died. People who held grudges against me. I still don't know if they were real or imagined. It might be that there is a gas in there like ether and that just makes one see things. Or it might be purgatory. The villagers here call it 'the Well of Souls'."

With that, he wished us luck and turned to leave. As he did, Mr. Wilde said to him, "You are to be a grandfather." Lloyd turned back to look at Wilde for a moment, then just nodded and left us holding a rope that disappeared into a dark cave.

Mr. Stoker took the lead, and I brought up the rear as we followed the rope into the cave.

After a minute or so of inching our way along, suddenly the damp darkness of the cave vanished, and we were in a misty, gray fog. At least that is the only way I can describe it. The heavy atmosphere of the cave was gone and replaced by a feeling of nothingness. There was no feeling of cold or hot. No breeze or even the feeling of air on one's skin. The lack of any sensation was almost as disorienting as not being able to see more than a foot in front of your face. Even Messrs. Wilde and Stoker were out of my vision, though I could feel them tugging on the rope and hear their voices.

"This is as terrible as Lloyd told us," Mr. Wilde said. "How are we supposed to find anything in here?"

Something made a whooshing sound as if it went over our heads, though I lacked all sense of direction here so it really could have been anywhere.

Mr. Stoker told us to keep moving, and it was only then I realized we had stopped. I felt him tug on the rope and then started to follow again, sliding my hand along the rope Mr. Stoker was keeping taut.

From the void, I heard someone call out to me. It was a child. "Help me, I am so lost."

I asked the others if they heard the voice and they did not.

"Please help me…Mommy," the voice called out. She was crying, and it was all I could do to keep myself from running to help her, but I resolutely kept moving forward.

I remembered the cotton Mr. Lloyd had given us. As I fumbled to retrieve it from my pocket with my right hand, the rope slipped out of my fingers. I frantically tried to grasp it again, but could not. I called out to the others, and they did not answer. I stopped walking and shouted again and again, but there was nothing, my voice just disappearing into the mist.

I was very much alone and felt like a frightened little girl. I recomposed myself, for I had no time for fear. The others would turn back for me when they realized I wasn't behind them. All I needed to do was stay put.

Then, through the mist, a little girl emerged. She was wearing a sleep shirt and clutching a rag doll. She looked familiar and at the same time was a stranger.

I didn't know what to do. She was most likely a spirit of some sort, but then maybe she had wandered into this place like we did. She looked real enough. And she felt real when she ran up and hugged my leg.

"You found me! I knew you would, Mommy."

A horrible wave of recognition sent a shiver up my spine. It couldn't be her.

I knelt down and the little girl threw her arms around my neck and hugged me tightly. I wanted to call out her name, but then I never did name her. The nuns told me it was best not to hold her and took her away to give to her new mother.

"Why ever did you leave me?" she cried.

"I could not take care of you," I said. I felt no sadness at this revelation. It was true. I was a child myself and living on the street.

"My new mother got sick and died," she said. "Then I got sick and ended up here. I am so very lost."

I started to cry, not just for her but for the me that might have been.

"Well, I found you now, and that is what is important," I said to her.

The mist swirled behind her and exposed a door. I was relieved to see it, somehow thinking it was a way out. It slowly swung open by itself. Through the door all I could see was a sky-blue color. Shafts of golden light glowed around the door's frame. I instinctively knew the door was for her and it was my duty to help her go through it. A warm feeling of peace and love emanated from our embrace, and I clung to her for a few moments more before gently breaking away.

A woman appeared in the doorway. She smiled at the girl, happy tears in her eyes.

"That's my other mother," the girl said.

I took her head in my hands and kissed her forehead. Smiling at her, I said, through my own tears, "Go with her. I'll be along soon." Even though I knew I wouldn't be following her now, I would someday.

She hesitated, torn between me and the other woman. "Run along, now," I said.

She smiled at me, turned and bravely walked into the blue void. The door shut and disappeared back into the mist.

Off in the distance, I heard Mr. Stoker frantically calling for me and I called back to him until he found me. He seemed shaken.

"Did you just see a spirit, one you had to help through a door?" he asked.

I told him I did. He said he had lost Mr. Wilde as well and then had a similar experience in the mist, where a spirit talked to him.

Moments later, Mr. Wilde emerged from the mist. He was out of breath and shaken as if he had seen something too. He said that he also had encountered a spirit, but did not offer details and we did not ask him about it.

Mr. Stoker held up his hand, which still grasped the rope, and said, "Shall we continue?"

FROM THE DIARY OF CONSTANCE WILDE, 22ND OF AUGUST 1884

As I write this, my world has been shaken yet again. We were all almost killed by someone who was supposed to protect us.

Oscar, Bram and Cora have gone into the Realm, but they would not have done so if we didn't have protection while they were gone. We have armed ourselves and had the additional security of Mr. Blackwood and Henry Irving.

Having our own vampire keeps Mueller and his monsters at bay, or at least gives them second thoughts about attacking us. In addition, we are hiding out in Oscar's secret flat. All of this made us feel very safe indeed.

However, tonight as the sun went down, Mr. Irving became agitated. He began pacing back and forth in our cramped living conditions. Mr. Blackwood was down in the building's foyer, standing guard.

Florence asked Mr. Irving what was bothering him. He grunted and continued pacing back and forth.

"I feel like a caged animal. I am tired of waiting. I should find Mueller and put an end to this, an end to him!"

Ellen was preparing sandwiches at Oscar's writing desk and cut her finger slicing bread. A tiny cut, but apparently that is enough to put blood's scent into the air.

Mr. Irving suddenly stopped in his tracks and whipped his head in Ellen's direction like a hound scenting prey. He fixed his gaze at Ellen as she wrapped a handkerchief around her injured finger. In an instant, his eyes turned red. His lips twitched into a snarl, revealing fangs.

"Henry?" Florence said calmly, stepping between him and Ellen. "When did you feed last?"

I have been told that he feeds from time to time on willing victims, mainly prostitutes. Lately he has been getting fresh blood from Dr. Seward.

"Let me get you some blood," Florence said. We have some in Oscar's small icebox, but Henry put up his hand to stop her.

"I can't eat any more of that cold, old blood," he said. He then shoved Florence out of the way and stepped closer to Ellen, stalking her. She put her cut finger behind her back.

"Henry, I am not on the menu," she said sternly. "Get a hold of yourself."

In a flash so quick I did not see him move, he was holding her from behind and he plunged his teeth into her neck!

Ellen let out a shriek. Florence rushed across the room with a silver cross in her hand and smacked him on the head with it. His hair sizzled, and he broke away from Ellen, who ran behind Florence for protection.

Florence held the cross out defiantly. "Henry, what has got into you?"

Mr. Irving glared at her malevolently. His muscles tensed as though readying for another attack. But then, with visible effort, he stepped back and took a deep breath. His eyes returned to their normal colour and his fangs retracted. He looked stricken, shame and horror mingling on his face.

In a blur he was gone, with the entry door slamming behind him.

Moments later, Mr. Blackwood came running up the stairs into the room.

"What happened? Was that Mr. Irving who sped past me?"

He noticed Ellen holding a cloth to her neck and rushed to her.

"Did he bite you?" he asked, guiding her to a chair.

"Just a nibble. I'm fine," she said as he took the cloth from her hand and tended her wound.

"You won't turn into…?" I asked.

"Heavens no, there is a whole process of draining a victim, then refilling with Henry's blood to sire a vampire."

I did not know Ellen was so knowledgeable on the subject, but I suppose it shouldn't be surprising, as it were.

We told Mr. Blackwood what had transpired.

"He hasn't been himself since that witch opened the Spirit Gate," Florence said. "He told us he was having trouble controlling his vampire nature. We should have listened to him."

"Without Henry, we have lost our biggest advantage," Ellen said. "It's only a matter of time before they find us. Lorna said they are searching the entire city for us."

With that, Florence took out her pistol and checked her bullets. She pulled out another pistol from her bag and handed it to Ellen.

"Then it is time we took the fight to them," Florence said.

"Your husband told me to keep you here, Mrs. Stoker," Mr. Blackwood said. "If there is any fighting to do, I'll do it."

"Ellen and I would be better suited for the task I have in mind."

I expected him to argue, but then he is a member of an organisation in which female agents are not uncommon. He merely asked, "May I at least know the particulars of this plan?"

"We are friends with Director Hammond's wife. It wouldn't be out of the question for us to pay a social call, especially while she is grieving the loss of her son. Then we will make our move to kidnap her husband. We will see how he likes it for a change. We will force him to tell us where Mueller and Wilkins are hiding."

Ellen asked what they would do if the director wasn't home.

"Then we kidnap his wife. That is how their side plays it, so we will have to be just as ruthless."

Mr. Blackwood protested, saying they have no training in such matters and weren't up for the task.

"I have killed vampires in the Wild West of America," Florence said. "Not to mention a four-armed monster of enormous size and strength. I think I can handle a petty little man." Before he could argue further, she added, "You'll find I cannot be persuaded once I make my mind up, Mr. Blackwood. Now, I need you to stay here and protect Noel and Constance."

She and Ellen pushed past Mr. Blackwood and went down the stairs to Ellen's carriage.

I wished I could have gone with them, but my bad leg makes me not much of a fighter. However, I have my pistol ready to back up Mr. Blackwood should the need arise.

LETTER FROM HENRY IRVING TO BRAM AND FLORENCE STOKER, 22ND OF AUGUST 1884

Dear Bram and Florrie,

It is with a most heavy heart that I must tell you I have left London. I can no longer fight my vampire urges, as Florence witnessed tonight.

I am not sure why now, after hundreds of years, I have lost control of my humanity. Miss Chase suggests it is because the Spirit Gate is open; more evil energy is coming into our world, so perhaps that is causing my vampire nature to take over.

It matters not. As you saw when I rescued you, Bram, and you when I lost control in the flat, Florence, the vampire is vicious and ravenous.

To my horror, I nearly killed Ellen. My shame is great, and I can no longer trust the human part of me to pull the reins on my vampire nature.

The hunger is so great for fresh, warm blood that I must take myself away for your protection.

Everywhere I go I hear the heartbeats of the living, smell the warm blood pulsing in their veins. It is too much to bear.

There is a monastery in Scotland that helps creatures like me. I will go there to try to master my impulses.

I am sorry to leave you in this time of need. Perhaps with some time away I will return, re-humanised.

In the meantime, I will have my solicitor transfer temporary ownership of the Lyceum to you, along with the power of attorney over all my financial assets.

Give little Noel a kiss from me and pray for my soul when you can.

Sincerely,

Henry

FROM THE JOURNAL OF BRAM STOKER, 22ND OF AUGUST 1884

Time: unknown

As I write this, I am on the steps of an ancient temple. It appears to be Egyptian in origin and made entirely of marble. It is the only building inside the Land of the Dead, according to Mr. Lloyd. This was where his rope led us.

The steps lead to a statue inside the temple of an Egyptian queen on her throne. It is quite large, I would say about forty feet tall. The only other things in the temple are four obelisks, one in each corner.

It is here Miss Chase says we are to perform the ceremony to close the gates. She is setting up the necessary elements now: outlining a star in salt on the floor and preparing a potion of some sort.

Oscar has his sketchbook out and is drawing the statue.

This land is shrouded in mists so thick that as we travelled, we couldn't see more than two feet in front of our faces. Lloyd's rope was our only lifeline. On our way in, somehow we all became lost in the mist, despite the fact we were all holding on to the same rope.

As we made our way through the Land of the Dead, I felt two tugs on the rope and I stopped. I called out to the others and heard nothing. I followed the rope back quite a way, but did not find Oscar or Miss Chase and I began to panic.

It was then I saw a figure emerging from the mist. For a moment I was relieved, thinking it was my travelling companions. It was not.

I was mightily surprised to see Dr. Hesselius, though somehow in this place it made perfect sense. He was the expert sent to us by Richard Burton to help put down the vampires that threatened us in London several years ago. Without his help, it is doubtful we would have survived the Black Bishop and his vampire minions.

Hesselius lost his life in the battle, killed by vampires in the theatre. I was not there at the time, but by all accounts he died valiantly. His death has weighed on my mind ever since. I feel great guilt for having pulled him into our fight and have thought of him even more frequently since Wilkins and Wotton have returned.

And now here he was, looking just as I remember him in life, with a tidy grey beard, his familiar rose-tinted spectacles and a neatly pressed, if old-fashioned suit. He walked up to me with a smile, grabbed my hand and shook it, though I made sure to keep my other hand on the rope.

"So good to see you again, my friend," he said in his Dutch-accented English.

I echoed the sentiment, though I am sure he saw the shocked look on my face.

He looked around and said, "Not much to look at, is it? I am not sure how long I have been here."

"It has been over four years," I said.

"Really? Fascinating. It seems like only a few days," he said, and I was happy to hear that as I would find this nothingness unbearable if I stayed for too long.

"So I am dead, then," he said. "I thought so. And you too, I am sad to see." I reassured him that I am not, and told him about Wilkins' return, though he knew Wilkins only as the Black Bishop.

"Ah, this explains much," he said. "I have sensed stirrings among the other inhabitants here for the last – well, it's felt like a few hours to me, though I suppose it is a matter of weeks back in the world. I did not know what to make of it."

"Spirits being drafted back into Wilkins' army," I said grimly.

"Not even death can keep that madman from his evil plans," he said. "But you beat him once and I know you can do it again."

There was a door behind him now. I hadn't noticed it before. He turned and looked at it too.

"That door appears now and then. I think I am supposed to go through it," he said. "But I can't get it open. I think I have unfinished business." He tried the knob, but the door wouldn't budge.

We stood there in silence for a moment. Then I said, "I guess there is an afterlife. This is proof of that, at least."

"Yes," he said. "So this must be some sort of purgatory, a waiting station before one moves on."

"Well, doctor, I don't know if this would be your unfinished business, but I want to apologise to you. Those vampires were my problem. I should not have got you involved. You would still be alive if I hadn't."

He laid a hand on my arm. "No, Bram, I was on my own path, and hunting vampires was my purpose. It was fitting that I should give my life in such a way. I was not one who was ever likely to die comfortably in my sleep."

As he said this, the door slowly swung open, revealing what looked like a blue sky on the other side.

"I see," he said. "It appears that *was* the unfinished business. I think your guilt is what was holding me here. The living can haunt the dead, it seems."

Now I felt doubly guilty! "Then even if we can't achieve our mission, it was worthwhile coming here," I said.

He gazed through the doorway for a moment, then said, "I do want to leave this place, and yet I must confess, I am frightened to go through."

Then a young woman appeared on the other side of the door.

"Elsje?" he said. He told me it was his niece, the one who had been killed by a vampire so many years ago. Elsje said nothing; she just smiled and beckoned him to come through the door.

He turned to me and said, "So this is it. I go on to one last great adventure. Farewell, Bram."

"Farewell, Dr. Hesselius."

With that he walked through the door, and there was a flash of blinding white light. He and the door had both vanished.

I continued to follow my rope back, calling for my companions, and finally heard Miss Chase returning my call. Moments later I found her, wiping a tear from her eye. She was relieved to see me and grabbed hold of the rope again.

I asked her if she'd seen a spirit and she said she had, but I did not press her about who it was, thinking it was a private matter.

"We should find Mr. Wilde and not get waylaid by these spirits," she said. "Living the life I have led, there are probably many ghosts here who want a word with me."

It was then Oscar came out of the mist. "Oh, thank heavens I found you! You will not believe what just happened to me."

He told us he'd encountered a spirit, and we told him we had as well. We then resumed following our rope forward until we reached this temple. The mists are not so thick here, which is heartening.

Miss Chase has prepared the ceremony and has called us over. I hope this closes the Gate and stops Wilkins and Mueller for good.

FROM THE JOURNAL OF FLORENCE STOKER, 22ND OF AUGUST 1884

Constance has written on the magic piece of paper Lorna gave us, asking her to come to our hiding place. We desperately need help that only she has the power to give. We must try to contact Bram, Oscar and Miss Chase in the Realm.

This evening, we went on the offensive. They won't be expecting us to take the fight to them, and so we decided to use that to our advantage.

Armed with two pistols and a dagger, Ellen and I hopped into her carriage.

We saw a curtain twitch as we approached the front door of the Hammond home, but when we knocked, nobody answered. We glanced at each other and quickly reached an unspoken agreement. Trying the knob, we found the door unlocked, and flung it open with 'guns blazing', as the cowboys say, or at least ready to blaze.

An empty entryway and parlour greeted us. At first we thought perhaps we'd imagined the curtain twitching, but moving cautiously from room to room, we soon found the director in his study. He had a bottle of whisky in front of him and his own pistol on the desk just inches away from his hand. Seeing the gun, we froze with our pistols trained on him.

He looked up at us with recognition but little interest or even surprise.

"Go ahead, shoot me. I deserve it. I was about to do it myself." He took a big swig directly from the bottle.

I cautiously approached the desk and grabbed his gun with my free hand while Ellen kept her own pistol pointed at him.

"Why were you going to do that, Mr. Hammond?" Ellen asked.

"I have ruined everything I have ever worked for," he said. "Everything I ever lived for."

It was then I noticed the young man dead in a chair on the left side of the room. You might think one would scream or faint at the sight of these things, but both of us had already seen plenty of dead bodies. This one had been shot between the eyes.

"Don't worry, he won't be dead for long. I'm sure they will bring him back." He took another swig and added, "They always come back. This one was posing as my dead son, returned from the afterlife. He had me fooled. But not my wife. No, she knew straight away he wasn't really Andrew. She asked him questions only Andrew could answer. It seems I didn't know my son well enough to ask such questions. She has left me for good."

I was in no mood for his self-pity. "You are coming with us, Director. We are taking you to Scotland Yard. You can tell them what horrible things have been going on."

"Bad idea, Mrs. Stoker. They have taken over the White Worm governing board, and likely have spies on the police force," he said, as he pulled an envelope from a drawer. He slid it across his desk towards me. "Here are the names of those I know of who are being inhabited by returned spirits. I don't know if the police will believe you, but I am sure these imposters will break under interrogation. I have made a full confession in the letter as well."

"You will be happy to know my husband and your Agent Chase are in the Land of the Dead closing the Spirit Gate for good."

He laughed. "No, dear woman, they are not. I knew Miss Chase was snooping around and I made sure she found false information. The ritual she took from my drawer will remove the veil completely. I am not sure what that will do, but I am certain it isn't good."

He opened another drawer, took out a large folder and laid it on top of the desk.

"For what it's worth, this is everything I've been able to gather about how to close the Spirit Gate. I am afraid it is rather complicated, involving lightning and Egyptian artefacts, four obelisks that once stood at the temple of Luxor. These were powerful magical items and deemed too dangerous to remain together. Three were relocated to different countries. Their power can only be activated by having them struck by lightning simultaneously. Even if we brought them back together somehow, we have lost the spell to summon lightning. It's all rather impossible, I'm afraid."

He picked up the folder and offered it to me. "But maybe you will find my research useful. It was what I was rather good at, studying ancient texts. I should have stayed a professor. How everything would be different. Andrew would be the son of a teacher and never would have joined the White Worms."

I set his gun down on his desk and took the folder.

"Please leave now," he said.

We left with the folder and his letter to Scotland Yard. As we exited the front door for the carriage, we heard a gunshot from his study.

I suppose I should have tried to talk him out of it – taken the gun at the very least – but I am afraid my goodwill was all used up for the day.

When we returned to the flat, it was Constance who came up with the idea to use Lorna to contact the others in the Land of the Dead.

She is here now and preparing.

"I have learned much since we spoke last," she said, showing us a book of spells her mother had given her. "And I have been reading up on the Land of the Dead in Mother's ancient scrolls."

I did not know how she could read such scrolls and didn't press the matter. I was just grateful there was some hope that we had a witch on our side for a change.

"I found something that could bring them straight home," she said, unrolling a scroll she had brought. "We just need a spirit to deliver the message. I'm pretty sure I can't contact live people, even in the spirit world."

She is now going to try to contact a friendly spirit who could help us. I pray we are successful.

FROM THE DIARY OF OSCAR WILDE, 22ND OF AUGUST 1884

Dear yours truly,

My life continues to go in the most extraordinary directions. Now, not only have I been to a rodeo in Nevada, I have travelled into and out of the Land of the Dead. Both places I would not recommend. They are both vacant of beautiful topography or interesting aesthetics.

After a gruelling trip to Cardiff, we entered a pleasant world inside the Realm, but we had no time to be tourists as we were just passing through on our way to the Land of the Dead.

I was rather hoping for some Dante imagery or having to cross the River Styx in some mythic fashion, something one could write about or regale one's grandchildren. Alas, it was but a grey void.

The trip did at least afford me the opportunity to meet my father-in-law. We were astonished to find him alive and well and seemingly uninterested in returning home, obsessively studying the Realm and its workings. He would not be the last person to surprise me on the trip.

Mr. Lloyd had explored inside the Land of the Dead and showed us how to get in and out again, which was most useful. He told us of its dangers. It is a void that has no landmarks, making it easy to get lost inside. It is a place of spirits that will pester the living. But despite his warnings, none of us was prepared to actually see and talk with those who had passed on.

We were on a mission and it was simple: get to a temple inside, perform a ritual (these supernatural things always come with these silly rituals, I know not why) and close the Spirit Gate – the veil between our world and the Land of the Dead.

We entered and followed a rope Mr. Lloyd had tied to a tree in his world and to the temple in that one.

"Don't let go of the rope until you are in the temple," he told us more than once.

Stoker was leading the way in front of me and Miss Chase was right behind me. As we walked on following the rope, the other two would disappear into the fog. Even a few feet ahead or behind me would put them out of view.

Still, I did not worry, for I could hear them talk and feel them tugging on the rope. I could even smell Stoker's sweat ahead. Not usually pleasant, but it somehow gave me comfort, and we went deeper, onward through the fog.

I wasn't conscious of it, but at some point I had let go of the rope, perhaps to scratch my nose. Cursing myself, I immediately reached to my left for the rope but could not find it. I called for the others, but got no response. A panic set in as I felt my way through the mist, searching for that damn rope.

I saw a figure coming towards me. It was too thin to be Stoker and too tall to be Miss Chase.

"We have to stop meeting like this, Oscar," he said, emerging from the fog with his most winning smile. It was Derrick. Not vampire Derrick. Not Derrick in someone else's body. The human Derrick, or at least his spirit-world equivalent.

"Oh, heavens," was all I could manage to say.

"Not quite," he said, looking around. "Maybe purgatory. Could be hell, I suppose, it is oppressively dull."

I remembered Lloyd had told us not to listen to spirits and fumbled in my pocket for the wads of cotton he had given us for our ears.

"Can you ever forgive me, Oscar?"

I stopped looking for the cotton. It was too late, anyway; nothing short of puncturing my eardrums would have got me to stop listening.

"Forgive *you*? I've killed you twice, Derrick. I should be furious if anyone killed me once."

He shrugged. "It was my own fault, both times. I was so obsessed with living forever, I didn't live at all," he lamented. "I didn't realise that it is the spectre of death that gives life meaning, makes it more precious."

He stepped forward, and I saw then that there was a door behind him. It was black with a large gold knocker in the shape of a lion. It was the door to my old flat.

He turned to see what had got my attention. "That door appears now and then. Other spirits tell me I will eventually see someone I knew in life, beckoning me to come through. They say it might be someone I barely knew, like an old aunt or uncle, but someone I knew nonetheless. But I don't know anybody who would come for me in this place."

The door slowly swung open on its own, revealing blue sky.

"I don't see anyone waiting for me, Oscar."

Then, to my astonishment, I saw my sisters, Emily and Mary, who had died in a fire. Derrick saw them too.

"I do not know these girls."

"No," I said. "But I do." I wanted to rush to them, but did not know what would happen if I did. Would I be drawn on to the next world? I was not ready for that.

"My dear sisters," I said. "I have missed you terribly. But are you here for me?"

"Because of you, Oscar, but not for you," Mary said. Or at least I heard the words. Her mouth did not move, but her voice echoed in my ears nonetheless.

"We came when we sensed your presence," Emily said. "But we see that you are merely a visitor here. If your friend needs help, we can see him safely to the other side."

I could tell that Derrick did not hear the voices. They were speaking only to me. I explained to him why they were there.

"It is time for you to go, Derrick," I said. "Time for you to leave this dreadful place."

He gave me a kiss, his lips warm and soft, and a last, regretful look, then turned and went through the doorway, disappearing in a flash of light. The door vanished, and I was once more alone and still lost.

I fumbled around in the mist and saw another figure coming to me. It was my father!

"No," I said. "No, no, no, seeing one spirit is enough for one day."

"Oscar, please help me," he pleaded with outstretched arms.

"No, be gone with you back into the fog." As I shooed him away, the back of my hand hit the rope. I grabbed at it like the lifeline it was and it jerked in one direction as if someone were pulling on it. I quickly followed and found Stoker and Miss Chase once again.

"You won't believe what just happened to me," I said. But I could tell by the flustered looks on their faces that they too had experienced something. We quickly compared notes, then continued in what we hoped was the right direction. Before much longer, to our relief, we found the temple.

It was like looking at Zeus's temple in the clouds of Mount Olympus, a structure of shining marble rising out of the mist. Large steps led inside to an enormous statue of a beautiful Egyptian queen seated on her throne. She clasped a golden sceptre in one hand and a silver lightning bolt in the other. The only other items were four obelisks, one in each corner. One of them was of white stone and shaped exactly like Cleopatra's Needle, the gift Greece gave England that now sits on the banks of the Thames. I have spent much time there looking at the hieroglyphics and writing poetry in Greek at its base. Seeing this one made me feel at home in this strange place.

Miss Chase told us to wait while she set up the necessary paraphernalia for the ceremony.

I took this time to make a drawing of the statue. She looked familiar to me somehow. I also made note of all the hieroglyphics I could find on the obelisks, thinking they may be important.

Stoker sat on the steps writing in his journal.

Miss Chase told us she was ready, and we all held hands, taking our place around a five-pointed star she had drawn in a pile of salt. There were black candles at each of the points of the star.

"Okay, here we go," she said.

"Stop!" a voice yelled from outside of the temple. We broke our circle and looked out through the pillars of the temple. A man was coming out of the fog and up the steps. He was passably handsome, in a rough-hewn sort of way, with a thick mop of black hair. I recognised him, but wasn't sure from where. I meet so many people in my travels, you see; it is hard to keep them all straight. Then it all came back to me. I had only met him once, in the company of Derrick.

"Coal!" Stoker yelled in anger. I remembered then that Bram had told me of his friend Lucy, who had been turned into a vampire by Coal, and how the fiend had met his end in a graveyard.

"Please, listen to me," Coal said, stopping just outside the entrance.

"I have a message from Florence." He turned and looked at me. "And from Constance."

"This man is a monster," Stoker told Miss Chase, who was looking on in bewilderment. "He was a vampire. He is one of Wilkins' thugs."

Coal shook his shaggy head. "I *was*. That was me in life," he said. "I am atoning for my sins. Your wife says that the ritual you are about to perform won't close the gates and will actually trap you here forever." He turned to Miss Chase. "She says the director made sure you found fake information in his desk drawer."

"Why should we believe you?" Stoker asked. He was tensed, his fists clenched, as if ready to fight (though I do not know if one could physically hurt a spirit here).

"I am talking with Lorna Bow right now," Coal said. "She says she can bring you home."

"I am sceptical as well," I said. "If you are really talking with Constance, tell me something only she and I would know."

He paused a moment then said, "She says, 'The night before you left, we did that thing you taught me in Paris.'"

My face grew warm. Stoker cleared his throat and looked away, but Miss Chase was clearly suppressing a smile.

"Yes, it is Constance," I confessed. "Now have Florence tell you something about Bram."

"You said something about getting us out of here?" Miss Chase asked.

"Lorna says for you all to lay your hands on an obelisk and she will use a spell to transport you to that obelisk's counterpart in your world."

We looked to the four corners.

"But which one?" Stoker asked.

I ran to the one I recognised. "This one," I told them. "It looks just like Cleopatra's Needle in London. It has to be this one, I am sure of it."

We reached for it, but before we could touch it, Stoker held up a hand to stop us. He turned to Coal. "Have you seen Lucy here?" he asked.

The man's face fell. "No. I hope that means she's gone on already. She didn't deserve to linger here like I do. She didn't deserve what I did to her."

Stoker still looked like he wanted to strike the man, but he merely nodded. "All right. Let's go," he said to us.

We laid our hands on the obelisk.

"Now what?" Stoker asked.

Before we could get an answer, we were no longer in the temple, but on the banks of the Thames, our hands planted firmly on the base of Cleopatra's Needle. This unfortunately was a good eight feet off the ground and we fell, sliding down the marble base to which the Needle is affixed. Miss Chase and I hit the ground hard. It knocked the wind out of us and surprised some passers-by.

There was a ruckus on the other side of the base and after dusting ourselves off we went over to investigate with the other onlookers, who were shouting and pointing towards the river.

It seems Stoker's landing was a bit off and he had landed directly in the Thames. No worse for wear, he was swimming to the Embankment where a set of steps was waiting.

So there, dear diary, was my trip into the Land of the Dead and my trip out of it.

We did not complete our mission, but Florence and Ellen have acquired the true way to shut the Spirit Gate for good, so all hope is not lost.

FROM THE JOURNAL OF BRAM STOKER, 23RD OF AUGUST 1884

9:15 p.m.

We have all gathered at Oscar's secret London flat. It is very crowded with us all here, but we don't dare return to the theatre without Henry there to protect us. Mueller and his monsters have completely taken over the White Worm headquarters. We are very much alone in our fight against Mueller and Wilkins.

We have Director Hammond's research into closing the Spirit Gate, or 'the Well of Souls', as it was originally called.

It was created thousands of years ago by an Egyptian queen, a powerful sorceress who wanted to capture evil souls on their way to the afterlife so she could feed off their power.

The queen was defeated by fellow sorcerers. Four magical obelisks comprised the source of her power, tapping into the elemental forces of nature. The sorcerers separated the obelisks and moved them to various parts of Egypt out of fear that keeping them close together could be dangerous.

Over the next few centuries, their magical power was forgotten, and they were treated like ordinary artefacts from a lost ancient kingdom.

Queen Cleopatra brought one of the obelisks from Heliopolis to Alexandria shortly before the time of Christ to decorate a new temple, but it was never erected. It lay buried in sand until presented as a gift to the British nation in 1819 by the ruler of Egypt and Sudan, Muhammad Ali, in commemoration of the victories of Lord Nelson at the Battle of the Nile and Sir Ralph Abercromby at the Battle of Alexandria in 1801.

Although the British government welcomed the gesture, it declined to fund the expense of transporting it to London. The obelisk remained in Alexandria until 1877, when Sir William James Erasmus Wilson sponsored its transportation to London from Alexandria at a cost of some £10,000.

Egypt gifted two other obelisks to France and America. A fourth one remains at the temple of Luxor, near Cairo.

The New York Needle was the first to acquire the French nickname, 'L'aiguille de Cléopâtre', when it stood in Alexandria, and to this day they are all referred to as 'Cleopatra's Needles'.

It would all be terribly interesting if lives weren't at stake.

"So, if these are hit by lightning, we close the Spirit Gate?" Oscar asked.

"Yes, but it has to be done simultaneously," I said. "Not a simple task, even if they were all still in one place."

Florence pointed out that we could coordinate now with modern communication. "Thanks to the transatlantic cable and other telegraph lines, we could pick a date and time to do it, if we could summon lightning somehow."

"Does it have to be natural lightning?" Constance asked. We all turned to look at her. She was looking out the window at the recently installed electrical arc lights on the street. "The London Needle is lit by electric light, is it not? It wouldn't be that hard to run a copper line to the stone itself."

"I believe the Paris Needle has nearby lights," Oscar said.

"That leaves New York and Luxor," I pointed out. I suggested we could contact the Roosevelts and see if they could help us with the New York end of things.

"Yes," Miss Chase chimed in. "The New York Needle is in Central Park. There must be electricity somewhere close by. But what about the one in Egypt? I doubt there is electricity near there."

"We have a countryman at Luxor at this very moment," Ellen said. She had picked up a newspaper that featured a story about the noted Egyptologist Flinders Petrie and his dig at the temple of Luxor.

"Perhaps he could use one of those kerosene generators to zap that one," Constance said.

"I believe Richard Burton is good friends with Petrie," Oscar said. "He was going to introduce me to the man in Egypt when I was travelling after Cambridge, but I grew distracted writing an epic poem in Greece and never made it any further."

"This could work!" I said. I sprang into action as the general of the mission.

I put Miss Chase in charge of contacting the Roosevelts in New York. Oscar would go to Paris to see to the operation there.

I would contact Captain Burton and get his help for the obelisk at Luxor, and I will also coordinate the work at the London Needle.

Once we secure the co-operation we need, all we must do is pick a date and time and shock each obelisk and the Gate will be closed for good.

Then it is just a matter of rounding up Mueller, Wilkins and their thugs. Hopefully, the letter we received from the director will convince Scotland Yard to help us in this endeavour, and without access to souls, Mueller's highly placed protectors will lose interest in him.

Yes, we have a plan!

FROM THE JOURNAL OF CONSTANCE WILDE, 23RD OF AUGUST 1884

Our band of warriors is busy planning the closure of the Spirit Gate that has brought so much trouble to our lives, but I am distracted. When Oscar told me today that he needed some time alone with me, I assumed romance was on his mind. Sadly, that was not the case.

It is difficult to find privacy in our current living arrangements, so we chanced a visit to a small park a few streets away. We sat on a bench in the shade of an elm tree and he took my hands in his.

"Constance, my darling, you know I was just in the Realm."

I smiled indulgently. "Yes, Oscar. I missed you terribly."

"Hmm, yes," he said. "Of course, I missed you as well. But the thing is, we got to the Realm using the instructions in your father's diary. So I suppose I should not have been surprised…and yet I was… to find him there."

It took me a moment to understand what he had said. "You met my father? He's alive?"

"Yes, and very much so," he said.

"Then why did he not return with you? Did you lose him again?"

"No, my darling. The thing is…he did not want to come. He knows the way out, and always has. He…is very busy. With research."

Again I stared at him, stunned. "You mean to say he could have returned to me, but he let me think he was dead?"

He only nodded, his arm around my shoulder to steady me. I took a deep breath and thought for a moment.

"I should have known," I said.

"What?"

"He was always like that. When he had a project, it was nearly impossible to get him to think about anything else."

"But still…."

"Oh, I'm not excusing him, Oscar. I am furious. I could have had a father all these years. I should have been the one to introduce you to him. Will he ever even meet his grandchild?"

"I did tell him," Oscar said. "Perhaps he will return to us. He can't stay there forever."

I laughed, but it was bitter. "You don't know him very well, Oscar."

Then I wept, and Oscar held me. But my tears did not last for long. I have a new life now, and it's one worth fighting for. We returned to our comrades and continued our work to make the world safer for our child.

FROM THE JOURNAL OF THEODORE ROOSEVELT, 26TH OF AUGUST 1884

Archivist's note: At this time Theodore Roosevelt was a New York State Assemblyman, placing him in a good position to help Mr. Stoker with his plan.

Agent Cora Chase of the White Worm Society has contacted me on behalf of Bram Stoker. He heroically helped us put down a band of vampires out in the West, and America owes him a debt of gratitude.

Now he needs my help, and by Jove I shall provide it!

His request is an odd one. He wishes me to electrocute an Egyptian monument in Central Park, precisely at noon New York time on a particular date, to be determined when all the necessary pieces are in place. Apparently, there is another lunatic on the loose meddling with supernatural forces. There is a ritual that can foil his plan, but it involves striking a number of monuments with lightning. Since we cannot as yet bend the forces of nature to our will, manmade electricity will have to do.

But it will not be easy.

Stoker is not sure how strong the current has to be or how long it has to last. Since it is replacing natural lightning, we assume it will need to be a few seconds at most. But the current of lightning can melt sand into glass; I'm not sure if manmade electricity will fit the bill here.

I decided to recruit Thomas Edison to the cause.

I visited him this morning. I have always found him to be cantankerous at best, and when I arrived at his office, he was in the middle of an argument with an employee.

"Out! You're fired!" Edison yelled as the man exited his office into the outer room. Edison turned to his secretary and added, "Go down to payroll and have them cut a check for Tesla's last day."

Without even acknowledging me, Edison returned to his office and slammed the door.

"Does he mean it this time?" the secretary asked Mr. Tesla.

"It matters not," he said in an Eastern European accent. "This time I quit!"

"Okay," the secretary said. She then turned to me and asked if I had an appointment. I told her I did, for ten o'clock.

"Well, have a seat until then. Mr. Edison is very strict about meeting times. I'll announce you when I get back from payroll." She turned back to Tesla. "Are you sure, Nikola?"

"Yes! I am through here. That old fool doesn't understand that DC power is not the future!" Tesla said. "Alternating current is the only way to electrify the world."

"So you've said," she replied with a patient smile. "I'll just get your check."

She left, and Mr. Tesla took a seat, still fuming from the argument.

After a moment, he looked up at me. "I am sorry that you had to witness that," he said.

"I am sorry you lost your job," I said, and introduced myself.

"As you heard, my name is Nikola Tesla." He told me he was an engineer at the Edison Machine Works, where he supervised research into dynamos.

Not looking forward to my conversation with Edison, I took the opportunity to ask the electrical engineer the questions I had. He was intrigued.

"So, why do you want to shock a stone in the park with electricity?" he asked.

I made up a story about an experiment, hoping to appeal to the inventor in him.

"Stone does not conduct electricity. Anyone could tell you that," he said.

"I have it on good authority that this Egyptian stone has special properties that react to strong current."

"How strong?"

"As strong as lightning, if that's possible."

"No, that's as hot as the sun, you see." He thought on it a moment. "Alternating current would give the strongest current available. You would need a dynamo or to tap into an arc lamp. And then you would need heavy-gauge copper wire to conduct the current, and it would have to be heavily insulated. You would, of course, also need thick rubber gloves to handle live wire. Even then, I couldn't guarantee you would not be electrocuted to death. AC is very dangerous."

I asked where one would get such equipment, here and in Europe.

"You are shocking stones in Europe as well?"

I said we were. And in Egypt.

He told me the Ganz company in Budapest has portable dynamos and the proper wiring and such.

"By portable I mean the size of a cow, but easy enough to get from place to place by boat and train."

I asked him if there was an easy way to get power to Cleopatra's Needle in Central Park.

He thought for a moment and told me the Brush Electrical Company has arc lamps on Broadway. I knew that was a good four miles from the park and asked how hard it would be to run a wire from there to the Needle.

He laughed. "That is much wire." He leant in and whispered, "I might have a better solution. I happen to know of a mansion on Park Avenue, only two streets over from the park, where an AC generator has been installed."

I smiled. "Do you now? Was this done under the auspices of the Edison Company?"

"Ah, it was not. Mr. Edison is not a proponent of alternating current, as you have heard. But what I do in my free time is, technically, my business. In any case, I have enough wire in my shop at home to make it that distance."

So, I canceled my meeting with Edison and took Mr. Tesla up on his offer.

I have cabled Mr. Stoker with the information about copper wire gauge and insulation requirements, as well as the recommendation from Mr. Tesla of where we could get such equipment in Europe.

FROM THE MEMOIR OF SIR RICHARD BURTON, 26TH OF AUGUST 1884

I am devastated to learn from Mr. Stoker that the White Worm Society is no more. It has been taken over by monsters or some such nonsense. I shall have to set that to rights, but first I have another mission to accomplish.

I am on a train from Budapest to Constantinople with a newly purchased electrical dynamo. There, I shall board a ship to Cairo, where I will take another train to the temple at Luxor. Flinders Petrie, the Egyptian archaeologist, has been generous in funding the purchase of the generator and its passage to Luxor. And his father is an electrical engineer, so Flin has some experience in setting up such things.

He will be happy to have power to light his night-time digs and I will have a source of man-made lightning to close something called the 'Spirit Gate', which Stoker tells me has been opened, causing general mayhem in Britain and elsewhere. We thought we were rid of the Black Bishop and his evil schemes, but alas he has returned and is bringing legions of his minions with him.

Cutting off souls to that maniac will not be enough, however. We will still need to round up his cohorts like we did the first time we did battle with him. A stern letter from me, on behalf of the Queen, should set Scotland Yard straight and give Stoker the fire power he needs to round up those bastards.

It will take me two days to get to Constantinople and another day to cross the Mediterranean on one of Cunard's steamships. Add to that yet another half day to take the train from Cairo to Luxor, if the train is even running the day we arrive, which oftentimes it is not.

Still, I will give it a go. My wife says I am too old to make the journey, but I told her there is very little exertion in being a passenger these days. Thanks to Lord Cunard, I have first-class passage all the way. My days of riding on top of trains and crossing deserts by camel may be behind me, yet I look forward to this one last adventure. Especially if we can send Wilkins to hell once and for all times!

FROM THE DIARY OF OSCAR WILDE, 26TH OF AUGUST 1884

Dear yours truly,

I have successfully recruited Willie to help me on my part of the mission. While he knows no more about electricity than I do, he is at least good for manual labour and, should the authorities catch us in our task, more likely to be mistaken for a drunken lout than a master criminal.

I was not certain he would agree to participate. The free trip to Paris would be appealing, but he has been very melancholy lately and was never as adventurous as I.

I went to the hiding spot I had arranged for him and Mother. When I arrived, I was surprised to find him in good spirits.

"Look what I can do, Oscar." He held up his hand and turned it into a paw. I must admit it would be a good party trick, but it made me afraid. We hadn't the time for me to chase him around London again.

He gave the paw a shake, and it was a hand again. "Soon I'll be able to control it fully, I think. Maybe even under the sway of a full moon." He tells me Mother has helped him learn to manage his wolfie powers. The last full moon he went almost two hours before transforming. It is hoped with strong herbal teas and Indian mantras, he can learn to control it completely.

That was good news. Even better, we will not have to put this to the test on this trip as there is no full moon for a fortnight.

I packed light: only two suits, four pairs of shoes, six ties, three shirts and two hats. I had a black jumper and matching wool cap for our clandestine work, along with a pistol, dagger and my trusty sword cane.

We are now on our way! We need time to assess the situation and plan our part of the operation so we'll be ready when the time comes.

Ah, to be in the thick of it again. At least this time I won't be running into any monsters, only rude French waiters. At last, the fight against evil has brought me to Paris!

FROM THE JOURNAL OF BRAM STOKER, 27TH OF AUGUST 1884

6:15 p.m.

Oscar and Willie are off to Paris.

Regular telegrams arrive from Teddy Roosevelt, detailing his progress, which has been substantial.

Burton is on a train to Constantinople with a newly purchased generator and will see it all the way to the Needle in Luxor. The trip will take him three or four days. He will telegraph us from Cairo so we can set the day of the operation.

And, of course, we are making preparations for the London Needle.

As an added measure, I have put Mr. Blackwood in charge of causing a distraction the day of our mission. Lorna has told us that Mueller's London lab is in the basement of the Grosvenor Art Gallery, of all places. Apparently they have quite a good electrical system, which Mueller needs for his grisly work. Mr. Blackwood suggested that we flood the lab hours before our mission. That should keep Mueller and friends busy.

I am hopeful now that we might be able to pull this off. As Mr. Roosevelt said, "Bully! We will send those monsters straight to hell!" (Seems expensive to say so in a telegram, but I do appreciate the sentiment.)

Then there is Lorna. She is pestering me to let her join the mission. We had sent her home so as to not raise suspicions she is helping us and to keep an eye on her mother's activities.

She showed up this morning to talk to Florence and me. She had a bag with her and I took that to mean she was planning on staying with us.

"Mother suspects something. It isn't safe for me there anymore. I think she can read minds."

"Bram," Florence said. "Perhaps it is better she stay with us until after the Needle ceremony?"

I agreed.

Then Lorna said she wanted a role in the mission.

"Absolutely not," I said. I told her we would not want her to put her life in more danger than it already is.

Florence agreed. "You have done enough for us, child."

"But you will need me!" she protested. "They know Mr. Irving has left and Mother is using a location spell to find you, Mr. Stoker. I've put a cloaking spell on this building, but I don't know how long it will last."

She went on to explain all the spells and magic her mother possesses.

"She can stop time, so she can easily stop you on the day, if I'm not there."

This was dire news indeed. I had no idea Endora was so powerful as all that.

"I can counter her magic," Lorna said. "I have been practising a dampening spell. It might not be strong enough to stop her outright, but I can slow her down. Let me show you what I can do." She took out a snake from her pocket, much to Florence's displeasure as she hates snakes. I am not too fond of them myself.

She set it down on the floor.

"Don't set it loose," Florence scolded.

Lorna went to grab it, but the damn thing slithered off at great speed and hid under the sofa.

"Maybe I can do it without the snake," she said, shrugging. "I think I have the gist of it now."

She held a hand out towards the drapes and said, "Calla benty moroto," or something like that. She repeated the incantation over and over and then the sash on the drapes began to move, untying itself and then slithering down the drapes and across the floor.

Florence and I looked at each other in amazement as the sash wrapped itself around a table leg.

Lorna sneezed, and the spell was broken. The sash snake dropped to the floor.

"Maybe I'll just practise the dampening spell," she said.

"Good idea," I said. "Because you are right, we might need you on the day."

"Bram, no," Florence said.

"I don't think Endora will harm her in any event," I said. "We will keep her hidden."

With that, a happy Lorna went outside to reapply her cloaking spell to the building.

Florence protested again, but I pointed out having Lorna with us would not only prove useful for her magic, but would give us our own hostage should we find it necessary.

"Oh, Bram, we can't use her as a pawn in all this."

But deep down she knew I was right. Lorna could be the ace up our sleeve, as the Americans say. Mueller has shown he will stop at nothing to continue his plans, and we must be just as ruthless.

FROM THE DIARY OF OSCAR WILDE, 29TH OF AUGUST 1884

Dear yours truly,

Willie and I are in Paris, staying in a small hotel under assumed names. If one is going to save the world, one should at least do it from Paris, though I would prefer to headquarter at the Hotel Continental.

We have examined the area around the obelisk to locate the nearest source of power. Ever the optimist, on the journey here I had dared entertain the hope that the Parisian authorities had installed electric lights to illuminate the Obelisque de Louxor, but alas, that is not the case. There are, however, electric arc lights not too far away on the Champs-Élysées, so we are lucky there. We brought copper wire with us, but it isn't nearly enough to span the distance. Luckily we found a tinker's shop that had a large reel of it, so we have acquired what we need.

We have formulated a plan: on Electrocution Day, we will disguise ourselves as workmen and Willie will shin up the nearest light pole to the Needle under the ruse of doing maintenance. I find that in the hustle and bustle of city life, people tend not to question such activities, and merely walk around them in irritation.

Willie will connect the cable per the instructions of Theodore Roosevelt's engineer friend, then we will run it to the Needle. Connecting it there is bound to attract some attention, as we will have to climb its base. Should anyone ask what we are doing, I will say that we need to stretch out the cable in order to test its integrity and that we need to attach it high up on the Needle to keep it out of the way of traffic. It's a ridiculous story, to be sure, but as I will also strongly imply that the cable may send dangerous sparks out at any moment, I am hoping that nobody will hang about for further questions.

Then we need merely wait until the designated time, flip our switch, unhook our wires and make a hasty escape.

We have prepared as thoroughly as we can. We have found deserted street corners at night where Willie can practise climbing light poles. We have rehearsed the connecting of the cable with spare bits of wire. We have walked our route repeatedly, timing out how long it will take us laden with a spool of cable, and encumbered by traffic. We have not practised climbing the obelisk, as we don't want to be arrested so close to 'show time', as it were.

I'm sure there are myriad ways for this plan to go awry, but for now I believe we are as ready as we can be.

FROM THE DIARY OF ELLEN TERRY, 1ST OF SEPTEMBER 1884

Today is the day! Our intrepid band of monster hunters is carrying out our carefully crafted plan to close the Spirit Gate. I feel so alive and invigorated as I find myself once again battling the forces of evil.

Bram tasked my beloved Brent with creating a diversion. Brent's plan is to flood Dr. Mueller's lab, causing much havoc for Mueller and his monsters. We hope it will not only keep them busy for a few hours, but destroy their research and laboratory equipment.

Lorna provided him with a way in, an entrance from the Underground train track to the sewer lines that Wilkins and his men have been using to move about the city undetected. Now we can use it for our own purposes.

I say 'our' because I tagged along on Brent's mission. He firmly told me not to come, but I followed him clandestinely from the Underground. He was dressed in all black and carried a black doctor's bag full of tools and such. I, too, dressed for concealment, in a black gown of lightweight silk that would not weigh me down excessively should I have to run for my life. It has a loose-fitting skirt and bodice that would not confine me if I needed to kick or punch an attacking creature. A veiled hat completed my ensemble. I could tell by the sympathetic smiles I received en route that passers-by took me for a recent widow.

Alas, as I followed Brent into the sewer, I accidentally kicked a loose brick and the jig was up. He saw me and ordered me to turn back.

"All the others have put their lives on the line and I want to help," I protested. He relented.

"You may come," he said. "But I lead the way and you must do what you are told."

"I am an actress," I reminded him with a smile. "I am accustomed to taking direction."

"And at the first sign of trouble, you will turn back," he said, as we pressed onwards with our lanterns in hand.

We went through a hole in the brick wall of the Underground into a sewer tunnel. It was surprisingly dry, only a trickle of water at our feet. The smell was atrocious, and I stifled a gasp as I saw rats scurrying about.

A few feet down we found another hole in a wall. This one had been smashed through from the other side, as the pile of bricks and rubble were in the tunnel with us.

"This must be it," Brent whispered. It was dark ahead, but we turned off our lamps for fear of being detected. We entered a large cellar, coming out behind a coal furnace. We cautiously went around the furnace and there was the laboratory before us. A single window high in a wall provided the only light. We were very much alone, aside from what I assumed to be two corpses under sheets at the near end of the laboratory.

Brent tapped a large pipe above our heads. "This should do it. I think this is the sewer line for the building." He tapped a smaller pipe running alongside the bigger one. "And this is a water main."

He took tools from his bag and started to unbolt a metal collar on the big pipe. By the time he had removed three of the six bolts, a tiny bit of sewage was leaking out.

We were interrupted by electric lights suddenly flickering on.

We took cover behind the furnace just as a red-haired woman and Mueller entered. From the looks of her, I knew straight away it was Endora, Lorna's mother.

"She's not here, either," Endora said. "Where has that child gone off to? This isn't good."

"Can't you use your powers to find her?" Mueller asked.

"I tried but cannot. Perhaps she is blocking me."

"We don't have time to find her now," Mueller said. "We have to stop Stoker. Molly says they throw the switch at five p.m."

They turned and went out the way they came. The light flickered off.

"They know!" Brent whispered. "We have to warn Stoker." We turned to leave, and Brent dropped his wrench back into his bag. It made an unfortunate clank.

The light came back on. "Who's down here?" Mueller shouted. "Show yourselves!"

We could hear footsteps coming towards our hiding spot.

Brent looked at me and shrugged, a small smile on his face. We both knew Mueller would be no match for him. He whispered to me, "Stay hidden," then stepped out from behind the furnace.

Mueller was holding a pistol, but before he could get off a shot, Brent disarmed him with a roundhouse kick to his hand that sent the gun flying. Mueller backed away, with Brent advancing on him.

At the far end of the room, I could see Endora, her eyes closed and her arms held out before her. She was muttering something that I could not hear.

I know I promised to follow Brent's direction, but I could not sit helplessly while he did all the work. I grabbed the wrench from his bag and continued loosening the bolts on the sewage pipe.

As Brent landed his first karate punch on Mueller, Endora lifted her arms and the corpses rose up on their tables. The sheets slid down, and I was horrified to see the bodies were headless. Spinal bones protruded from their necks, and the flesh and veins around them were desiccated and rotting. They stiffly climbed down and shambled towards Brent and Mueller.

"Brent, look out!" I shouted.

He looked up just as the corpses reached him and started to pummel him. He was forced to back away.

The bolt I had been working on finally came free, and the collar could not hold any longer. The pipe burst open, pouring out sewage.

Brent looked at me, grinning. "Nice work," he said, then grabbed the wrench from my hand and smashed the smaller overhead pipe, and it too burst.

We fled back through the wall into the tunnel.

I could hear Endora shouting some sort of incantation. The air around us felt charged, like a jolt of electricity being carried on a hot wind.

All the water and sewage that had been spilling into the lab was suddenly a torrent behind us.

"It is no use!" Mueller yelled. "My men are on their way to the Needle to stop all this nonsense."

The river swept us up, knocking us off our feet. We were being pushed along by the surge of the putrid-smelling water.

It receded a bit, and we stumbled back onto our feet.

We made it back into the Underground tunnel and across the track just as a train came through.

If they had been following us, we were safely cut off from them as we made our way out of the tunnel and into daylight.

Oh, the humiliation of being covered in sewage and walking down the street. My veiled hat had been knocked loose in our escape, and I prayed I would not be recognised. Our stench and appearance parted the crowd on the pavement like Moses parting the Red Sea.

Cabs refused to stop for us.

As luck would have it, a fire hydrant was being flushed into the street. We thankfully let the water wash over us. It was frigid but took away most of the filth.

"I will go to the Needle to warn the others," Brent said. "You go back to the flat and tell Mrs. Stoker and Mrs. Wilde what has happened. See if they can gather some reinforcements."

I did as I was told. Florrie and Constance are marshalling stagehands, shopkeepers, and anyone else they can find. I bathed quickly and am tending Noel while they are out.

I take courage from Florence's words as she left to round up the troops.

"It takes a mob to fight a mob," she said. "We are not going down without a fight!"

FROM THE MEMOIR OF SIR RICHARD BURTON, 1ST OF SEPTEMBER 1884

I arrived in Cairo half a day late due to inclement weather. I oversaw the unloading of the dynamo by crane onto an open railway truck that would take it the rest of the way to Luxor.

Oh, such a pleasure to be in an exotic foreign land again! The heady smell of spices and coffee in the air, colourful locals going about their day in the market, the braying of camels; I have missed it so.

The train ride was quite pleasant. I had a lunch of pita, hummus and olives, with mint tea. It wasn't too hot that day, and the wind from the open window cooled me nicely. I thought of the fact that it might be the last time I see the desert and made the most of the view.

Flinders Petrie greeted me when I arrived in Luxor. He has not changed a bit – same penetrating dark eyes and devilish black beard.

He oversaw the loading of the generator onto a trailer. I was surprised to see it had skis instead of wheels.

"She is a beauty," he said, patting the side of the dynamo. "With this we will have lights to work night and day. Runs on kerosene, I see."

I had, of course, brought plenty of the fuel with me. There is no time to waste trying to locate supplies here in Luxor.

I enquired as to how far away the site was and how we were going to make the final distance.

"Wait until you see, Burton." He waved his arms and a loud contraption started heading our way, making much noise and belching smoke from behind. It was an automobile of some sort. It had four wheels and not three like the other automobiles I have seen. The wheels were wrapped in wooden treads, presumably to traverse better on sand.

A driver backed it up to the trailer, and other men attached the trailer to the automobile. They covered the generator with large tarps and tied them down to the trailer.

Flin tapped the treads with his walking stick. "These treads let us glide over the dunes as if they are water." He pointed off to the west. "The site is about two miles that way."

The driver hopped out and Flin took the driver's seat. I got in beside him. "Hang on, this thing can reach speeds of nearly ten miles an hour."

With the weight of the trailer, however, there was no chance of reaching such a speed. At first I feared we would not even budge, but with a bit of a push from Flin's workers, we were off. We left the paved road and headed out into the desert. It was slow-going, but faster than a camel, and we made our way towards the temple site.

He asked me once again what it was we were going to do, and I told him. He has dealt with magical objects before (and has even seen a mummy come to life) so he was not as incredulous as one would think.

"It won't hurt the monument?" he asked.

I told him Bram informed me it would not, but truthfully I was not sure myself what would happen. "But no matter what, Flin, it has to be done. The future of the Empire depends upon it."

We were puttering along, and Flin seemed preoccupied with the gauges above the steering wheel. "Oh, drat, we are overheating. That thing might be too heavy for our motor."

I asked how much further and he said the temple should be in view now; however, it was not. When I pointed this out, he looked up and to the horizon. An immense cloud blocked our view.

"Oh, heavens. That's not good," he said. He stopped the automobile, ran around to the boot and pulled large canvas tarps from the trunk. "It's a sandstorm! Help me get this over the car."

The wind hit us as he said that, making covering the car difficult, but we did it and got the tarps tied down just as the worst of the sand started to pelt us, ripping flesh off our skin as these things often do.

We re-entered the car and sealed it up the best we could from the onslaught of wind and sand. The force of the wind snapped off the automobile's driver-side mirror. The sound was deafening, which mattered not since there was nothing we could say.

I checked my pocket watch: two hours until we had to shock the obelisk. I knew these storms could last for days.

FROM THE DIARY OF OSCAR WILDE, 1ST OF SEPTEMBER 1884

Oh, yours truly,

What a dreadful day! We are to zap the obelisk at 6:00 p.m. Paris time and it is looking like we will fail.

When we showed up at our chosen lamp post today, there was a podium and seats filled with people set out beneath it. A ceremony of some sort is happening. By the looks of it, they are giving out awards to police officers.

We dare not shin up a lamp post in front of them and are waiting for the festivities to be over before we try. In the meantime, there is nothing to do but fret.

Dear yours truly,

It has been nearly an hour and we are still waiting. The ceremony, according to a flyer I found on a chair, appears to be going on well into the evening! The clock is ticking. If our team cannot manage to electrify four obelisks at the same moment, our efforts will be for naught. I do not want to be the weak link in this global operation.

REPORT FROM WHITE WORM SOCIETY AGENT CORA CHASE

Date: 1 September 1884
Subject: Operation Needle – London

We had carefully coordinated with our teams in New York, Cairo and Paris to simultaneously shock our obelisks. In London, our time was to be 5:00 p.m. sharp.

At 3:00 p.m. GMT, we shut the power off at the closest lamp post and ran a cable from the arc light to Cleopatra's Needle. The cable was taut from post to obelisk, a good eight feet off the ground. We then had only to wait to throw the switch.

Captain Burton had come through on his end, not only getting a generator to the Luxor site, but persuading Scotland Yard to help us. Inspector Abberline was there with six of his men, armed and ready for a fight if needed. Six was all he could bring whom he was sure were loyal to him and not the newly corrupted White Worms, who have infiltrated law enforcement. They roped off the area around the Needle, giving us room to work undisturbed.

There are two black marble lions on brick pedestals flanking the obelisk, and this is where Abberline's men were concealed. It provided excellent cover.

Mr. Roosevelt had cabled that he was ready in New York. We hadn't heard from Mr. Wilde in Paris since that morning, but knew he had arrived and was on the job.

At 4:40 p.m., a very wet Mr. Blackwood joined us. He was out of breath from running to warn us that Mueller and Wilkins knew of our plan and were on their way to stop us.

We took refuge behind the marble lions just as Mueller and Wilkins showed up with twenty of their thugs. It seems Mueller had been very busy with his resurrection business, despite Lorna leaving his ranks. Lorna did tell us her mother could pluck souls from the spirit world herself, as she had been gaining necromantic power with every soul brought to this world.

We were at a standoff. Wilkins' men were across the boulevard (Victoria Embankment) taking cover behind a large garden wall.

We were greatly outnumbered. As one police officer set out to get reinforcements, they shot him dead. This sent nearby pedestrians and carriages fleeing the area. We could only hope that they reported the incident to the police and more help was on its way.

Lorna was hidden in the brush near the lamp post, ready to throw the switch at the appointed time. All we needed to do was stall them until 5:00 p.m.

"Just stop what you are doing, Stoker!" Wilkins yelled. "This doesn't have to end badly. Join us and live forever or fight us and die now!"

"How did he know we are trying to close the Spirit Gate?" Mr. Stoker wondered, as did I. I feared our running around town gathering copper cable and supplies may have attracted some interest, but Mr. Blackwood told us Lorna's friend Molly let the cat out of the bag.

Dr. Mueller emerged from behind the wall and walked to the middle of the path, holding up his hands to show he was unarmed.

"Mr. Stoker, Inspector Abberline, I implore you not to do this. More police are not coming. We have friends in high places to make sure that doesn't happen. We will stop you. We can do that with violence or you can join our work and everyone will be spared."

"I will never help you!" Mr. Stoker yelled back.

Endora popped her head up over the wall and pleaded for Lorna to join them. "Lorna, you know what I am trying to do. Please, do not abandon our work. It is your destiny."

When that didn't work, Wilkins perched Lorna's friend Molly on top of the garden wall.

The girl yelled, "Lorna, come home! We miss you."

Lorna remained silent and stayed hidden; good girl!

Seeing the futility of turning Lorna back to their side, Wilkins sent his men to attack the monument, guns blazing. We fired back, but with their greater numbers, Mr. Blackwood, some of the officers and I were forced to jump over the wall into the river to escape. By the time I made it back to dry land, it was all over.

FROM THE JOURNAL OF THEODORE ROOSEVELT, 1ST OF SEPTEMBER 1884

The day had arrived for us to do our part to close the Gate. Mr. Tesla had provided us copper wire necessary to traverse the thousand yards across Park, Madison and Fifth Avenues to Cleopatra's Needle.

I have called in a few favors from my contacts to get the traffic on those streets rerouted, making the laying of cable easier.

We arrived at the Park Avenue home of Mrs. Hoeting, a wealthy widow whose late husband owned several flour mills in the Midwest.

"Nikola!" she greeted him warmly, and he introduced us. Her entire home was lit with incandescent bulbs, and electric fans brought a pleasant breeze. The light was unnaturally bright, and I did not care for it.

"Please, you must join me for apple tea," she said.

Mr. Tesla politely declined and said we had to get straight to work. I suppressed a smile, remembering that he had warned me that her tea is mostly apple brandy.

"I am sorry, dear lady, but we will have to turn your power off for several hours," Tesla said.

"No matter," Mrs. Hoeting said. "It is a lovely morning."

With that, we went to the basement where Mr. Tesla and two of his friends went to work on the dynamo. It was powered by gas, which I found amusing since Mrs. Hoeting could just use that for light. This electrical rigamarole seems a foolish expenditure on her part, but it does suit our purposes quite nicely.

"Gas burners under this tank heat water into steam," he said. "The steam drives the turbines that turn the magnets inside a copper coil, and that generates the electricity." He explained his breakthrough that allowed him to electrify the house is a 'transformer', to 'step the power down', and make it safe for Edison's incandescent bulbs, which require a lower wattage.

"But today, we want all the power we can get. We will bypass the transformer and take full power to the stone," he said. "I will supervise the unrolling of the cable and the attachment to the obelisk." He pulled down a brass-handled switch and the humming dynamo came to a stop. "At the appointed time, simply pull this switch up and in less than a second we will have power to the stone."

He asked me again why we were doing this. With all the help he was providing, I found no good reason not to tell him the truth, so I did.

For a moment he seemed genuinely dumbstruck.

"This is true?" he finally asked. "There is a spirit world?"

"Apparently, it is so," I said. I then regaled him with tales of vampires I had hunted out West and other supernatural shenanigans I knew Mr. Stoker and Mr. Wilde have gotten into.

He confided in me that Mr. Edison had built a device in hopes of talking with the dead. "We all thought him mad, of course, but now, who knows?" He said Edison never got it to work and like many of his inventions he abandoned the idea for a new one.

Tesla and his two workmen went outside to the large spool of insulated wire he had left on the lawn. They rolled it straight down the sidewalk of Eighty-First Street toward the park.

I waited for the appointed time of noon, nervously checking my pocket watch every few minutes. I had over an hour to wait so I took Mrs. Hoeting up on her offer for some apple 'tea' when she came downstairs and offered it again.

She had chairs and a small table brought down and we sat and chatted while we waited. I sipped slowly, not wishing to dull my faculties at such a crucial time.

Mr. Tesla returned twenty minutes before noon and told me everything was ready on the other end.

He went to check on his dynamo and I heard what I assumed was swearing in some foreign language as he went into a panic. "The gas, it is off! The boiler is not producing steam!"

He checked a few more valves and such when the gaslight on

the wall flickered and went off. We now only had the light coming through the basement window. There was a clattering on the stairs, and we turned to see one of his workmen rushing down them. "Bad news, boss!" he exclaimed. "A gas line blew a few streets over. Gas is out for blocks."

"Oh dear," Mrs. Hoeting said. "Shall we have more tea while we wait for it to be repaired?"

I noticed another tank under the boiler and asked Tesla what it was for. "Kerosene," he said. "That was what originally fueled the generator before I modified it for gas."

"Mrs. Hoeting, do you have any kerosene in the house?" I asked.

"No, I don't think so."

"Anything else we could use for fuel, cleaning spirits, perhaps?" Tesla asked.

Then I looked at our teacups. "Brandy! Do you have more applejack?"

"There is some in the wine cellar behind you." She opened the door to reveal a large quantity of liquor barrels.

I grabbed a nearby bucket and filled it from one of the barrels.

"You see, my doctor has prescribed it for medicinal purposes," she said. "That's why there is so much on hand."

I was not one to judge. "Well, that is fortunate for us, madam, and we will certainly replace what we take," I said as I filled the tank. Tesla lit the wick to fire up the tank, and flames danced under the boiler. But would it produce steam in time?

"Come on, come on!" Tesla yelled, opening up some valves.

I checked my pocket watch – it was two minutes to noon! We had synchronized our watches as best we could via transatlantic telegraph that morning, but I wasn't sure how synced we would stay. We could have been a minute or two off already.

Fortunately, the water had not cooled off significantly, and finally we saw a puff of steam and the turbines started to spin up. Tesla inserted a rod in one end of the turbine and started to hand-crank it. He called me over to help.

"We will give it a head start," he shouted, as it began to whine and hum.

We cranked, and as the steam built up it took over and did the work.

At the stroke of noon, maybe a second or two after, Tesla threw the switch and the connection of the cable gave off a spark and filled the room with an acrid smell.

"Yes!" he yelled. I am not ashamed to say I hugged him and whooped in delight.

We ran upstairs and out onto the front lawn where we were treated to an amazing sight. A bright green shaft of light was emanating from the park and shooting straight up into the sky. A hole opened up in the clouds through which we could see night sky, even though it was high noon.

In less than a minute, it was all over. The beam vanished as quickly as it had appeared, and the hole closed itself up.

"I think it worked," I told Tesla.

"This is a cause for celebration," Mrs. Hoeting said. "I shall get us all some more brandy. I mean, tea."

I excused myself for a brief visit to a telegraph office to inform Miss Chase of the success at our end. Tesla quickly reversed the work he had done that morning, rerouting the power back through the transformer to power Mrs. Hoeting's lights. We were all soon toasting with our teacups and had a jolly time that afternoon.

I am currently waiting for Miss Chase's reply. I hope and pray that the teams in the other three cities have succeeded as well.

FROM THE DIARY OF OSCAR WILDE, 1ST OF SEPTEMBER 1884

Dear yours truly,

What a night! Again I found myself in jail. At least the jail food is decent in Paris, and I didn't have to listen to Stoker complaining the whole time.

I was also covered in blood, which I worried would be difficult to explain to the police. However, many people saw the rabid dog attack that man and I was only doing my part to save him.

At the Needle site, Willie and I had finally decided that we could wait no longer. The fate of the world was at stake, so if we had to inconvenience a few Parisian police officers, so be it. Dressed as workmen, we brazenly rolled our wire reel up to the lamp pole where Willie shinned up and made the connection. We had brought thick rubber gloves with us that we were told by the salesman would insulate us from shocks. I fretted when I saw a few sparks fly into Willie's face, but they did not kill him or knock him from the pole. A few of the people watching the ceremony took notice, but remained in their seats.

The man handing out awards at the podium turned to me and asked if we 'had to do this now?'

I told him in French that of course we did and if we did not the whole of Paris could burn down. That seemed to satisfy him, and he went on calling names and hanging medals around policemen's necks.

Willie climbed down and attached the live wire to a switch box on our spool. More sparks flew as he connected it. We rolled our spool of copper wire away towards our Needle. It was 5:47 p.m., and we had no time to spare!

We reached the base, which is just outside of Place de la Concorde. Fortunately, there weren't many people passing by. All we had to do was wait for the appointed time.

It was then everything went pear-shaped.

Willie had scaled the base with a free piece of wire, so we were good there. We had a loose plan about how we would attach it, but weren't sure if it would actually work. But he managed to make a loop of the wire and lassoed it over the pointy part of the Needle. He did it in one throw, and I told him I had not even seen cowboys that skilled in ropin', as the Americans call it. He seemed pleased.

My joy at our apparent success dampened, however, as I felt something cold and hard being jammed into the small of my back. It was a familiar feeling, the barrel of a pistol. I knew at once who it was. I have a sixth sense about these things.

"What the hell are you up to, Oscar?" Wotton said. I turned slightly to look at him over my shoulder. He was wearing the body I had seen him in previously.

"Just admiring this beautiful Egyptian artefact," I said.

He had a new eye that didn't seem to be the same colour as the other one, but it was hard to tell in the fading daylight. It seemed to bother him as he kept rubbing it with his free hand.

"I've been following you since you left London," he said. "I would have killed you earlier, but I was truly curious to see what you were up to. Tell your brother to come down here."

"Oh, Willie," I yelled. He had already finished, however, and was climbing down. "Mr. Wotton here is about to kill me. And, I suppose, you as well."

"That's Lord Wotton to you," Wotton said in my ear.

"Not in that body," I replied.

Willie hit the ground with the copper wire in his hand that still needed to be connected to the live wire on our spool's electrical box.

Willie eyed the situation. "Is that so? Well, a resurrected villain is a better end than I had predicted for you, Oscar. I sort of figured you would meet your demise at the hands of a jealous husband. Hello, Wotton," he said. "I never thought we'd meet again. Pity it's not at a full moon."

I frantically wondered what time it was. The last I had looked at my pocket watch it had said 5:53 p.m.

Willie, also aware of our deadline, made a break for the spool.

Then the monster shot Willie! He hit him in the leg. I instinctively tried to run to him, but Wotton grabbed me and wheeled me around.

"Not even death can keep me from killing you," he said. "That is how much I hate your smug, pompous face."

"Smug and pompous mean the same thing. You are being redundant."

He looked over my shoulder and seemed confused. "Where did he go?"

I turned to see Willie was no longer there. He had dragged himself off into some nearby shrubbery. *Good for him*, I thought. *Let's not make it easy on this vile toad.* And with that I lunged at him, grabbed his wrist and started wrestling the gun from his hand. He was incredibly strong, however, and all I managed to do was twist the fabric around his sleeve as he laughed at me.

He slapped me hard across the face, and I fell to the ground.

Fortunately for me, Wotton was never one to get down to business if he had a chance to bloviate first.

"First, I'm going to shoot out your eye. Then a few shots into your fat stomach so you bleed to death slowly. Then…." He paused, his attention drawn to a rustle in the foliage. And then…a growl.

Willie sprang from the bushes in his wolf form. Wotton fired bullets at him but, not being silver, they merely bounced off his hairy hide.

I had no time to fear for my own life as Willie pounced on Wotton and started tearing him to shreds with his teeth and claws. Blood and viscera splattered everywhere. Fortunately, I was wearing workman's clothes so none of my actual apparel was ruined.

I heard passers-by on the nearby street scream.

When Willie had his fill of Wotton, he turned to me!

"Now, Willie," I scolded. "One person is quite enough for tonight."

I heard police whistles and men running towards us as I stared into Willie's red, lupine eyes.

I swear he winked at me.

Then Wolf Willie just ran off, frightened Parisians scattering from his path. Police ran after him, shouting and blowing whistles.

My pocket watch rang out. I had set its alarm to 5:59 p.m.! I ran to where Willie had dropped the wire.

I connected the Needle wire to the electrical box.

Some of the police officers had circled back and were very curious as to what I was doing, standing close to what was left of Wotton's mangled body, covered in blood and holding a wire running to a national monument.

They yelled at me in French to stop and put my hands up.

I had no time even to use my carefully crafted cover story. As my watch chimed its last bell, I held my breath and flipped the switch. I jumped back as it sparked heavily.

Angry policemen charged at me, but stopped as the entire obelisk lit up with a bright green glow.

"*Sacré bleu*," the one nearest me yelled. We all stood mesmerised at the light emanating from the stone, and more so when it pulsed and a super-bright beam shot into the heavens.

I laughed and danced a bit, knowing I had done my part. I hope it has gone so well for the others.

In a few minutes, at least three I would guess, the light show was over. The coppers grabbed me and hauled me away. One asked me what I had done.

"*Je dirige et expérimente. Je suis un scientifique.* (I am conducting an experiment. I am a scientist.)"

He grunted and told me that he was sure that requires a permit.

"*Parfois, il est plus facile d'obtenir le pardon que la permission.* (Sometimes it is easier to get forgiveness than permission.)"

They hauled me into the station, but after witnesses gave their testimony, the police let me go. They couldn't find a law that said I needed an 'experiment permit', but they did fine me for trespassing.

I returned to the hotel to clean up and change, knowing that I would need to mount a search for Willie. But to my delight, as I entered the room he was emerging from the bath, towelling his hair dry.

"Willie!" I cried, embracing him. "You are safe! I hope you didn't eat anyone besides Wotton."

"No, he was filling enough. Besides, it's not a full moon. I was able to switch back to human form without too much trouble. The tricky part was finding my way back here while naked. Fortunately, I snagged a tablecloth from a pavement café."

"What about your leg?" I asked. "Wotton shot you before you turned."

"Yes, that smarted. But when I turned into a wolf, the bullet was pushed out and the leg healed itself," he explained. "Just a waste of ammunition on Wotton's part. Serves him right for getting me bit by a werewolf in the first place."

I cabled Miss Chase to let her know we were successful. We went out for a brief celebration, where I toasted my brother, the true hero of this operation, then returned to our room, exhausted. We will be on the first train back to London tomorrow.

FROM THE MEMOIR OF SIR RICHARD BURTON, 1ST OF SEPTEMBER 1884

Archivist's note: Continued from previous entry.

The sandstorm raged for an hour and a half, then dissipated as quickly as it had come on. We pushed our doors open through drifts of sand and got out of the automobile. It was half buried and it would take hours to dig it out and be on our way again.

The trailer had fared better; it was only buried a foot or so. With the cloud of sand gone, I could see we were frustratingly close to the obelisk, but two men could not pull it there alone.

To my surprise, four sand dunes in front of us began to move, the sand slowly falling away from blankets as Bedouins and their camels emerged. The animals and men shook it off as if it were a normal part of life.

Flinders and I ran over to them, shouting in Arabic that we could pay them handsomely for the use of their camels.

After a brief bartering session, they attached their camels to our trailer and pulled it out of the sand and easily hauled it the few hundred yards to the temple.

Once it was in place, we bid our Bedouin friends goodbye and got to work firing up the kerosene engine on the dynamo and running the wire to the obelisk, per the instructions we had received from some chap in New York, via Stoker in London. Oh, the wonders of modern communication technology! We had just enough cable to wrap it around the base, as the Egyptians looked on in confusion. The generator was making a racket, what with the puttering engine and the high-pitched squeal of the dynamo.

A man, who appeared to be a local magistrate, came to ask what we were doing, but after a few words with Flinders, he let us continue our work. Flin is well known around these parts and has many contacts with the local government.

It was then I noticed my pocket watch had stopped. I am not sure if it was the sand or if I had simply forgot to wind the damned thing.

Flin was wearing something called a 'wrist watch' and told me we only had minutes left. We waited until the stroke of 7:00 pm and threw the switch. I could only hope that his watch was reasonably accurate.

"How will we know if it worked?" Flin asked.

I was about to say that I had no blessed idea, but before I could, the stone started glowing and shot a bright beam of green light into the sky!

"That's how," I said.

The locals fled and, to be honest, I wanted to follow them, but I stood my ground.

It was still daylight, but the beam of light was cutting a hole into a night-time sky. Stars twinkled above us.

Then an even more remarkable thing happened. The temple in front of us started to glow as well, and the wall closest to us shimmered. The wall appeared to vanish and we could see through to the interior of the temple, but not as the dry, dusty relic it is today.

Inside we could see a beautiful queen sitting on her throne. She was holding a gold sceptre that had a glowing green gem on the end. She wore the most colourful, beautiful robes I had ever seen, and a golden crown adorned her head.

The courtiers surrounding her looked to be dressed in ancient Egyptian garb as well.

Flin and I just stood there, frozen in awe. What was it we were seeing? Was it the past?

The queen and her court could see us as well. Some took up a defensive position before their queen. Others were frightened by what they saw, and cowered before us, or bowed as if in supplication.

The queen, however, showed no fear or reverence. With a look of rage on her face, she pointed her sceptre at us and shouted. My Egyptian is rusty at best and this was an ancient form, but even still I could tell she was threatening us.

The tip of the sceptre started to glow and a beam shot out, just as our beam into the sky abruptly ended.

The hole into the temple of another time slammed shut, and we were once again alone in the present. I wonder what that beam blasting out of her sceptre would have done to us and was glad I did not have to take the brunt of whatever magic she wielded.

We dug Flin's automobile out of the sand, attached the trailer and drove back to Luxor, where I cabled Stoker to let him know we had succeeded in what he and Wilde wanted us to do. I hope it was in time, and that the others completed their bit. The part about the Egyptian queen will have to wait until I can speak to him in person, or at least set it down in a letter.

FROM THE DIARY OF LORNA BOW, 1ST OF SEPTEMBER 1884

Today, I helped Miss Chase and Mr. Stoker in their fight against Wilkins and Mueller. I thought I would feel guilty about betraying Mother, but I did not. Still, I do feel bad about how it all turned out. So many people are dead, and for what? Because a madman wanted to cheat death and take power that was not his to wield? I want nothing to do with ghosts or magic after today.

I already feel like it was all but a dream, or sometimes a nightmare. It is almost as if it happened to another me. I am having trouble shedding tears for all I lost today, but Mrs. Stoker says I will in time, when the shock wears off.

Why are things so confusing? I was so happy to meet my mother, yet at the same time angry that she had abandoned me so long ago. I loved contacting spirits, but it also felt like what I was doing was wrong.

Constance says life is often that way. Your path is never clear like it is in stories. Knowing right from wrong is not as apparent as one would think.

Miss Terry says our hearts protect us from the pain and to hold on to all my good memories, even of things that turned bad later. I like that. I honestly didn't know Dr. Mueller was an evil man, at least not at first. I would like to remember him as the kind man he seemed to be in the beginning, the man who made me feel important and useful. A man who loved my mother.

Miss Chase wants me to write down what happened. She says it is not only important for the authorities to know, but it will help me remember this bad day and, while I don't know it now, someday it will be important to read my own words.

My part of the mission, as Miss Chase called it, was a small one, but very important. I was to hide in the bushes near the lamp post where our wires were connected and throw the switch when the time came. A second too soon or too late can make all the difference where magic is concerned. And, if Mother showed up, I would do my best to dampen her magic.

All was going swimmingly, as Mr. Wilde would say. Then Reverend Wilkins arrived with his gang of reanimated corpses. All those hateful souls I had helped put into other people's bodies.

It was my fault that they knew what we were doing. I realise that now. Foolishly, I told Molly about the four obelisks and the global mission to get them lit all at the same time. I had no idea she would tell Mother.

So, there we were, surrounded by two dozen monsters. Mr. Stoker, Miss Chase, Mr. Blackwood and the police sent to help us were pinned down, hiding behind the obelisk and the two sphinxes that guarded it on either side.

Mother raised her arms and put her palms out towards our people. I knew she was going to freeze time, but that is one I could counter!

I put my own palms towards her through the leaves of my hiding spot and said the protection spell she had taught me. It is more of a magic-dampening spell, really. I felt a bubble of energy surround me and spread out. Being so close to the Needle seemed to make magic easier; I was drawing power from it.

Mother felt the bubble bump up against her and put her hands down.

I saw her saying something to Wilkins and shaking her head.

Mother called to me, pleading with me to come out, then they trotted out Molly to do the same. But I stayed silent and hidden. I even wore green that day to hide better in the bushes.

I wanted the Spirit Gate closed. Every day, I felt more and more energy running through me as I brought spirits into the world. I liked it at first. Mother showed me how to do magic with the elements of nature, but as my power grew I felt more of me slipping away. The magic was calling to me to do bad things. I can't describe it more than that, but the magic was trying to use me just like Mother had.

Suddenly Wilkins sent his men to attack the monument. They were firing guns. Chips of stone were flying everywhere as the bullets struck the step and base of the monument.

I was afraid that I would be hit by a bullet, by accident if nothing else, and flattened myself on the ground.

To escape, Mr. Blackwood, Miss Chase and some of the policemen jumped over the wall into the river, which is very far down! I worried that they would drown, but dared not get up and go look over the wall.

Mr. Stoker stood and left his hiding spot, walking straight out into the open.

"Hold your fire," I heard Dr. Mueller yell. "We need him alive."

Then Mr. Stoker did something astonishing. He raised his gun and held it to his own head. "Stand down, Wilkins, or I will end myself right here. You will have no more blood from me."

I hoped he was only stalling for time and did not intend to really do such a thing.

"You're bluffing," Wilkins said.

"Try me."

Wilkins also stepped forward, smiling. "You forget, Bram, how well I know you. I do not think you would take your own life. Leave your wife a widow and your son fatherless? No, Bram, that's not you."

He continued to walk forward, while his men advanced alongside him towards the obelisk.

"You're right," Mr. Stoker said, then pointed his gun at Wilkins. "But nobody will miss you. Not even Mueller needs you."

He pulled the trigger, and Wilkins flinched, but the gun only clicked. Empty.

Wilkins' men rushed towards the obelisk and climbed it like apes, and grunted like apes too as they disconnected the cable and it hit the ground.

I looked at the pocket watch Mr. Stoker had given me. It said 4:56 p.m. It was only four more minutes until I was supposed to pull the lever. There was no hope in reconnecting the wires.

Dr. Mueller came over to the men and yelled at them to disconnect it from the lamp post as well. The lamp post I was hiding under!

There was no place for me to run. I couldn't go over the wall, since I can't swim.

I looked up at the cable attached to the lamp post. Two of Mueller's stooges had the other end, the bare part of the cable that was wrapped around the Needle. Four or five others were following the rest of the cable right to me.

I reached up and pulled the lever. I still am not sure why I did it; panic I suppose. It turned out to be a good move. The junction box sparked and the two blokes holding the other end lit up like Roman candles as a thousand volts of electricity flowed into their bodies. Their muscles jerked violently and their hands started to smoke.

The others who had been running towards me ran back to help them. They managed to yank the insulated part of the cable to pull it from their friends' hands, but not before the two were fried to a crisp.

They dropped the cable, and it continued to spark and jump around like a hissing viper, as the men fled from it. It was alive with current and so snakelike that it reminded me of the spell I had used on the rope.

It took a moment for Mueller to even realise what was happening, and he shouted again for someone to pull the cable from the lamp post.

A calm came over me, even as Mueller and his monsters ran towards my hiding spot. They were only a few feet away, but I already had control of the cable. The electricity flowing through it gave me more power, helping me wield it. Sparks danced off my fingertips as I commanded it up the base of the monument and curled it around the obelisk. For a moment the world fell away, and I was the cable; I was the obelisk; I was the electricity. I felt the magic flow through the stone as it flowed through me.

Then one of the brutes grabbed me out of the bushes, abruptly breaking the connection. A second found the junction box and turned off the current.

The monster dragged me towards Mr. Wilkins, who was grinning as if he had beaten us.

"Don't hurt her," Dr. Mueller ordered.

Mother ran towards me.

"Stay where you are, Endora!" Wilkins yelled.

I could still feel the magic channelling through me. Perhaps the switch didn't matter now. The monster was still holding me around the waist. As Wilkins advanced towards me, I raised my hands again. My whole body was humming with power. I sent that power towards the obelisk, which absorbed it like a sponge soaking up water.

Before anyone could do anything else, the stone of the obelisk began to glow. Then a bright green beam of light split the sky. I had done it!

Wilkins, Mueller and their henchmen just stood looking at the beam like the dumb apes they were. The light show lasted a good minute or two. At the top of the beam we could see night sky. This was indeed powerful magic.

Then it stopped, as though the light was being sucked back into the obelisk. The hole in the sky slammed shut.

I knew it had worked, that the Spirit Gate was closed, its tether to this world snapped like broken piano string. There even was an audible *boing* in my ears. I felt a drain of energy. I could see that Mother felt it too; her knees buckled a bit, but she regained her footing.

"Put her down," Mother commanded. She raised her palms to the thing holding me, about to cast a spell. He gripped me tighter around the waist with his left arm, sliding his right arm around my neck. "Stay back or I'll snap her neck!"

Wilkins walked up to me and my captor.

"We are all family here. All is forgiven. We welcome you back into the fold, Lorna."

We were interrupted by an angry mob marching towards us. They carried guns, clubs and meat cleavers and were being led by Mrs. Stoker! Her army was made up of theatre workers, butchers and other local shopkeepers. The mob took cover behind the same garden wall Wilkins had used earlier.

"I have brought reinforcements!" Mrs. Stoker shouted. "You are outnumbered and I order you to stand down."

"It's over, Wilkins!" a man shouted from behind us. We turned our heads to see Mr. Blackwood standing by the right sphinx statue. He was furious and dripping wet.

"It is not," Wilkins said calmly. "We can reopen the Gate. We still have our new followers." He gestured at his monsters all around him. "And, best of all, we have you, Bram."

He nodded to one of his followers, who grabbed Mr. Stoker by the arm, and Wilkins and his other minions took cover behind the monument, while the one holding Mr. Stoker stood his ground, using Mr. Stoker as a shield.

"We meet again, Stoker. This time you don't have a vampire to kill old Dripp," he said, as Mr. Stoker tried to struggle free. It was no use;

the monster was too strong. "Stop wiggling about or I'll crush you like an egg."

Wilkins' men started to fire at Mrs. Stoker's people, and this forced them back behind the wall.

Mr. Blackwood suddenly leapt from the sphinx statue and attacked the man holding Mr. Stoker.

Mr. Dripp let go of Mr. Stoker to fight off Mr. Blackwood, but Blackwood gave Dripp a swift karate kick to his face. (Who knew a person could kick that high?)

To my surprise, and I am sure to the surprise of all, Dripp fell back dead. His face was caved in, a mess of blood and bone. It looked as if Mr. Blackwood hit him in the face with an anvil instead of a foot.

Wilkins' creatures all around us started to fall to their knees. They must have been weakened by the closing of the Gate, and their souls were having trouble staying attached to the bodies.

I could actually see their spirits being pulled away from them and into the ground, as if hell itself were swallowing them up.

The creature holding me let go and fell to his knees. I kicked him hard in the face and I watched his soul slither out and disappear into the ground.

Mr. Stoker turned his attention to Wilkins. "You and I have a score to settle!"

Wilkins threw a punch at Mr. Stoker, who dodged out of the way. Wilkins came around with his left hand, but Mr. Stoker blocked it and Wilkins' whole arm fell off! It landed with a thud at Mr. Stoker's feet.

"I see you're finally starting to feel that colloidal silver I drank to poison my blood," Mr. Stoker said, as he rolled up his sleeves and began to pummel Wilkins in the face. Each blow took off huge chunks of now-rotting flesh! Stoker pounded and pounded him until he was a quivering heap on the ground. Wilkins protected his face as best he could with his remaining arm. "Please stop!" he cried like a whimpering baby.

Mr. Stoker did stop, but it was too late for poor Reverend Wilkins. I watched his soul drain into the ground, leaving behind only the lifeless corpse, which began to rot before our eyes.

Mrs. Stoker's gang was making quick work of what was left of the minions. The spirits of those that still had them were easily knocked out with a single blow.

I was so caught up in the spectacle of it all, I hadn't noticed Dr. Mueller sneaking up behind me. He grabbed me and put a pistol to my head.

"Stop! Or I will shoot her!" he screamed. There wasn't anything to stop at this point. All his creatures were dead or dying.

Mother rushed to my aid with her palms out. She did not even try to negotiate with Mueller, just said a brief incantation (one I did not recognise) and his head snapped back hard.

But Mother hadn't taken into account his finger on the trigger of a gun. As he spasmed, his gun went off. He shot me through the neck.

I fell to the ground.

I remained conscious for a moment, long enough to think I was dying.

I blacked out and then awoke with a start as Mother's hands were around my neck. She was using all her power to save me. I felt life surge back into me. I felt the wound in my neck sealing up.

I grabbed Mother's wrist to tell her to stop; I was healed. But she did not take her hands away and kept passing her life force to me. I watched her skin wrinkle, her hair turn white and, finally, watched the light fade from her eyes.

She collapsed dead in front of me. I hadn't the strength or the skill to bring her back, and I started to cry.

Mrs. Stoker came to my side and embraced me. She said nothing, but then what could she say?

Dr. Mueller was dead as well. Mother's spell had broken his neck. There would be no one to bring *him* back.

That is my account of this terrible day. The day I lost my mother, all the things she could have taught me, and the whole future we could have had together.

FROM THE JOURNAL OF BRAM STOKER, 16TH OF SEPTEMBER 1884

6:18 p.m.

Yet another astounding day. I have come to hate astounding days. I long for a simpler time of boredom and routine.

But it is not to be. A man came to the theatre today and told me Queen Victoria wished an audience with me and Oscar.

I was dumbfounded, of course, and then sceptical. This was just the sort of thing I should learn not to do, getting into cabs with strange men. It could have been a ruse of some sort. Maybe Wilkins was somehow back for a third time.

But the man showed me a letter from the Queen herself. We have received correspondence from the Palace before, on theatre business, so I had confidence it was quite real.

When I got into the carriage Oscar was already inside, giddy at the prospect of seeing Her Majesty once again.

We had met her once before, of course. She personally thanked us for saving the life of her grandson during Wilkins' first reign of terror.

Oscar thought we would be knighted, but I told him that would almost certainly be arranged with more ceremony and our families in attendance.

The carriage took us to Buckingham Palace, and a waiting footman led us into the Queen's receiving room. She was sitting behind a desk, looking more like a clerk than royalty. Papers and books littered the desk, and she had a pair of reading glasses at the end of her nose.

When we entered, she rose and crossed the room to us, and we bowed. "Please, be seated," she said.

Once we were all settled, she said. "It is a pleasure to see you both again. We wish it was under better circumstances. We are very saddened by the destruction of the White Worm Society. It has a long and valiant history of keeping the Empire safe from supernatural forces."

Oscar and I offered our condolences.

"We are in the process of rebuilding the home office," she said. "We are bringing together agents from field offices across the Empire to form a new board of directors and select a new director. In the meantime, we would like the two of you to serve as board members, at least on a temporary basis."

What were we to say? It was our Queen asking us. As much as I wanted to scream that I wanted no part in the White Worms, I did not dare say no.

"What sort of salary is involved?" Oscar asked.

"We are not sure," Her Majesty said. "We are certain a small stipend could be arranged, in any event."

Oscar stood up, saluted and said, "I accept! Does something like this also involve a knighthood?"

"We must regretfully refuse," she said. "This is a clandestine operation and knighthoods are much too public."

"Ah, I see. Yes, of course," Oscar said. He sheepishly sat back down.

"We just need some old blood to welcome the new members, someone to see to the restoration and re-cataloguing of the library, things like that."

I did like the idea of restoring and reorganising the library. Brings me back to my clerking days in Dublin Castle.

"Bram's your man for that," Oscar said, clapping me on the shoulder. "Wrote an entire book on it, you see."

"Yes, we know. We commissioned it. We have cleared everything with your employers and you may take a day to talk it over with your wives," she said. "And rest assured, we promise you that you will never again be called upon to hunt monsters. This will purely be administrative work and part-time at that. And, perhaps, advise the monster hunters, as it were."

The administrative part sold me on it, of course, and I agreed.

Florence is all behind the Queen on this, telling me I am the best man for the job.

"It's the perfect combination of your managerial skills and your supernatural acumen," she said. I must admit she's right.

My first order of business is to record all the events Dr. Mueller and Wilkins set in motion. Those involved, including Lorna Bow, will donate their diaries and journals for the project. We have shut down Mueller's London laboratory and confiscated his notes and journals.

I, at last, feel as though all my monsters are in the past and my eyes are on a more pleasant future.

REPORT FROM WHITE WORM SOCIETY AGENT CORA CHASE

Date: 18 September 1884
Subject: Reconstruction of the White Worm Society

I, with help from Queen Victoria, have convinced Mr. Stoker and Mr. Wilde to temporarily oversee the rebuilding of the White Worm Society.

A new board of governors will be created, and a new director hired.

I am returning to America and have been promoted to Director of the North American branch, where I will oversee operations in the United States and Canada.

It seems my first order of business will be to hunt down and kill a Wendigo that is terrifying the Great Lakes region.

I hope to persuade Bass Reeves to come out of retirement for this, as he was so helpful in putting down the vampires out West.

This should be fun.

LETTER FROM HENRY IRVING TO BRAM STOKER, 24TH OF SEPTEMBER 1884

Dear Bram,

As I write this, I am in the monastery in Scotland. It is a special place with others of my kind, other supernaturally afflicted souls seeking cures.

The friars here have taught me how to control my evil urges and how to continue to use my power for good. It helps that you and the others closed the Spirit Gate. I did not realise how much effect the increased supernatural activity was having upon me.

I am almost ready to re-enter society. I will return to the theatre in a fortnight and look forward to resuming my acting and directing duties.

Thank you for being my friend and helping me in my darkest hours.

Yours,

Henry

FROM THE DIARY OF OSCAR WILDE, 5TH OF JUNE 1885

Dear yours truly,

Oh, heavens! It is a boy. A healthy, beautiful baby boy. I never thought I would see another soul as captivating as myself, but here he is. We have named him Cyril, and he is perfect in every way and, thank goodness, looks just like his mother.

Now that I am a father, I have vowed to put all monster hunting aside for my family and my art. I know that will be hard to do as long as I associate with the Stokers, but I shall try.

I must go. My perfect child is crying and his mother deserves a rest.

FROM THE DIARY OF LORNA BOW, 25TH OF JUNE 1885

Archivist's note: This is an entry a White Worm operative copied from Lorna's second diary.

This is the first page of a new diary. I gave the last one to the White Worm Society as a record of all that has happened. It was almost full anyway.

The girls and I are back in the séance business. Mostly fake ones these days as I don't really care to call forth real spirits very often anymore. I have tried to contact Mother, but haven't been able to find her. I hope she's moved on and found peace.

Oddly, just as I put my magic days behind me, I got a strange visitor today. This exotic-looking woman came into the parlour asking to see Mother.

She looked Egyptian, with olive skin and beautiful hair as black as coal. She wore a large gold necklace in the shape of an eagle, and a gold ring that looked like a beetle.

I had to give her the bad news that Mother had died. She shoved an old book into my hands, then told me she was a priestess of Isis and they wanted help resurrecting their mummy queen, Hatshepsut, so she could take the world back from men.

I told her I was out of the magic business, and my powers were never as strong as Mother's to begin with, aside from contacting the spirit world. I could never transfer the souls like Mother did. I tried to hand the book back to her. She refused to take it, so I tossed it onto the table.

She then put a warm, metal object into my hand. It was a beetle, a scarab I guess. It was gold, like her necklace and ring.

When I held it, power surged through me like the night Mother had performed the ceremony at the obelisk. All my fading powers came rushing back. I was fully charged once more.

I suddenly realised why I have not been able to contact Mother's spirit. It isn't in the afterlife – she is somewhere else. The parlour fell away, and I was standing in a field of poppies and Mother was hugging me.

"You have the power to change the world," she said. She let go, and I popped back to the parlour.

"You *are* your mother's daughter," the woman said, smiling. With that, she just left.

As I clutch the golden scarab in my fist, images of all the men who have treated me badly flicker through my mind.

The book on the table calls to me.

FLAME TREE PRESS
FICTION WITHOUT FRONTIERS
Award-Winning Authors & Original Voices

Flame Tree Press is the trade fiction imprint of Flame Tree Publishing, focusing on excellent writing in horror and the supernatural, crime and mystery, science fiction and fantasy. Our aim is to explore beyond the boundaries of the everyday, with tales from both award-winning authors and original voices.

•

Other titles in the *Stoker's Wilde* series:
Stoker's Wilde
Stoker's Wilde West

Other horror and suspense titles available include:
Snowball by Gregory Bastianelli
Thirteen Days by Sunset Beach by Ramsey Campbell
Think Yourself Lucky by Ramsey Campbell
The Hungry Moon by Ramsey Campbell
The Influence by Ramsey Campbell
The Wise Friend by Ramsey Campbell
Somebody's Voice by Ramsey Campbell
The Haunting of Henderson Close by Catherine Cavendish
The Garden of Bewitchment by Catherine Cavendish
The House by the Cemetery by John Everson
The Devil's Equinox by John Everson
Hellrider by JG Faherty
The Toy Thief by D.W. Gillespie
One By One by D.W. Gillespie
Black Wings by Megan Hart
The Playing Card Killer by Russell James
The Sorrows by Jonathan Janz
Will Haunt You by Brian Kirk
We Are Monsters by Brian Kirk
Hearthstone Cottage by Frazer Lee
Those Who Came Before by J.H. Moncrieff
Creature by Hunter Shea
Ghost Mine by Hunter Shea
Slash by Hunter Shea

•

Join our mailing list for free short stories, new release details, news about our authors and special promotions:

flametreepress.com